KU-406-376

Miss Austen

NEWHAM LIBRARIES

90800000152216

ALSO BY GILL HORNBY
FROM CLIPPER LARGE PRINT

All Together Now

Miss Austen

Gill Hornby

W F HOWES LTD

This large print edition published in 2020 by
W F Howes Ltd
Unit 5, St George's House, Rearsby Business Park,
Gaddesby Lane, Rearsby, Leicester LE7 4YH

1 3 5 7 9 10 8 6 4 2

First published in the United Kingdom in 2020
by Century

Copyright © Gill Hornby, 2020
Map © Darren Bennet

The right of Gill Hornby to be identified as
the author of this work has been asserted by her
in accordance with the Copyright, Designs and
Patents Act, 1988.

All rights reserved

A CIP catalogue record for this book is available
from the British Library

ISBN 978 1 00401 277 0

Typeset by Palimpsest Book Production Limited,
Falkirk, Stirlingshire

Printed and bound by
T J International in the UK

MIX
Paper from
responsible sources
FSC® C013056

To Holly and Matilda

Men have had every advantage of us in telling their own story . . . the pen has been in their hands.

Jane Austen, *Persuasion*

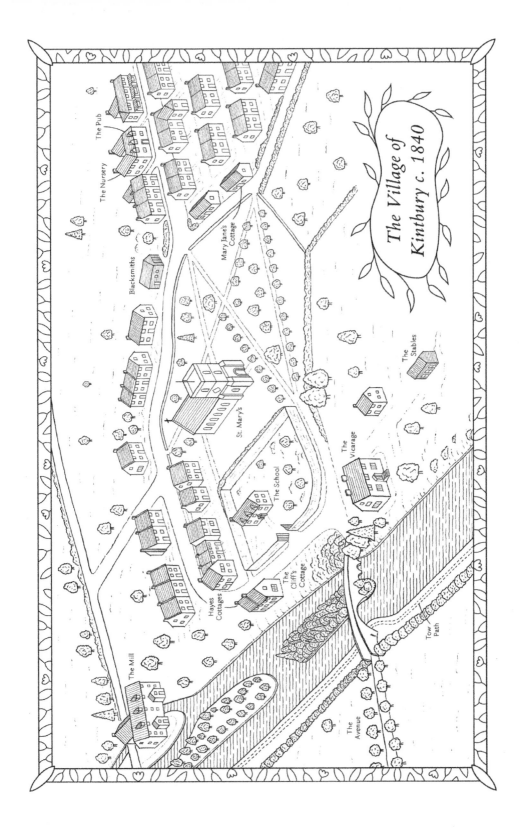

The Village of
Kintbury c. 1840

The Pub
The Nursery
Blacksmiths
Mary Jane's Cottage
St. Mary's
The Stables
The Vicarage
The School
The Cliff's Cottage
Hayes Cottages
The Mill
Tow Path
The Avenue

THE FAMILIES

The Austens

THE REVEREND GEORGE AUSTEN, Rector of Steventon, and his wife, MRS (CASSANDRA) AUSTEN: the couple had eight children, one of whom, named George after his father, was disabled and lived away from the family. Of the rest:

JAMES succeeded his father as Rector of Steventon. After the death of his first wife, he married MARY LLOYD. He had three children: ANNA, JAMES-EDWARD and CAROLINE.

EDWARD was adopted by wealthy relations in his youth, and lived the life of a landed gentleman. He was married to ELIZABETH and together they had eleven children. His eldest daughter FANNY was a particular favourite of his sisters Cassandra and Jane.

HENRY was first a soldier, then a banker and finally a parson. The cleverest and most worldly of the brothers, he helped Jane find a publisher and acted as her agent.

CASSANDRA was engaged to Tom Fowle; in later life she became the executor of her sister's literary estate.

FRANCIS, known as Frank, joined the navy, rose to the position of admiral and was eventually knighted. On the death of his first wife, who left him with eleven children, he then married MARTHA LLOYD.

JANE wrote six full-length novels, two of which were published posthumously. She died in July 1817.

CHARLES was also a sailor.

The Fowles

THE REVEREND THOMAS FOWLE, Vicar of Kintbury, and his wife MRS (JANE) FOWLE had four sons:

FULWAR CRAVEN succeeded his father as Vicar of Kintbury, and married ELIZA LLOYD. They had three sons and three daughters, MARY-JANE, ELIZABETH and ISABELLA.

TOM was betrothed to Cassandra.

WILLIAM became a military physician, and CHARLES a lawyer. Both died young.

The Lloyds

ELIZA was the wife of Fulwar Craven Fowle.

MARTHA was a close friend of Cassandra and Jane Austen. She married Frank Austen in later life.

MARY was the wife of James Austen.

'Let us take that path.'

He closed the garden door behind her, and gestured towards the Elm Walk. She pulled her shawl close and drank a deep draught of the new, green air. The year was 1795, and the day seemed to assume itself to be the first of that spring. Birds high in the oak tree sang out their relief; a new stickiness shone from the twigs. Together, they walked up the slope at the back of the rectory, through the gap in the hedgerow and, there – out of sight of her family – he stopped and took her hand.

'My love,' Tom began. Cassy smiled: here it was, at last. She had been waiting so long for this moment. 'Oh—' He stopped, shy suddenly. 'I think you know what it is I am about to say.'

'Do I?' She looked up at him, encouraging. 'Well, I should dearly like to hear you say it, whatever it may be. Please. Do go on.'

And so he spoke. It was not a polished declaration, considering how much time there had been for the planning of it. It was a little halting, in places – he had loved her since, well, he could not quite remember . . . she was the only woman whom he could ever contemplate . . . um . . . sharing – and so on, but she was charmed all the same. It was entirely in his dear character, and both as wonderful and as ordinary as these moments should be. When it seemed that all words, even the inadequate, were beginning to fail him, she accepted to spare him the struggle. They kissed, and her whole body was consumed by a surge of – what was it exactly? – yes: satisfaction. This was her destiny. Her life was in place.

They walked for a little, her arm in his, and discussed the terms of their engagement. In fact, there was only one term that could concern them: it would be long. And those dread words 'two hundred and fifty pounds' and 'per annum' did have to be mentioned – how they wearied them both! But be mentioned they must. He asked for her patience; she promised it without thinking. Cassy was just twenty-two; they had years yet to play with. And patience was, famously, one of her many virtues. They turned back to the house to spread their glad news.

It was met with all the exuberant delight that they could have wished for, though not even a pretence at surprise. For this engagement – between Miss Cassandra Austen of Steventon, and the young Revd Tom Fowle of Kintbury – had been settled as a public fact long before it was decided by the couple in private. After all, it was the perfect match, of the sort that would bring such pleasure to so many. So it must be their future, their one possible happy ending.

The universe had agreed on that for them, many years before.

CHAPTER 1

Kintbury, March 1840

'Miss Austen.' The voice came from behind her. 'Forgive me.' She turned. 'I did not know you were there.'

Cassandra managed a smile, but stayed where she was on the vicarage doorstep. She would dearly like to be more effusive – she felt the distant, familiar stirrings of effusiveness somewhere, deep down – but was simply too tired to move. Her old bones had been shaken apart by the coach ride from her home in Chawton and the chill wind off the river was piercing her joints. She stood by her bags and watched Isabella approach.

'I had to go up to the vestry,' Isabella called as she came down from the churchyard. She had always cut a small, colourless figure, and was now, of course – poor dear – in unhelpful, ill-fitting black. 'There are still duties . . .' Against a backdrop of green bank dotted with primrose, she moved like a shadow. 'So many duties to perform.' The only distinguishing feature about her person

1

was the hound by her side. And while her voice was all apology, her step was remarkably unhurried. Even Pyramus, now advancing across the gravel, was a study in reluctance with a drag on his paws.

Cassandra suspected that she was not welcome and, if that was so, could only blame herself. A single woman should never outlive her usefulness. It was simple bad manners. She had come uninvited; Isabella was in difficulties: it was all rather awkward but quite understandable. Still, she once might have hoped for some enthusiasm from a dog.

'My dear, it is so kind of you to let me visit.' She embraced Isabella, who was all cool politeness, and fussed over Pyramus, though she much preferred cats.

'But has nobody come to you? Did you not ring?'

Of course, Cassandra had rung. She had arrived with great commotion and business in a post-chaise so that nobody could miss her. The coachman had rung and then rung again. She had seen people, plenty of them: a steady traffic of labourers balanced on carts coming back from the fields and a group of boys, wet to the knees, with a newt in a bucket. She longed to speak to them – she was rather fond of newts, and even fonder of boys in that fever of innocent passion – but they did not seem to see her. And the house had stayed silent, though that difficult maid – what was her name? Cassandra's memory, always prodigious, was beginning to fray, if just at the edges – must know perfectly well she was there.

'I came at a bad moment. Oh, Isabella' – Cassandra held her arms and looked into her face – 'how are you?'

'It has been difficult, Cassandra.' Isabella's eyes reddened. 'Really most difficult.' She struggled, but then composed herself. 'But how does the old place seem to you now? Have you been looking around?'

'Exactly as it has always been. Dear, dear Kintbury . . .'

The vicarage had been a landmark – familiar, oft-times sad, always beloved – in Cassandra's life for forty-five years. A white, three-storey building with a friendly face set east towards the ancient village; garden falling on one side down to the banks of the Kennet, rising on the other to the squat Norman church. It stood testament to everything that she valued: family and function, the simple, honest, good life. She rated this happy piece of English domestic architecture over anything grander – Godmersham, Stoneleigh, Pemberley even. That said, she dearly would like to be inside it – by the fire, in a chair, getting warm. 'Shall we—?'

'Of course. Where is everybody? Let me take that.' Isabella reached for the small black valise in Cassandra's hand.

'Thank you. I can manage it.' Cassandra clutched the bag to her. 'But my trunk . . .'

'Trunk? Ah.' Though Isabella's face remained

pale and blank of expression, her piercing blue eyes flashed bright with intelligence. 'I am sure it is my fault. I have had so much on my mind.' One eyebrow arced. 'And your letter arrived only yesterday – was that not odd?'

Not odd at all; indeed, it was entirely deliberate. Cassandra had never before been so discourteous as to arrive without proper notice but, on this occasion, had simply had no choice. So she gave a vague smile.

In the absence of any explanation, Isabella went on: 'I did not grasp quite how *long* you are staying. Do you plan to be with us a *while?*'

Isabella's displeasure at her arrival was now perfectly plain. Beneath that mild, quiet exterior, there was, perhaps, a stronger character than had previously been witnessed. Nevertheless, Cassandra would stay here as long as was necessary. She was determined not to leave until her work here was done. She muttered about possibly travelling further on to a nephew, affecting an uncharacteristic indecisiveness brought on by advancing age.

'Fred will bring in your trunk. Please.' Isabella signalled towards the door, which opened at once from the inside. 'Ah, you are there, Dinah.'

There. Dinah. She must remember that. She might be needing Dinah.

'Miss Austen is with us.'

Dinah squeezed out a negligible bob.

'Shall we go in?'

*   *   *

4

Cassandra had first crossed this threshold as a young woman. She was tall then, and slim; many were kind enough to say handsome. Was time playing its tricks or had she worn her best blue? A crowd of family had assembled to greet her; the servants – excited, admiring – jostled behind. She had stood still and thrilled at it – the power of her position! The force of that moment!

Oh, she still looked in the glass, when she had to. She knew she would not be called slim now, but spare. Her spine, once a strict perpendicular, was kinked and shortening; her face so gaunt that her once proud nose – the Leigh nose, the stamp of a distant aristocracy – more like the beak of a common crow. And the people who loved her then were gone now – as she herself was gone, almost. Those receiving her today – poor Isabella, difficult Dinah, Fred who now passed through the vestibule, grunting and dragging her trunk – of course knew the facts of her history, but had no sense of the *truth* of it. For whoever looked at an elderly lady and saw the young heroine she once was?

They moved through to the wide, wood-panelled hall. Cassandra followed them meekly but, once there, was suddenly seized with alarm. She made for the generous stone fireplace, clung on for support and looked with horror at the scene around her.

She could hear Dinah mutter: 'Lord save us. She's turned up and lost 'er senses. As if we don't have enough on our plate.'

And Isabella whisper: 'Perhaps it is more sorrow or sentiment that affects her. After all, this must be the last time that she will ever come here.'

Cassandra knew better than to acknowledge them. It was one of those conversations conducted as though she could not hear it, in which the young so often indulge around the old. But as if *she* could be overcome by sorrow or sentiment, when for decades they had been her constant companions. No. It was not the fact that this was the last visit – she gasped for air, her hands shook – it was the fear that she had left it *too late*. The house was already in a chaos of removals.

'My dear, are you sure you are quite well?' Isabella, softening, took her elbow, giving her something to lean on.

A portrait of the Fowles' benefactor, Lord Craven, had hung above that fireplace ever since she could remember. Now it was gone from the wall.

'That coach was too much for you.' Isabella talked loudly as if to an imbecile, while untying the ribbon around Cassandra's chin. 'All that way in this cold weather.' Her bonnet was removed. From where she was standing, Cassandra could see into the study where the shelves had been emptied. Which books were gone? They had had the whole set of Jane's. Who had them now?

'And she's come alone then, I can't help but notice.' Dinah was behind her, loosening off her cloak.

6

The furniture still in place looked abject, humiliated, like slaves in the market place.

'Perhaps her maid is away?'

'Which leaves who looking after 'er, may I ask?' Dinah flung cloak and hat over her arm. 'Me and whose army?'

A vicarage without a vicar was always a sorrowful sight. Cassandra had borne witness to it more often than most, yet it still affected her every time. The Fowles had lived in this house for three generations. It had been handed on, father to son – all good clergymen, all blessed with fine wives – but that chain was now broken. Isabella's father was dead, and her brothers had refused it. No doubt they had their reasons and, to squander all that family heritage, Cassandra sincerely hoped they were good ones.

Church tradition allowed the relics of the family two months to vacate the house for the next incumbent. And, although it was not anywhere written, Church tradition seemed somehow always to rely on the vicarage *women* to effect it. Poor Isabella. The task she had before her was bleak, miserable, arduous: just two months to clear the place that had been their home for ninety-nine years! Of course, she had to start on it at once. But still, the Reverend Fulwar Craven Fowle had been dead but a few weeks. Cassandra had come as soon as she could. She was shocked to see that the work was already this far advanced.

To think that journey – so tiring, so uncomfortable, so shamefully expensive – might not have been worth it! To think that for which she had come might already be gone!

Cassandra felt nauseous and dizzy. Kindly Isabella smoothed down her hair – she must look dishevelled – and led her through the hall.

The Kintbury drawing room was a thing of simple beauty: a perfect cube with walls of deep yellow which caught and held the setting sun. Each of its windows, on two sides, looked out over water: you could stand and watch the fishermen on the river or barges glide along the canal to east and west. Ordinarily, it was one of Cassandra's favourite places. It satisfied her soul. But on that day, she approached it with nervous trepidation, consumed with a dread of what she might find.

She need not have worried. Even as she entered, before setting a sensible shoe on the needlepoint carpet, she felt herself safe. The atmosphere here was one of calm and repose. The air was quite undisturbed. And all the furniture was here, just as it had always been. So she had not come too late! Her knees almost buckled with the relief. She turned back to Isabella, her voice and authority returned to her at once.

'Now, perhaps I may repair myself before we dine?'

Cassandra had often privately observed that when the gentleman of the house died, fine dining died with him. It was a thesis that evening's dinner was determined to prove. Their mutton was just that: mutton, with no sauce, potatoes or pudding, its only companion a cabbage that had loitered too long in the ground. She smiled as she compared it with the meals she once enjoyed there. Isabella's father was always a man of high standards and immoderate reactions. If Dinah had dared serve him something like this, he would have made his displeasure known.

But they were two ladies, so they politely thanked their Lord, with some effort cut their mutton, and chewed with a dogged determination. The only other sound was the loud ticking of the clock. Silence at that particular dinner table was another unwelcome innovation, one that Cassandra was finding more tough than the meat.

'I see from the labels on everything that you are already well ahead in dividing up all the effects.' Cassandra eyed the decanter, which was empty for the first time in its history. She tilted her head and read that Mr Charles Fowle had already claimed ownership. It could look forward to a busy future with *him*.

'The will was read last week and my brothers were able to make their decisions.' Isabella betrayed no emotion as she said this. Her face was turned down, those bright eyes studied her plate.

Cassandra, though, could not help but be more forthcoming. 'And your brothers are to have *all* the goods and chattels?' She could hear the sharpness in her own voice and was at once all regret:

she was well aware of being too sharp for some tastes, and did try to blunt her own tongue. But really, this business was too vexing. The Fowles were like the Austens in so many ways: both large families, blessed with sons and daughters, and by a great good fortune which seemed only to run down the male line.

'My father did leave some novels to my sister Elizabeth.' Isabella gestured at the bookcase, which had one blank and dusty shelf. 'Particular favourites, which they read together.'

Cassandra lit up. 'Ah!' At last, they had struck upon her favourite conversation. She asked, teasingly: 'And they were by whom, may I ask?'

'By *whom?*' Isabella seemed at once baffled by the question, as if books were books and their authors of no matter. 'Why, Sir Walter Scott, I do believe.'

Cassandra gripped her fork and stifled all natural expression. Sir Walter Scott. *Sir Walter Scott!* Why must it always be *him?* How she wished that just once, she too could let fly with an immoderate reaction. Instead, she sat silently brooding – on the injustices of fame; the travails of true genius; the realisation – and this came to her quite spontaneously – that she had never particularly warmed to Isabella's sister Elizabeth. And then her thoughts were suddenly interrupted. What was this? Isabella had at last found she had something to say.

'It is my opinion that his books are very . . .'

There was a pause while she looked around her, searching for the bon mot. '. . . very . . . very . . .' And then, as if by a miracle, it came to her: '. . . *long*.' She drew breath to continue. Having thus broached the unlikely territory of literary discussion, she was somehow emboldened to journey yet further therein. 'There are many, many words in them,' she carried on, with some bitterness. 'They seem to take up too much of everybody's time.'

Cassandra was generally used to a higher level of discourse, but still she could only agree. In other company, she might have argued that he was a fine poet and joked that his work as a reviewer was quite unsurpassed, but could sense that this was not quite the forum. 'And what about you, Isabella? Do *you* like novels? What are your particular favourites?'

'Novels? Me?' Isabella was back to being baffled. 'Favourites? No. None at all.'

The debate was over. Cassandra surrendered. Dinah bustled in and slapped down a compote and they supped in a silence broken only by the continued ticking of that clock.

'Do take Mama's place,' said Isabella when dinner was over. Cassandra accepted at once, as the chair happened to be nearest the fire.

The evening in the drawing room yawned before them, the latest challenge in a challenging day. Pyramus padded in, and stretched out on the carpet: it had always been one of those houses of

11

which dogs had the freedom. Cassandra did not mind this dog in particular, but did not quite approve of the practice in general. She tucked in her feet, opened her valise and took out her work. How useful it was to sew, to fuss about with a needle, to keep your eyes on the stitch. It was always her armour in difficult situations, the activity itself a diversion from the awkwardness of the company. She often wondered how men managed, without something similar. Although it did seem that they were so less often stuck for words.

She had only brought with her patchwork. Her eyes were no longer good enough for anything finer by lamplight. 'Do you not have work, Isabella dear?' She slotted the paper behind the shape of sprigged cotton and started to stitch around. 'Nothing with which you are busy?'

Isabella, staring into the fire, shook her head. 'I was never terribly good at that sort of thing.'

Cassandra, who could patchwork with her eyes closed, looked up with some surprise. What an odd little creature Isabella was. She had known Isabella since birth – how the years blurred and fell away – and yet, she realised, she did not know her at all. She studied the woman before her: her figure was neat, though ill served by her mourning; her features could pass as delicate, had sorrow not robbed them of prettiness. Isabella had neither the beauty of her mother, nor the intellect of her father – though those arresting blue eyes were certainly his. And even after forty years of acquaintance, any sense of character or personality still seemed elusive. Cassandra could hardly stay here in the vicarage without establishing some sort of relationship, but it was as if she was in the dark, feeling around a thick blank wall in search of a secret doorway. It was hard to find a way in.

And then inspiration struck her: 'I hope death was kind to your father when it finally came for him?'

For what else do the newly bereaved want to discuss but The End?

Isabella sighed. 'It was clear about ten days before that his time was coming. He had a seizure after dinner and when Dinah went in the next morning, he was too weak to rise . . .'

The lock had been sprung. The door to conversation now opened.

'The pain that afflicted him, with which he lived so bravely, was finally . . .'

Cassandra worked on, listening to stories of ice baths and poultices, and suddenly felt much more at home.

'On the fifth day, his spirits were so low that we were able to admit the doctor—'

'The doctor was not consulted *before*?' This smacked of negligence!

Isabella sighed. 'Mr Lidderdale is a fine surgeon and we are lucky to have him. He is popular with everyone – everyone, that is, except Papa. My father had doubts on the very idea of a doctor in the village. He worried it could encourage illness in those who could least afford to be ill. But then, when he himself was past objecting . . .'

Cassandra reflected that dying must indeed have been a torment to the good Reverend: to have to lie there mute and have his irascible demands ignored.

'. . . and I, of course, was so grateful to have Mr Lidderdale there with me. Oh! The relief that I was no longer alone—'

'But your sisters, Isabella,' Cassandra interrupted. 'Surely they both took their turns?'

'Well, Elizabeth is now so busy with her work with the babies in the village. And of course they must not suffer. We do not see much of her here.'

Elizabeth! Frankly, Cassandra expected no better. 'But Mary-Jane? She lives just across the churchyard.'

'Mary-Jane of course has her own establishment to concern her.'

Ah, the tyranny of the married woman, thought Cassandra – even one now a childless widow.

'Then they should be grateful to you for shouldering that burden alone.'

'I did not mind it.' Isabella shrugged. 'And did not mind it at all, once the doctor was with me. It is such an odd time, when someone is dying but you cannot tell when. Mr Lidderdale says deaths are like births in that regard.'

Cassandra had much experience of both and

14

well knew their trials. She had run out of thread, and reached into her bag for a new length.

'. . . and then, just before the end, he said he was hungry and I remembered we had a good raised pork pie. He does like a pork pie. And this one had an egg in the middle. He is quite unusually fond of an egg—'

'Fulwar was after pork pie even on his own deathbed?' Cassandra threaded her needle and shook her head: he really was the stuff of legend.

'Not my father! Mr Lidderdale. Mr Lidderdale is often hungry, even hungrier than Papa. He is not a tall man, but broad in the shoulder and he does work so very hard.' For a moment, her eyes caught the dance of the firelight. 'Where was I? So, yes, there we were, sitting one on each side. He could not decide if he would prefer beer or tea. We were discussing it. The meals get so confused when one stays up all night. And he suddenly grasped my father's hand and said, "Oh Isabella!" Those were his words. "Oh Isabella." And I knew that was it. It was over. Never again would I sit by his side.'

Cassandra had already heard reports of Isabella's distress at Fulwar's passing. According to the family, she had been brave during his illness but quite beside herself when it came to the end. Even after the funeral she had had to be put to her bed. The evidence was still there – the tears in the eyes – but Cassandra still found it a little surprising. Of course all parents should be *mourned*: that was the duty of all offspring. But were they all to be *missed* in the same way?

She began to pack away her work. Isabella's new-found loquacity had quite seen off the evening. At last it was an hour at which they could respectably retire.

Isabella went first up the shallow oak staircase, holding the lamp for Cassandra, who took the steps slowly, one at a time. She had to stop for a rest on the half-landing and caught the draught coming in through the curtain at the north-facing window. What a trial it was going to be, staying in a bigger, higher house when she was so used to her cottage in Chawton. May her progress be swift so that she did not have to stay here too long.

They made their way down the corridor. The door to Isabella's mother's chamber was ajar, and Cassandra glimpsed just enough to assure herself that it too had not yet been cleared: that was most promising. They passed what she still thought of as Tom's room – what a relief not to be put in there! – and at last came to the end. Cassandra knew this room. It had been for many years the only home to poor Miss Murden, that friendless, captious burden on the family. 'All Contents Herein to Go to the Workhouse' said the sign pinned outside it. Any hopes Cassandra might have once had for her own comfort were adjusted at once.

Isabella ushered her in, lit the lamp by the

bedside and bade her goodnight. The significance of being put in here was not lost on Cassandra. It was chilly and unaired, the furniture basic. There was water in the washstand, but that too was cold. She passed a hand over the bedcover; there was no brick or bottle in there to warm it, and thought: There we are, then. I am their friendless burden now.

Her trunk stood unopened, but she would not yet unpack it. There was a flicker of life in her yet: no time like the present. She would begin her search for the letters. Cassandra moved back to the door, waited for the footsteps to fade and the house to fall silent, opened it and slid back to the landing. Through the shadows, she crept towards Isabella's mother's room; she had almost gained the threshold when a voice came from behind her.

'Can I help you, Miss Austen?' Dinah, lit from below by a weak tallow candle, stood at the foot of the stairs to the attic. 'Lost are we, m'm?'

'Oh, Dinah. I *am* sorry.' Cassandra put on a show of confusion. 'How strange. I cannot remember why I came out here.'

'It's tiredness, I'm sure of it. Best get to bed, m'm. Over that way, we are.' Dinah watched her, unsmiling. 'That's it. Goodnight then, Miss Austen.' And stayed in position until Cassandra was back in her room.

CHAPTER 2

Kintbury, March 1840

A white sky rushed past the windows; the bare branches of the big beech waved high in the wind. The two ladies watched it all from their table, at which Cassandra was enjoying her breakfast. This was always the meal to rely on when visiting; even the worst of kitchens found it hard to go wrong. And she needed all the strength she could muster for the day that lay ahead.

'This jam was made by my mother.' Isabella spooned out just enough for a scraping. 'She was so productive right till the end. We are still, even now, enjoying her food.'

Cassandra took another bite and Eliza was conjured up before her. She could taste her in the fruit, see her picking and stirring and laughing and pouring and thought: these are the things by which most of us are remembered, these small acts of love, the only evidence that we, too, once lived on this earth. The preserves in the larder, the stitch on the kneeler. *The mark of the pen on the page.*

'Now, my dear. What are your plans for the day?' Cassandra put down her muffin, all appetite gone. 'Am I right to hope that we might see your Aunt Mary this morning? I know that now she lives so close by, she calls here quite often.'

Isabella, who had until that moment seemed almost relaxed and nearly cheerful, adopted again her woeful air. 'Yes, really quite often. And I am sure it will be oftener still if she knows that *you* are here.'

'In fact . . .' Cassandra picked up her cup and, quite casual, as if it were nothing out of the ordinary, said: 'I do not know what is the matter with me. I am becoming so hopeless and forgetful. I do believe that I failed to write and tell her that I was.'

Isabella's blue eyes met hers. 'And I have not had a chance to mention it, either. Your letter arrived so late, there was not the time.'

'Then she does not yet know of my arrival.' Cassandra turned back to study the weather through the window. 'That is a shame.'

'And we cannot hope that my aunt might call today.' Isabella reached back to the jam and took a hearty dollop. 'On Tuesdays, Aunt Mary always takes tea with Mrs Bunbury.'

They smiled. There was a new sympathy between them. In the unlikely figure of Mary Austen – a woman not previously associated with the promotion of social harmony – they had found a common bond.

'Ah!' Cassandra felt a new lightness in her person. 'Then we cannot hope to have the pleasure before tomorrow at the earliest.' That she might be left in peace was now all that was required. 'While I am with you, I would dearly like to be of service. Having been in your position, I know how very much there is to do. Please. Let me be useful.'

There are women who offer to help, do everything required of them and can be relied upon to do so well. Historically, Cassandra was one of these. But there are also women – of whom she knew plenty – who appear to want to do everything for everyone, to put themselves in the centre of all operations, but whose excellent intentions are always to be met with some obstruction particular only to them. They are generally to be found on a sofa doing nothing, while the rest of the household flurries about. And on this day only, though it might rub at every fibre of her make-up, for the purposes of her mission Miss Austen was determined to be one of those.

'There is so much to do that I know not how to begin it,' sighed Isabella. 'It is all organising . . . arranging . . . sorting through. These are not the things that best suit my talents.'

Which were what exactly? Cassandra wondered. They were thus far mysterious. But she had an unshakeable belief in God's design of humanity: we all have our uses. She looked forward to Isabella's being revealed.

'Perhaps you might be so good as to help Dinah go through my mother's clothing?' Isabella continued. 'I confess I have not been able to touch any of her possessions, and nor could my father, from the day that she died.'

Dinah, who was at the sideboard with her back to the ladies, gave a loud sniff that was heavy with some sort of meaning.

'Of course!' Cassandra sat up in her chair, the picture of enthusiasm. 'Although' – as if the thought had suddenly occurred – 'I cannot be on my feet for too long. That would require so much standing and stretching.' She held out an arm, and then retracted it, wincing. It was quite the performance. Dinah turned and looked on with approval. 'Let us think. What else can I do?'

And so breakfast continued. Isabella served out suggestions; she batted them all back – her knees would not bend, her hands could not hold, the very mention of dust made her break into sneezes – until their napkins were folded, the table was cleared and the morning was set.

As the church bell chimed ten, Cassandra was at repose in the yellow drawing room. Tucked up with her valise in the corner of the sofa, work in her lap, needle in hand. It was all most satisfactory except for one thing: she had not yet been afforded the privacy she craved. The household was flurrying, certainly; unfortunately, it seemed only to flurry about her.

First, it was Fred come to lay a fire, a task to which he brought much resentment but no kindling. Cassandra watched him set a few logs smoking, gave generous thanks and waited until he withdrew. Might she now put down her needle? Dared she get up and begin her investigations? The bureau in the corner must be the first object of her attention. It was where Eliza, Isabella's mother and her own dear friend, sat at her correspondence each morning. Surely anything of importance would be in there . . . She moved to the edge of her seat. And then Dinah came in.

'Are you quite comfortable then, Miss Austen?' Having been spared the fate of a morning in the closet and left to her own slovenly devices, Dinah was suddenly all friendliness. Cloth in hand, she flicked dust hither and thither – from candlestick to clock to ornamental vase – and chattered on. 'It's quiet enough in here.' She picked up the cushion on which Cassandra's elbow rested and thumped it. 'Nobody to disturb you in whatever it is you're busy with.' Moving to the glass above the fireplace she added a smear to its impressive collection. 'Quiet everywhere in this house, since Mr Fowle departed, God rest his soul.'

Cassandra made noises of sympathy and reached for her thimble. She was clearly not to be left alone for a while.

'And we don't get the visitors now, either. No

parishioners coming here with their problems. No men from the Hunt or the Kennel traipsing through with mud on their boots.'

Dinah moved to the bureau and gave it an aimless rub. Would she now open it and reveal its contents? Cassandra sat up in anticipation.

'Oh, yes. Very quiet we are now. Quite filled the 'ouse with his presence, did the Reverend. Those rages of his! You could hear them in the village.' She shook her head, smiling fondly, and polished on – though without any beeswax. Cassandra had to suppress the urge to go and find some herself. 'Used to fair bellow at Miss Isabella. Bellow!' With a chuckle, Dinah turned her attention to the casement of the window. 'It was throwing his stick at her head that brought on that seizure. The exertion of it did for 'im, they say.' She stopped and gazed around at the product of her labours. 'Oh yes, it's a terrible loss, Miss Austen. A terrible loss for us all.'

With her work there done, her standards met, Dinah departed. But before Cassandra could begin to reflect on the horrors she had heard – that a man so fond of his dogs could mete out such treatment to his daughter! – Isabella herself sank down beside her with a sigh. Oh, Isabella! What had the poor woman been through? 'Are you all right, my dear?' Cassandra laid a hand on the younger woman's knee.

'I suppose so.' Isabella fiddled with a tassel on a pillow. 'It is just that I do not seem to know which way to turn. I was wrapping the china that is to go off to my brother, but then I took to wondering if there was not something else I should do . . .' She looked around her, helpless.

'But surely', said Cassandra, 'your sisters are helping you now?'

'Well, Elizabeth is so busy at her nursery . . .'

Cassandra held up her hand. 'Yes. I do understand.' It was always the same. No matter how big the family, the mantle of caregiver-organiser-helpmeet is only ever laid upon one. 'It is as if Nature can only throw up one capable person to support each generation. In my family, that has always been me.'

Isabella was a picture of misery. 'Then we are equals in our misfortune.'

'Not at all!' exclaimed Cassandra. 'Our fortune is to have families who need us. It is our duty, our pleasure. Our very worth!'

'Oh, Cassandra. I fear you have always been so much more useful than I will ever be.'

Cassandra had not been many hours in the vicarage, but she had been there long enough to assess the domestic skills of her hostess. So it was hard to argue, and almost impossible to control her desire to promote competence and order, to combat this depressing inefficiency. In kind and encouraging terms, she dispatched Isabella back to the china cupboard to finish what had been started and Isabella, sighing heavily, did as she was told.

Cassandra sat still and listened until the footsteps diminished and the door shut on the offices. Seizing the moment, she fastened her needle into the fabric, struggled out of the sofa and moved towards the corner.

Miss Austen was not used to intruding upon the privacy of others. Her heart hammered at her ribs. The unfamiliar discomfort of guilt was enough to halt her in her tracks. For a moment, she simply stared at the bureau. This delicate piece of walnut, with a lid that folded out into a table and three drawers below, had been Eliza's only private corner in these big, busy rooms. Fulwar, of course, had his gracious study, which no one would ever dare enter without permission. Did he keep any secrets in there? His own perhaps, but he would hardly be chosen as the guardian of others'. Eliza, though – the excellent Eliza – was a woman of boundless sympathy. They all knew they could trust her with any sort of confidence.

How many words of advice had been dispatched from that desktop? How many most personal matters had been read about there? It was impossible, now she studied that small piece of furniture, to imagine it could contain all Eliza knew . . . She began to doubt the course of her own actions; she almost determined to stop at that moment, to find a more decorous approach to the problem, one that she could take with her head held high. And then she collected herself. This was Austen business. Family always trumped all.

Both she and Jane had once written many intimate letters to this vicarage. They could still be there. Cassandra was the executor of her sister's estate: the keeper of her flame; the protector of her legacy. In the time that was left to her, she was determined to find and destroy any evidence that might compromise Jane's reputation. It was simply imperative that those letters did not fall into the wrong hands.

Emboldened, she stepped forward and pulled down the lid. She saw only ink and paper, a pen. She shut it and opened the first drawer: locks of baby hair, first teeth, a handful of childish sketches. Footsteps approached. She pulled out the next one: laundry lists, menus, membership details for the circulating library. Someone was crossing the hall. The last held just records of charities and village good works. All of it orderly, neatly arranged; none of it that which Cassandra hoped she might find. She closed it as Fred crossed the threshold. 'I was just stretching my poor legs.'

Fred nodded, uninterested. He had not come to see her, but to check his own handiwork. The fire, which had started out so disappointing, was disappointing still. He assessed it with some degree of professional satisfaction, as if disappointment itself was the one true ambition, and, with a limp bow, left Cassandra alone with the chill.

She returned to the sofa, gathering her work and her wits about her. She must not despair.

26

After all, what had Isabella said over breakfast? That they had not been able to touch any of Eliza's possessions from the day she had died. Everything could still be here somewhere: she just needed more information before continuing her search.

There was not long to wait. Within minutes, Isabella was back with her. 'I have done it. I have finished most of the china. Well' – she twisted her hands in her lap – 'some of the china. I have packed *all* the sauce boats – every single one.'

Cassandra had lived all her life with or around the country clergy. She was well aware how many sauce boats the average parsonage might hope to accumulate and the answer was: few. 'Ah. Well, that is indeed something.' This was rather like dealing with the children in the Godmersham nursery. 'So that leaves only the dinner plates, the dessert plates, the bowls, all the dishes . . .?'

'And the tea and coffee sets and so on,' Isabella added, her shoulders sinking. 'There is so much of all that, I thought it might wait for another day?' She paused, as if Cassandra – of all people – might endorse such procrastination. Then she confessed: 'The truth is that I find, now I have arrived at the moment, it pains me to part with it.' Tears came to her eyes. 'I have used this service every day of my life. It suddenly seemed so' – she sniffed – 'so significant. And I know you must think me pathetic – I see myself as pathetic – I can hardly bear to think I will not see it again.'

27

Cassandra reached out her hand and grasped Isabella's. Oh, the power of small things when the larger ones – the home or the family – proved fragile! She remembered Miss Murden polishing her little blue shepherdess, and Jane clutching her writing box, not wanting to let go.

'I do know, Isabella. Leave that till last and now, do sit and chat for a while. I have been feeling so guilty lounging here while you have been *labouring*. Is there nothing I can do for you that involves more sitting, less lifting? Anything in your father's office, for example?' Though she did not want to be in his office at all.

'That is all in order, as far as I know. For the past year, Papa was making his arrangements and, of course, he had his curate to help him. Such a conscientious young man, so thorough in his work.' She looked wistful. 'It is most useful to have a curate, Cassandra, is it not? Indeed, now I think of that too, I have never lived without a curate around.' The pallor returned. 'I suppose I shall have to get used to it now.'

Cassandra again was all sympathy. For the family – and most especially for its single women – to leave a vicarage was to be cast out of Eden. There was only trial and privation ahead.

'And, of course, Papa had due warning. He knew the end was coming. Poor Mama just left us. It was the work of a moment.'

'So very sad.' Cassandra reached down for her sewing. 'And her papers? Could I help you with

28

those? It would not be an intrusion. We were such friends and for so many years.'

'Thank you, but no. Aunt Mary has expressly requested that she do all that. Her son, James-Edward, is developing a keen interest in the family history, I gather. He talks even of one day writing a book on the subject!' She raised her eyes to the ceiling at such folly. 'As if the world does not already have too many books in it.' She smiled, confident of finding total agreement. 'And as if anyone would want to learn about *Austens*, indeed.'

Cassandra smiled back. 'My dear, I could not agree more. As you know, I could not be more devoted to my family and its memories, but even I must admit we are a quite splendidly dull bunch, to whom nothing of interest occurred.' This was just as she feared. It was imperative that Mary did not get to those letters first.

Isabella continued: 'My aunt feels very strongly that it should be her responsibility to go through the family papers and decide what to keep – her responsibility alone. She still grieves for my mother most deeply. She says it is infinitely more painful to lose a sister than a parent, but I would not know.'

Cassandra stabbed at her patchwork to release her irritation. No matter whose body lay in the coffin, Mary Austen would always appoint Mary Austen chief mourner. 'And has she yet begun?'

'Not quite yet, no. She certainly means to, but is, of course, horribly busy. Somehow she has so much more to do than the rest of us. Something seems always to get in her way.'

With a renewed energy, Cassandra suggested that Isabella set out into the village: a reward for her hard morning's work. There was the briefest attempt at resistance – Dinah was already out running errands; it would be so rude to leave their guest all alone – but one easily conquered. Isabella was soon off in search of her cloak and her bonnet. And at last it seemed that Cassandra might just have the house to herself.

She packed away her things, picked up her valise and went out into the hall. All was quiet. Halfway up the stairs, she stopped to look out of the window. There was nobody in the garden or down at the riverbank. Up on the landing, she listened again – was there a daily maid who had not yet been made visible? Someone at work in the upstairs rooms? Cassandra could not feel an extra presence, though there was clearly much to be done. She crossed over and into the old day nursery; then she peered out of the back window. There was Fred, in a sheltered corner of the once glorious poultry yard. Scrawny birds pecked in the dirt, while he chewed on tobacco and whittled a stick.

Cassandra had long admired this vicarage as the very model of domestic efficiency. It had always been run just as she herself would have run it, had her life worked out in that way. So she was quite shocked by the new sloth and general indifference of everyone left here, the ease with which the household had simply fallen apart. She itched to get control of it: for the sake of Eliza's reputation, it could not be handed on to the next incumbent in this sorry state. And she would do so – but later. For now, this chaos suited her purpose. With a more confident step, she set off for the mistress's room.

The door was open, as if Eliza had just left it. The bed was still made with her patchwork quilt, her nightcap waited for her by the lamp on the drawers. Brushes and combs were laid out on the dressing table by the window; ribbons trailed down from the pedestal glass; a nightgown hung over the back of the chair. Cassandra sat down heavily on the ornate oak settle against the wall, quite affected by the tableau around her: of living life paralysed; a frozen, suspended moment in time.

She studied the samplers on the walls that Eliza had chosen to wake up to each morning: simple prayers and mottos stitched by childish hands. 'There is no place like home', she read, and shook her head: so trite, and really, very poorly sewn. How very odd of Eliza to first mount and then live with them. But then these were the indignities that motherhood entailed: women of taste forced to cherish that which did not deserve to be tolerated. One of the many blessings of the spinster state was that at least one's walls were one's own. The thought quite revived her. She rose and continued her search.

There was nothing under the bed but dust balls.

31

Nothing in the wardrobe but moths and clothes. Though the ottoman held promise, it contained only bed linen. She looked around and her eye was caught by that settle. What an old, ugly piece it was. It was surely brought into the house by the first generation of Fowles, but a big, heavy bench made from such a coarse dark wood was quite out of place in the bedchamber of a cultured, modern lady . . . and with a flash, Cassandra understood at once why it was there.

She crossed the room, took the long flat cushion from the seat, put it on the floor and, with some awkwardness, knelt on it. The strain of lifting the lid was almost too much for her. She had to press hard, harder than she once believed herself capable. Her pulses throbbed. Then, suddenly, her struggle was rewarded. With a loud creak, it surrendered and revealed to her its contents. The search was over. She gripped the wood and looked down.

Laid out before her were the letters of a lifetime.

Dinner that night was hard to identify – uniformly pale and not at all pleasant. Cassandra suspected she had witnessed its last moments in the filth in the Kintbury back yard, but otherwise took little interest in what she was eating. She had only one concern for the evening and that was to get to her own room as swiftly as possible, lock herself in and return to the letters.

'I cannot think why I am so tired.' She placed her cutlery down on a plate as empty as she could manage it. 'I have done very little today, compared with you, Isabella. And yet I fear I shall soon have to turn in.'

She did not anticipate any objections. After all, silence and absence passed as politeness in unwanted guests and friendless burdens. Poor Miss Murden spent most of her life pretending to be happy alone in that room. So she was taken aback by Isabella's reaction.

'Oh, please not yet, Cassandra! I shall not sleep for hours and that will leave me all alone!' Isabella had returned from her trip to the village flushed and merry and her new mood had lasted right until that moment. Now, she was slumped once more in dejection. 'I am very bad on my own with nothing to do.'

'Forgive me, my dear. How thoughtless. Of course, I shall sit with you if that is what you would like.' Cassandra would manage it all somehow. One required so much less sleep in old age; she would stay up reading all night if needs must. What worried her more was this new evidence of Isabella's dependency. Very bad on her own? She was a single woman! Solitude was an inescapable part of her very condition.

They rose from the table and walked through to the drawing room, and tea. 'I have been meaning to ask you, dear Isabella. What arrangements have you made for your own future?'

'It is not yet quite decided what is to become of me.' Isabella poured, and passed cup and saucer.

'But you will, of course, be living with one of your sisters.' Cassandra could not help but be irked by this abject self-pity. Not every single woman was blessed with family to rely on. 'I merely wondered which one and where?'

'Oh, they will take me in, I suppose, if that is what I decide. I shall squash into Mary-Jane's cottage or together Elizabeth and I could take a small house in the village, which I shall keep while she never comes home. That was my father's last request, most explicit. His feelings were very strong on the matter. His feelings were, as you know, very strong in general and I have not once, in my history, done anything that might displease him. But in this instance alone, I – well – I, for once, have my own feelings to consider.'

Cassandra was aghast. To deny a father's dying request? And to what possible end? After all, these women were *sisters*. There was no closer bond on this earth. 'Either appears to me to be the most splendid solution, for which you should be perhaps a little more grateful.'

'*Grateful!*'

'Indeed. And if you can add to your own comfort the knowledge that you are there in accordance with your dear father's wish for you, then the outcome can only be a happy one – for everyone concerned.'

'Yes, there is the rub: my dear father's wish for

me. I have no real choice but to comply. But I confess it is not a future to which I can look forward with any enthusiasm. What a pitiful scene we shall make.'

Cassandra sipped at her tea, quite lost for words. It was not the first time that she had heard this assumption: that the divine blessing of a male presence somehow made a household more desirable, superior. But to hear it from a woman who had suffered sticks to the head? Now, that was a novelty indeed! Isabella had clearly not grasped the truth of her own situation: her sisters *were* her future; single women have *only* each other. For many, mutual support was their only means of financial survival, but for most it brought other riches with it: a whole wealth of comfort, companionship and joy. Isabella must learn this; Cassandra must teach her. It was something else to be accomplished before she left here.

'It will all fall into place, I am sure of it. Now' – Cassandra was bright but firm – 'let us read together to take our minds off it all. I am not convinced these long, silent evenings of unemployment are entirely good for you. There are no spirits so low that a good novel cannot raise them.'

'A novel?' Isabella put down her saucer with a rattle. 'I believe I already mentioned: I do not enjoy novels.'

'I am not suggesting we drag ourselves through *Peveril of the Peak*. That is no remedy for anything at all. I was thinking of one of my sister's. You already know them, I am sure.'

Isabella shook her head, and showed no enthusiasm. 'I believe my mother read and enjoyed them. But Papa did not permit them to be read aloud – or not that I remember. He had heard they were not of much interest.' She thought, and added: 'But then I never found much of interest in Sir Walter Scott.'

'My dear Isabella.' Cassandra reached down, opened her valise and brought out the one book that never left her. 'Now your father is no longer here to offer guidance and wisdom in all the many matters on which he was so *very* expert, I think it may be time for you to embark on the development of your own tastes.' She opened it at the beginning. 'Of course, I am prejudiced, but I believe you might enjoy this.' It did not now matter that her eyes were old and the lamplight was dim. Cassandra knew every word of it by heart:

'*Sir Walter Elliot, of Kellynch Hall, in Somersetshire, was a man . . .*'

Isabella sat, studying the flames in the fireplace and listening, but with no outward sign of enjoyment. The Baronetage clearly bored her. She fidgeted, sighing loudly from time to time.

Undeterred, Cassandra went on: '*Three girls, the two eldest sixteen and fourteen, was an awful legacy for a mother to bequeath; an awful charge rather, to confide to the authority and guidance of a conceited, silly father . . .*'

Pyramus showed his belly to the fire and let out a snore. But her human listener, Cassandra noticed with some satisfaction, had grown still.

'. . . *she was only Anne . . .*'

Isabella's eyes were now upon her, she could sense it.

'. . . *her bloom had vanished early . . .*'

It might have been fond imagining, but Cassandra was almost certain that her reluctant little audience was now quite in her grasp. Nevertheless, the act of performance was tiring and there was still much to do before she could rest. After four chapters, she put down *Persuasion* and looked up: the Enemy of the Novel did not seem quite as ferociously hostile as before.

'Are we to stop there? Oh! Well, thank you, Cassandra. To my surprise, I found it rather enjoyable. Anne is a very pleasant sort of person, sensible – quite the right sort of heroine to my mind. There is not so much drama about her as in other books. I do not appreciate too much drama myself, and fail to understand why it should be so often written about. After all, there is so little drama in life, is there not? Please, before you go up, do reassure me: does it all turn out well for her? Is there a happy ending in store?'

'My sister did not write desultory novels, Isabella – that was just one aspect of her genius.' Cassandra put the book back in the valise. 'But what would constitute a happy ending, in your view?'

'Well, marriage, of course!' Isabella retorted. 'What other sort is there?'

Cassandra looked up, raised an eyebrow and paused. She could now protest and proclaim, saying: Look at me, Isabella! I have known happiness. Without man or marriage, I found a happiness, true and sublime! But who would believe her? She was now an old woman and such proclamations were really not in her style.

'Ah.' She spoke mildly instead, using the arm of the chair to push herself upright. 'Then what a tragedy that the world has so many unmarried women in it, if there is no route to any possible happiness open to them.' She took the hand that Isabella offered and together they walked through to the foot of the staircase. 'Goodnight, my dear. We will pick up Anne's story tomorrow evening. And I promise all will be revealed before I leave.'

In bed – washed, changed, her long grey hair plaited – Cassandra leaned back with relief upon the tough bolster and took a minute to luxuriate in the privacy of her bare little room. She was tired from the day, and quite exhausted by Isabella. But there would be little sleep that night. Work must be done.

Cassandra had been relieved, when she went through the settle, to see dear Eliza had done most of her work for her: all correspondence had been individually arranged, tied into packets with a pale blue ribbon. On the top were all the letters from Eliza's many children. Cassandra had rummaged beneath. She came, in passing, across those from her own mother, but was sure there would be nothing in there to detain her. She knew the detail without even looking: expert notes on animal husbandry, helpful tips for confinement, dramatic details of her many, minor illnesses. She had leaned in further, hands delving deeper. A huge bundle from Martha – dear Martha! – formed an obstruction. She lifted it out, put it to the side; revealed was a hand that was both immediately familiar and yet hard to place. It was a long moment before the force of the truth hit her: that she was face to face with the evidence of her own happy, girlish self. She shook a little, and sighed. They must be examined at some point, but were not her main quarry. She took them out, and there below – a rich rush of love flooded through her – was the writing of Jane.

She had touched it and gasped. Her sister had been dead for so many years; in Chawton all her effects were cleared long ago. There had been a time when Cassandra – grief raw and still smarting – would stumble across some little trace and the slow-healing wound would break open. Then, for hours, she could do nothing but cradle and weep over some inanimate object, as she had once cradled and wept over the corpse. But all that had passed. The pain had abated. The practical was here her concern.

Cassandra had sharpened her wits, gathered everything of interest and come up with a clear plan of action. She returned to her room and hid it all under the mattress. Her own correspondence could stay there until she had time to peruse it. First, and as soon as was possible, she would deal with the letters of Jane.

But now the moment was upon her, she found that her resolution was dwindling. Cassandra reached over the coverlet and picked up the packet. Surely this should be a joy, to spend hours basking once again in the company of her sister? And yet she quailed at the prospect. She fell back onto the tough bolster. How much easier it would be to spend her last years in the present, rather than to confront her whole life in the round. Oh, to be allowed to dwindle away in Chawton, worrying about nothing but the roses and the chickens and the church.

Alas, there was not that option. This, her last duty, was the very cost of her privilege. Cassandra steeled herself, prepared her mind to be carried back through that mist of forgetting to the world that had once been their own.

She unfolded the paper, and began to read.

CHAPTER 3

Steventon Rectory
1st May, 1795

My dear Eliza,

You must find it in your heart to forgive the tardiness of my reply to your letter. The truth is that our once peaceful Rectory has lately been consumed by such a riot of celebration, that it is hard to find a quiet place in which one can write. I have just now crawled into the corner of the dressing room, which – for the moment, at least – is mercifully free of members of my family, noisily embracing and shedding tears of pure happiness. And I have shut the door firmly, in the vain hope of keeping the rioters at bay. Really, Eliza: there is so much joy and delight about as to make me feel quite sick and wicked.

I cannot quite remember how I once passed my time in the days before my sister's engagement. But it appears that, from now on, nothing more is required of me than to congratulate others, as often as my poor

41

breath will allow – my mother and father on the perfection of the match; Cassy on the perfection of her future husband; Tom Fowle on the perfections of his bride. Then when I have finished, it seems, I have to start all over again . . . And it occurs to me that, before I die from the exhaustion of it all, I should be congratulating you, too, my dear Eliza.

After all, once this momentous wedding has finally taken place, then Cassy will be a Fowle, and you will share with me the honour of calling her your sister. And you cannot know what delights are in store! She is the best, the cleverest, the kindest and most caring sister on this earth. And, should you occasionally be minded to say something witty, I guarantee that she will laugh until she is spent.

Of course, our insufferably happy couple must suffer a long engagement. A curate must always be patient; a curate's bride even more so. Economy is as ever at war with Romance. But one day, Tom's luck must change and they will be wed. I shall be so pleased for them then – but more than a little sorry for myself. For if there is a drawback to this perfect arrangement – and I should not dare to mention such a possibility in the hearing of my triumphant family – it is that I now have somehow to live without her. So felicitations to you, Eliza, and to all the Fowle family.

For you are the victors. Yes, we have the comfort of knowing that Cass will always be happy. But <u>you</u> will have her – and she is the best of us! – close by you, always.

Do look after her. She is so precious to me.

Yours affectionately,
J. Austen.

It was a deeply ordinary Wednesday afternoon in the Steventon Rectory. Cassy was intent on her embroidery, Jane on her letters at the table by the window, Mrs Austen nodding off over a sock yet undarned, when Tom Fowle burst without notice into the parlour.

'My love, I have news,' he announced, breathless, to his astonished fiancée. 'Great news! And I have come to tell you in person.' Tom grabbed Cassy's hand, greeted her family, begged for their privacy and pulled her through the house to the garden.

It was now September, the day brisk and brittle. Cassy had to skip to keep up with his stride.

'Well then, am I to hear it?' she asked of him, delighted and laughing. 'Dearest? What is this great revelation?'

In truth, she was not expecting to be told of any important development, but was merely indulging his mood. Her Tom she knew to be more tortoise than hare, not known for his shocks and surprises – or, at least, not hitherto.

'Wait just a moment.' Tom steered her further

up the Elm Walk. 'Wait until we are under our tree.'

Six months had passed since he had proposed to her there: months that Cassy had spent at the peak of contentment. She had discovered that favour in the family and fame in the neighbourhood which an engagement entailed, and was basking in it. She knew patience was required of her, and she delivered it without effort. There was no great imperative to rush on to the next stage, as far as she was concerned.

But Tom felt quite differently. The prospect of marriage had engendered within him the first stirrings of ambition. And it transpired that he did not, after all, share her appetite for waiting. He was suddenly keen to get on, get his hands on a living to which he could take his young bride.

They reached their spot. Tom stopped and turned to face Cassy.

'Last week, I had an interview with Lord Craven' – Tom seemed to inflate as he spoke – 'in which he agreed – oh, my dear love! – he agreed to act as my patron!'

His own family had nothing to offer him. Tom had, early on in life, committed the cardinal sin of being born second and for that he was now keen to atone.

'Tom! That is great news indeed.'

Cassy had often heard talk of Lord Craven, a neighbour of the Fowles and some sort of relation. He was young, rich and landed, with a powerful personality, or so it was said. Of course, she had not had the privilege of ever seeing him in person. But this she did know, for by now she had read a great many novels: such august creatures, born so entitled, could not always be trusted.

'And has he made you an offer?'

'Yes! He has made me an offer.'

Cassy's heart leaped. 'A living?' Already! So soon! 'We are to have our own vicarage?'

Tom smiled down at her. 'My love, yes.' He then paused to gather his words. 'In time. But first, he has asked me – and I have agreed – to accompany him on his next expedition.'

'Expedition?' Her mind conjured a few weeks stalking in Scotland, or sailing, perhaps, in the Solent.

'His lordship is leading a contingent of his regiment to the Windward Isles, shortly. I did not quite grasp his business down there. At the time, as you can imagine, I was quite overcome by the whole situation. Never before have I been alone with a man of such—'

'The Windward . . . But, Tom' – fear gripped her – 'they are in the West Indies.'

'So they tell me. I should not be gone more than a year.'

'Gone for more than a year . . .' Cassy repeated, her voice trailing away.

'I will be paid very well; beyond anything I can make if I stay here. And he has promised an excellent position on our return. We shall be set! In just a year! Cassy, without this, we should have waited much longer.'

'Yes, indeed. We had agreed, we were prepared to . . . It would have been hard, but at least we would have waited in safety. Surely there are risks involved in this scheme?' Had he promised all this without thinking? Simply because *Lord Craven* had asked it?

'I am to go as his private chaplain. Not too onerous a task, I am sure you agree!'

Cassy was struck dumb. His was not a naturally adventurous spirit. She had accepted a curate. Moreover, she was *happy* with a curate. Who was this new, seafaring, Romantic hero?

He kissed her hand. 'My Cassy. See this as my investment in our future security. The ship leaves from Portsmouth in a fortnight. I have come to say my goodbyes.'

The Austen family was sensitive to the young lovers' situation and, where possible, afforded them the privacy they deserved. On Tom's last morning, Cassy came down to a household that was already hectic. She knew her work for the day. She went straight to the parlour where her sister was sewing. Their brother, Frank, was now in the navy and needed new shirts. The two girls had been stitching their finest and fastest to get them done in time. Cassy made for her usual chair, but Jane, laughing, shooed her away.

She went through to the offices and her next

pressing task of the morning: the bottling of the orange wine. If it was not done soon, there would be none for Christmas. This was urgent work indeed. Her mother was already there – apron on, face flushed, hair escaping from under her cap. And Cassy's friend Martha was with her!

'You are not needed here, Cass.' Mrs Austen took a measure of muslin. 'I have a fine helper come from Ibthorpe for exactly this purpose.' She peered through the scullery window. 'There is a good morning out there. You and Tom should seize it.'

Dear Martha – who always got the most happiness from enabling the happiness of others, who had never once known the pleasure of a walk with a young gentleman in crisp winter weather – first embraced and then directed her out of the room.

The day was, in fact, a little unsettled, but they wrapped up well and did as they were bid. The garden was sodden, the fields unpassable, but, though the mud was building, the Church Walk was still just good enough. Cassy balanced on her pattens. Once out of sight of the rectory, Tom gave her his arm.

It was a poignant outing for both. Tom Fowle had come to live with the family in his sixteenth year, to be educated by Mr Austen. Here he had learned and grown up and become loved by all at the rectory. But from the beginning, his one, particular companion, with whom he shared an especial sympathy, was Cassy. For years, they had been walking these lanes together, since she was a girl and he only on the cusp of manhood. As they grew, Cassy's beauty bloomed to the point at which she was just the more handsome; her height stopped short of his at the requisite number of inches: they appeared to any beholder as the perfect young couple. Tom was already thought of as part of the family. Steventon was his home almost as much as it was hers.

'I shall miss this place,' he said grimly.

'Oh, Tom. It – we – I shall miss you.'

And then they talked – as they always talked when they were alone, without anyone else to tease them – about their joint future in minutest detail. Her favourite topic above all was their children. How she longed, how she ached for her arms to feel the warmth and weight of her own babies. It was what she was born for, she knew: to be surrounded by infants; to nurture; to care. They went through the naming process – her first girl would be Jane, after her sister, which she thought perfectly reasonable; his first son would be Fulwar, after his brother, which she rather did not – and moved on to the place that would be home to these offspring. And here the conversation took a more awkward turn.

'Unless we are in Shropshire, of course,' Tom was saying, quite casually.

'Shropshire!' Cassy could not stop herself gasping. The skies had turned grey; there was a smattering of rain. They were sheltering under the oak in front of the Digweeds' house. Water dripped around them from the few remaining leaves.

'Why, yes. Lord Craven said so himself.' He inflated again. 'Are there no limits to his influence? Not content with half Berkshire, he also has an estate out there, too!'

Since the moment of their engagement, Cassy had been planning her future in Berkshire. In all her fond imaginings – in those whimsical sketches a romantic young woman must somehow produce in her few idle afternoon moments – there had always been brick and flint cottages, gentle undulations, a parsonage solid and square. And in the background, off the page somewhere, there were Fowles close by and – this was important – Austens not *too* far. Surely that was the arrangement? She felt quite unsteady.

'It is good country around there,' Tom offered, but then immediately doubted it. 'Is it not? Yes, I am sure someone has told me . . . Who was it now?' Cassy knew that Tom had never developed a particular attachment to detail. 'I *think* I believe I *have* heard that said.'

'Yes. I think perhaps I too have heard that.' In fact, nobody around Cassy had ever testified to the goodness or otherwise of the country in *Shropshire*, not once in her life. She was certain of it. 'It is just that . . . surely . . . the very great thing you are doing in joining the expedition . . . the prize would be . . . Well, we will be a little further away than I had imagined, that is all . . .'

'Ah!' He brightened. 'Yes.' He was triumphant. A fact had suddenly occurred to him. 'I do know the living to be convenient for Ludlow.'

Convenient for Ludlow. Cassy thought for a while, and did try to find that consoling. She was always amenable, never known to be difficult, but even she could not find much consolation in *Ludlow*.

'Well, reasonably convenient, at least.' Tom looked vague again; confidence in his great fact was quickly diminishing. 'Quite how convenient I am not at all sure.'

Cassy had lived all her life in Hampshire: to her it was God's own country. She had been brave about Berkshire, accepting of her fate. Of course she must marry, Tom Fowle would be her husband – it was her destiny; indeed, her own good fortune – and so Berkshire it must be. That was quite exotic enough for Cassy. That was the limit of her own adventurous spirit. But Shropshire! That was foreign indeed.

A loud sigh escaped her. 'I was just thinking of my family – our families – and the possibilities of visiting.'

'Ah, of course. Yes. Our families . . .' Tom pondered, while Cassy marvelled that he had not thought of this sooner. 'Well, with God's blessing, we will soon have our own family to concern us. Wherever we live will become our home, will it not?'

'But we will still love them all! Even though we

will have each other, and – God willing – children of our own. I cannot imagine how we will ever see our families again regularly, for we shall be several – many – days away.' Cassy's mind, as always, turned at once to the practical. Her talent was for finding solutions, but on this she could see only difficulties – or, worse, realities, harsh and insuperable. How could her sister ever come to visit her? Which brother would give up all that time to escort her there? They could face years of separation! How could they bear it? What would Jane *do*?

Tom held out his upturned palm to check the rain was abating. 'It may not come to that,' he said. 'Let us not even discuss it. After all, I do have to get to and from the Windward Isles first.'

Immediately she was chastened, horrified, overcome by the force of her own selfishness. How dare she quail at the imaginary perils of England when he was off to face the real perils of heavens knew where?

He led her back on to the lane. 'We should not pick away at our own contentment, even before it is achieved. And I know myself to be happy anywhere, with you by my side.'

Cassy resolved, again, not to think about it, nor mention it to Jane. It would be bad for her sister's nerves, cast down her spirits. Why worry her with rumour before it had become fact? They joined arms, walked and their conversation picked up again: they would like one cow for the household, a pony for the children; Tom would no longer hunt, once married with a living: it meant too much time away from his work – and *his wife*. She blushed, and melted: dear, *dearest* Tom. He would still like to fish, though, if she would not mind it. She gave him her blessing; he thanked her. For he felt a particular peace on the riverbank, with a rod in his hand.

It was a cheerful party that gathered in the evening. The Austens were always cheerful, in the face of whatever life fancied to throw at them. Cheerfulness and good humour were the Austen way.

'That's a fine pair of sea legs you have there, Tom Fowle, so you need not fret on their account.' Mrs Austen, who had earlier dispatched a full plate of veal pie and dumplings, was now swelling gently in the chair by the fire. 'I merely have to look at a man to judge him a sailor or no. It is a talent I have, never once known to fail me. And you will have no trouble. I shall stake my reputation upon it. You, my boy, are a sailor. I can see it at once.'

'Oh, I assure you I have no concerns on that score.' Tom was also flushed and benign after the feast that had been prepared for him. Cassy looked at him sharply. Since signing up, he had assumed a new masculine swagger – expected in most men, quite ill suited to him. 'After all, I have lived *by* water all of my life.'

She felt quietly mortified. Her sister, beside her,

was stifling her giggles. And her brothers just loudly guffawed.

'You live on *the dear old River Kennet*!' cried Henry, slapping his thigh.

'It is not known for its high tides and breakers,' James added.

'Oh, but do remember, Brother, that day we had punting.' Henry, when he met with an opportunity for comedy, was always reluctant to let it move on. 'Those water lilies we came up against were the very devil itself!'

'Well may you tease, boys,' cut in their mother, reproaching. 'I went on a punt once on the Cherwell and quite feared for my own life. And my point was', she went on, determined to get the conversation on to a kinder, happier note, 'that Tom will sail there and back with no difficulty. And before we know it, this beloved young couple will be wed and in a house of their own.' She shifted uncomfortably in her seat. Cassy feared for her digestion later. 'I always knew you would not be a curate for ever, dear Tom. Fate never stands in the way of the promotion of happiness. Mark my words: the Lord doth provide.'

'If not *the* Lord, a lord – my esteemed patron,' Tom replied proudly. 'And indeed,' he looked across, smiling at Cassy, 'we shall be established – in Berkshire or Shropshire – ere too long.'

'Shropshire?' Jane's voice came out at a strange high pitch. She looked alarmed, then self-conscious, and shrugged carelessly. 'But – Oh, please, remove Cassy as far as you want, Tom. Why settle for Shropshire? Surely you can pick somewhere even more wild and inconvenient? Go further north! You can take her to Ireland, for all it bothers me.'

'Oh, no!' Tom leaped in at once, looking worried. 'Not Ireland! I should not like the snakes there. I am really quite fearful . . .'

At that, even the young ladies could only erupt into laughter and – because their mother preferred they did not laugh too loudly in company – collapsed into each other to smother the noise.

'Dear Tom.' Henry slapped his shoulder. 'You never fail us. Let me be the first to break it to you: it is said there are no snakes in Ireland! Is that not excellent news?'

James, a parson too now, with a healthy, if ponderous, appetite for preaching, cleared his throat and began in lugubrious tones: 'Legend has it that Saint Patrick—'

Henry at once cut him off. 'Thank you, James. We are all well acquainted with the saints and their miracles. Ha! All except one of us, that is. Who in this room will claim responsibility for Tom Fowle's education?'

Mr Austen, in his seat by the window, looked up from his book. 'I did my best,' he said mildly. 'We got you to Oxford, Tom, did we not? Fortunately, the dons cared less about the geography of reptiles and more for his Latin.'

Tom smiled over at Cassy again. 'And you helped

me so much with that.' Cassy blushed back at him. They used to work for hours together, after Tom had spent the morning in the attic schoolroom. The gerund would elude him, while she grasped it at once. But how touching of him to speak up and give her the credit. Not all young men would be so generous. This was the old Tom she knew.

Mrs Austen took another sip of wine, and the pink of her cheeks deepened. 'It has all worked out splendidly,' she proclaimed with great satisfaction. 'We could not be more pleased for you both. We are so very fond of you and your dear family, Tom, as well you know. And – remember this, when you are off crossing the Seven Seas – you will never find a better peach to pick than our Cassy. She is a wonder, make no mistake. Such an accomplished young lady as my *eldest* daughter will always be an asset to any young man.'

'Here it comes,' Jane said to Cassy, under her breath.

Cassy whispered back, with a tragi-comic countenance, impersonating their mother: 'But poor Jane . . .'

'But poor Jane,' began Mrs Austen with a sigh. Delight burst out of her daughters. Her voice had to be still further raised: 'We are not so sure what will become of her.'

'Mama,' urged Cassy gently, through her laughter. 'Jane *is* with us. Here. In the room.'

'I am merely saying that when a young woman is exceptionally competent—'

55

'Oh, Mama,' Jane protested. 'One can have a surfeit of competence.'

'Quite so, Jane, quite so. *If* one happens to marry a man on ten thousand a year. Should one fail to find such a thing, should even *you* end up like Cassy and myself, married to a man of the Church with a large family and limited resources, you will not have the luxury of dismissing those qualities. Your father will tell you how often I, through my hard work and efficiencies, have kept the wolf from our door.'

Mr Austen, now closing his book and rising to his feet, was in no mind to do any such thing. 'We are blessed with two brilliant daughters, Mrs Austen – if perhaps that brilliance manifests itself differently in each. And I should think any man would feel lucky to have either.'

'Thank you, Papa, for that glowing testimonial.' Jane nodded up at her father.

Tom beamed. 'I certainly am.'

'And now,' proclaimed the Reverend George Austen, as if from his pulpit, 'we have but a few hours left with our future son-in-law. I believe some music is called for, do not you agree?'

Jane leaped to her piano; the men moved the sofa. And Tom and Cassy danced their last dance for a while.

It was still dark when the coach came the next morning. At the doorway, George Austen shook Tom's hand briskly, wished him Godspeed and

– ever the schoolmaster – urged him to record in a journal all those wonders of the world he was to be lucky enough to witness. Was there envy in those older eyes? Cassy fancied she could see it. Her father had himself once had a lust for adventure that life had not chosen to satisfy. How she wished, for his sake, that Tom Fowle was made of the same cloth! Was there ever a man less suited to ship life, to campaigning in strange, far-off islands, than her beloved, cautious young curate? What a cruel twist of fate that he – of all of them – should have been chosen for this.

Her father withdrew and, pulling her shawl around her, Cassy stepped out into the cold for the final farewell. It was tender, and poignant: an awful moment that each pledged to remember for ever. She closed her eyes as he kissed her hand for the last time. And at once he was in the coach, the door was slammed and the horses were trotting. Cassy watched them all disappear. Yes, she was moved. She was a young woman bidding farewell to her fiancé. Of course the lump was in her throat, the tears in her eyes. And yet she also – much to her relief – felt a rush of confidence for which she had not dared to hope. Cassy was already a woman of strong and firm instincts. And she felt then, somewhere deep in her marrow, in the blood that was now warming her cheeks, that he would come back to her. She *knew* she would one day see him again.

The wind got up soon after he left. The Austens

watched the storm from the rectory window and thought of that young man at sea in cruel weather for the very first time. Lord Craven and his Buffs set off as agreed, but the conditions were terrible; they faced disaster. After sleepless nights, which Cassy passed listening to the gales roaring around her and doubted, cursed, her – and in particular her mother's – earlier assurance, a letter arrived. Addressed to Miss Austen. In Eliza Fowle's hand.

Fingers trembling, Cassy opened it.

CHAPTER 4

Kintbury Vicarage
24th November, 1795

My dear Cassandra,

I know you must be consumed with worry, as have we – oh, the horror of it – so let me tell you at once: we have this minute had news of Tom. My dear Cass, he is safe! And even now on dry land. The household is all jubilation, grateful prayers and relief.

We had heard such stories – of the hurricane hitting the fleet in the Channel, the ships scattering, the bodies washing up on the shore – and we had quite given up all hope that Tom might be delivered back to us. But we – and you, and our Tom of course – are the lucky ones. The Buffs somehow – we know not yet the ways and the wherefores – limped back into Portsmouth and disembarked yesterday. All the men are unharmed – thank the Lord! – though the poor ship has suffered. The voyage is perforce abandoned while she is repaired, and they will set sail again in January.

And so we are doubly blessed! Tom will be home again in Kintbury as early as next week. I have spoken to Mrs Fowle and it is agreed, if your own family will permit it: we would be so happy if you, Cassy, would be so kind as to join us here for the festive season? To have both you and Tom with us . . . It would be our own Christmas miracle! Please write and tell me you will.

Your hopeful friend,
E. Fowle.

Cassy was spinning. One week she was in Steventon and the next suddenly in Kintbury, with no sort of notice at all. Never had she known life to move so fast. By the moment of arrival, she was quite beside herself. Was this what they called giddiness? She had never knowingly been giddy before.

It had been decided that her brother James should escort her, and he was delighted to do so. For all the Fowle boys, not just Tom, had been educated in Steventon and played together with the Austens like a litter of puppies. As soon as their coach hit the Kintbury gravel, the Fowles had all swarmed out to greet it. James swung open the door and jumped down even as the horses were slowing. There was a lot of loud welcome, hearty hand-shaking and ragging. Cassy watched from within and laughed at them: in each other's company, they at once returned to boyhood, even now they were grown men.

While waiting, she took in her new surroundings and, to her great satisfaction, found them perfectly charming and exactly how she had imagined. Here, to the side, were brick and flint cottages, behind them were gentle undulations and before her a parsonage, solid and square.

'Here she is!' James turned back – Cassy could not help but notice the pride in his eyes – and offered his hand to her. 'Mr and Mrs Fowle, may I present to you my sister, Miss Austen, the next Kintbury bride?'

'My dear.' The older Mrs Fowle pressed forward and took her hands. A neat, tiny woman to have borne four such strapping sons, she was all warmth and determined on friendship. Cassy knew Mr Fowle well already – he was a great friend of her father's from their own days at Oxford – and here he was now, sober as ever, though most correct and polite. They each took her side and guided her in.

The hall was so busy she was almost over-whelmed by it. As well as Tom – hanging behind, shy, at the back – Charles and William were home for the season. The eldest son, Fulwar, and his wife, Eliza, lived there all the time now, with their three children. The two small boys were both attractive and charming; little Mary-Jane, who had

– what a shame – taken after her father, now wore a cross look and clung to her mother's skirts.

The whole household gathered to take a look at Cassy: she was quite the main spectacle. Someone took her claret pelisse, and in all her (modest) glory she was revealed to them. In a wild act of romantic abandon – it was not entirely suitable for travelling and she was nothing if not practical – beneath it, she wore her best blue. Their approval was audible. It was a magnificent moment.

And that was it: the high point of the fortnight. Poor Cassy: this was her first solo visit – a great rite of passage for any young heroine. But she had come to a household in the grip of misery and fear.

The last time she had seen Tom, he had been embarking on a year at sea in a spirit of blithe ignorance. One week in the Channel and he was now gaunt, hollow-eyed, quite haunted by the horrors he had seen. His parents, who had always held reservations about the whole enterprise, were now dismayed at the prospect of his leaving again the following month. Even Fulwar's wife, Eliza, on whose companionship Cassy had counted, was not quite her happiest self. She was exhausted by her young family and in some suffering with the new child she was carrying.

Christmas at Kintbury was more sombre than Cassy had ever known any Christmas to be. After beef and pudding – she wondered, had the pudding at home in Steventon turned out well? And how was the orange wine? – they gathered in the drawing room, a subdued little party. William and Charles set out the chess pieces, the ladies their embroidery; Tom sat with his parents by the fire in silence and studied the flames.

Just one person alone was in festive mood. Like nature – and there was something of the elements about him – Fulwar abhorred a vacuum. He strode into the middle of the silence and pierced it with a loud, cheerful peroration on the one topic in the world about which they did not want to hear.

'I do envy you, Tom.' He lifted his jacket a little to warm his seat further, blocking the fire from the rest of the party. 'Oh, how I envy you! Out there on the waves with the men. The camaraderie of a ship – that is second to none. Or so they tell me.' He gazed ahead, misty-eyed, at the horizon of the warm yellow wall. 'The sea air! The shanties! Fellow in the Hunt was on the *Victory*, you know. He was saying the japes are quite something. Puts the Meet Supper completely to shame.' He chuckled at this second-hand memory.

What a pity it was, Cassy reflected, that Fulwar himself had made the decision to forgo the thrills of military combat. What a shame that, instead, it was *his* fate to take over this charming country church from his father.

Mr Fowle pulled himself out of his musings to

remonstrate: 'I do not think Tom enjoyed much in way of *japes* when the ship was near wrecked a few weeks ago. Nor did he much like the waves crashing over his head.'

'Oh, it was not as bad as all that,' retorted Fulwar, who had seen out the disaster marshalling the parishioners of Kintbury through the challenges of Advent. 'And the fact that they abandoned ship shows how seriously Lord Craven takes the men's safety. Errs on the side of caution, I sometimes think.'

Cassy looked over at her fiancé from under her lashes, and studied his calm exterior. Why was Tom himself not protesting at all this? Of course, she well knew his temper was remarkably even. It was one of the many ways in which they were well suited. But she had never before noticed that his equilibrium could not be disturbed even when, surely, it should.

Eliza leaned towards her. 'Perhaps you find us – the majority of us – a little quiet in the evenings, compared to your own family?'

'Oh no!' Cassy blushed. Was she wearing her thoughts on her face? 'Not at all. It has been most pleasant. Could I perhaps borrow a pin?'

Eliza smiled, passed her work bag and asked, kindly: 'What will they be doing now in Steventon, do you suppose? I hear from my sisters that you are often playing games.'

'Yes,' Cassy could feel her own distress building. She hid herself in her work. 'I expect they will be on the charades by now.' Jane was, no doubt, being slightly too clever; her father roaring with laughter at the things she dared say. It was best not to think about it. 'Do you not do that here? Of course, I quite understand the present difficulties – I mean in happier times?'

'We tend not to,' Eliza replied, dropping her voice further. 'My husband does not take kindly to losing. Though some of us do enjoy a hand of Patience when we can find the time.'

Mrs Fowle spoke up. 'It is not the sea that worries me as much as the climate and fevers.' She patted Tom's arm. 'One does hear talk of such exotic illnesses out there.'

'Ha! Dear Mother, have you not always worried? And look at us! Look at the four indestructibles you have inflicted on this world.' In fact, Fulwar was of a build completely different from his brothers. He was short and squat and ruddy; the others were taller, yes, but Tom was rather slight. 'I would sooner worry about those unruly savages down there before I will worry about our Tom,' Fulwar continued. 'And they will not take a moment's sleep from me in a hurry. I shall tell you for why.'

Cassy steeled herself for what she knew was coming, and tried to focus again on her needle.

'The insurrection that is now upon us, in all four corners of the globe . . .' He gestured to the corners of the drawing room.

It occurred to Cassy that Fulwar was quite a

different person in his own home. Certainly, he was not like this with the Austens. Her family had no truck with pomposity or dominance. He would have been teased into submission as soon as opening his mouth.

'It is of vital importance that our men pick up their weapons . . .'

Charles and William, quietly hunched over their chessboard, were not quite the men she thought she knew, either. In Steventon, they were lively and mischievous; they threw themselves into all games, the louder the better. Here they were permanently subdued.

'The interests of our landowners must be protected . . .'

And her Tom: was he not altered in this environment? He must be preoccupied with the voyage. She understood that; they all were. And he was never gregarious, which was clearly a good thing. She looked over at Fulwar. Who would choose a gregarious husband? For the first time, though, she was noticing just how very quiet Tom could be.

'Those rebels must be prevented from getting their hands on that property . . .'

Cassy did not much care for the direction Fulwar's argument was taking. Her mind moved to what might be happening back home. Perhaps by now they had started the dancing? Jane playing the piano, the furniture pushed back. She turned again to Eliza. 'What about music?'

Surely, some music was just what was needed. 'Do you still get the chance to sing?'

Eliza looked at her with surprise, as if somehow forgetting she was born with a heavenly voice. 'Oh no! I am so tired in the evenings now I have the children. And anyway, we have no instrument here.'

No music. No games. No reading or good conversation! This was the first time that Cassy had ever stayed anywhere without another member of her own family beside her. She had always known that the Austens were remarkable; now it occurred to her that they were simply unique.

'The economy of this great country, the rule of our king, must be defended – yes, to the death, if it comes to it. Death is a small price to pay!'

And she decided that other families must be one of life's most unfathomable mysteries. It was no use sitting as an outsider and even trying to fathom them. One could have no idea of what it must be like to be in there, on the inside. She would share that thought later in her letter to Jane.

The Hunt met the next morning and, as Cassy left her room to go down to breakfast, the house felt abandoned, as if all the men had suddenly been called up to war. Crossing the landing, she saw the door to Tom's room open and, on the spur of the moment, without a thought to the propriety of her own actions, she went in.

The bed was unmade; a dirty shaving rag lay,

tossed, on the washstand; old soap formed a crust on the inside of the bowl. The strange, particular, not altogether pleasant scent of a man still hung on the air. She looked around at his property: a Bible, old Latin primers, not even one novel. No mementoes from school, nor from Oxford; one print of hunting was the extent of his intimate effects.

She stood alone, looking around her, and was overcome by a sense of Tom's otherness. This was a man she had known since a boy! At Steventon, he was familiar; yet here, here he was . . . who was he exactly? Cassy was no longer sure that she knew.

For the first time, she found herself looking beyond their engagement – that match they had made to the satisfaction of all – and gazing into the reality of marriage. She thought of them both, alone in their own vicarage, convenient for *Ludlow*. Miles from everybody; most particularly, far from Jane. Cassy must surrender her rights to the only world she had ever known: the bedroom she shared with her sister. There would be no more laughing or whispering or endless confiding. She might hardly see Jane in person again – their relationship would have to be conducted through letters from then on. Instead, Cassy would have only Tom. And, in the place of all that feminine prettiness, she must look upon a shaving rag, an indifferent hunting print . . .

Her heart tightened. At home in Steventon,

there was always talking and laughing. And so many jokes! She herself did not make many; though Cassy might be one of the cleverer Austens – her mother was often kind enough to say so – she was not one of the wittiest. But she laughed with them. Oh! How she loved to laugh with them. And Tom had laughed, too, there. Of course he did: who could not? But just them, alone? She tried to imagine, but her mind could not conjure it. What would they talk about? Would *they* play games, enjoy music? Whom would they laugh with? At what?

She was homesick already, and her marriage not yet even begun.

'My dear, you seem deep in thought.' Cassy turned to find Eliza – eyes warm with kindness, resplendent in pregnancy, a child at each hand – and felt some reassurance. Her friend had appeared just at the right moment, as if in a vision, an angel come to tell her that here was the essence of it: the construction of a family; the building of a life together. That was the point of us all.

She picked up Mary-Jane, who squirmed and protested, and laughing together the women and children went down to breakfast.

The visit flew by, as visits must do. In Kintbury, the young couple enjoyed few intimate moments; no consideration was given to their privacy. The parsonage bustled as a parsonage was wont to, and it was hard for them to find a quiet corner.

The climate, too, was against them: it was no sort of weather for walks. And Mrs Fowle – poor Mrs Fowle, one could not but feel for her – got more distraught with every day that brought the departure nearer. She was loath to leave her boy's side.

But in the last light hour of Tom's final afternoon, they were, finally, alone together. Cassy was trying to capture a likeness of Tom with her colours. It was not as easy as she had found it before. She did not want to include the grim set of his jaw, the dark circles around his eyes or that fear deep within them, but already could barely remember what he looked like without.

One of life's dreamers – though who knew what exactly he dreamed about? – Tom was always content to sit in an armchair and do nothing, so she was surprised when he suddenly stirred.

'There. You have had long enough to work on my indifferent appearance.' He rose and came round to look. 'Oh, yes. So clever. It quite defeats me, my love, how you can be so excessively good at everything to which you turn your hand.' The thought did not seem to make him anything like cheerful. 'I do wonder that such an extraordinarily gifted and accomplished young lady would even think of marrying a hopeless case like myself.'

'Oh, Tom!' Cassy started to pack up her brushes. 'This really is not one of my better efforts. It is not very clever at all.' She swung round to face him. Their eyes locked for a long moment. Her response – poor, ill judged, inadequate – seemed to echo around them.

With a grim smile, he reached down and took her hand. 'Let us walk. We have spent long enough sitting. I have a small piece of last business to attend to. Please. Come with me.'

They dressed up well – Mrs Fowle fussing around them, insisting they not be too long – and set out into the gloaming. It was a short walk, up a walled path that was glassy with cold, to the church. Tom looked neither left nor right – he could not feel quite comfortable in a graveyard at twilight – and tightened his grip on Cassy's arm.

'It turns out I made a slight hash of things when I was helping my father. The new curate spotted it. Odd little chap. Eyes like a hawk.' He stepped into the church porch and opened the heavy oak door for her. 'Got rather excited about it. Is that all that there is to God's work? I was minded to ask him. Do a few little dates matter, in the great divine scheme?'

Cassy half listened, but her mind was still in the drawing room: she was consumed with her own reproach. Why had she behaved so, to this man she loved so deeply, whom she had loved for so long? It was so unlike herself she could not explain it. All her life, she had always, instinctively, said the right thing at the right moment. Why would she slip now, on his very last day?

They entered the cold church, lit a candle and walked over to the register. 'I failed to write the year in one of the banns, and a Christian name in a burial, so the new curate told me.' Tom found the right pages, and dipped his pen.

While he did so, Cassy cast a quick eye over the other entries in his familiar handwriting. 'This christening here' – she marked the ledger with her finger – 'I may be wrong, but should there perhaps – possibly – be a birthdate for the baby?'

Tom looked over. 'Ah, yes. Good, Cass – correct as ever. You have sharper eyes even than that curate. How much more competent I will be at these and all other matters when I have you to guide me through every day.'

She smiled, left his side and moved to the head of the aisle while he did what he had to. It was a pretty church, small and plain, though its windows were stained. She looked up as the last winter light filtered through, sank into the quiet of the moment and communion with her Maker – oh dear Lord, keep him safe; let her be strong – until Tom appeared by her side. They stood quietly together, the betrothed young lovers, in front of the altar. He turned towards her and took her hand.

'My dear Cassandra,' he began, 'I know I am not the most eloquent of men. But there are things I must say before I leave you.' His face was grave. 'Things I want you to know, in case I never come back.'

In all those weeks of preparation, even in those spacious days of that first farewell visit, they had been careful never to embark on this conversation.

'Oh!' Cassy was not sure she could bear it. 'You *will* come back. I am depending on it. Please let us not have to discuss, to consider . . . It is too dreadful—'

He gripped her arms. 'We must. I want you to know that I have made my will, and left you the bulk of my – well – of what little money I have managed to accumulate.'

'Please do not tell me—' She fought with her tears, but she lost.

'I want you to have it. You are paying me the compliment of constancy in my absence. You should be . . . reimbursed if I fail to return.'

'But we are betrothed. This is my choice.'

'It will give you a little security, though not much,' Tom continued. 'And I want you to promise me that this bequest will not make you beholden to my memory.' He was urgent. 'That if you do not marry me, you *must* feel free to marry still.'

Her face was wet. When she spoke, her voice was broken. 'I promise you,' she forced out, 'Tom, I promise you . . .' And, mostly because she had always believed that he was her destiny, and a little because of how she had behaved earlier, she found her strength and declared: 'I promise you faithfully, here before God. I will never marry any man other than you.'

★   ★   ★

At dinner, they could hardly ignore that this was Tom's last, but no one knew quite what to say.

Fulwar, favouring distraction, began a recollection of hunting heroics of which, it just happened, there was only one hero. 'I was out on Biscay. Do you know why I called him that?'

Everyone knew; no one answered.

'Because he was a great, roaring bay! We had been out front since the set-off' – Fulwar had no regard for the virtue of novelty in anecdote – 'hounds in full flight, fella came up on my left as we were taking the hedge—'

Even Cassy knew this story backwards.

'Broke m' left leg and lost half m' teeth!'

Tom was not even pretending to listen.

'Did I take to my bed?'

The whole table seemed sunken in misery.

'Drank a bumper at supper that very same night!'

Then Eliza – sensitive, intelligent Eliza – introduced the perfect formula with which to discuss the imminent departure: 'I wonder how old this new baby will be before Tom meets him?' she pondered, looking down into her lap as she spoke.

Mrs Fowle immediately brightened at the thought of her new grandchild. 'Oh, still in the cradle, I hope.' She was emphatic. 'It will not be a long voyage, I am quite certain. Lord Craven will not take you away for much more than a year.'

'I quite agree, Mama. Swift and glorious does it. You will be making short shrift of those natives, I know,' said Fulwar.

As Tom's sole duty was the guarding of souls, Cassy sincerely hoped, and believed, that her future husband would make no sort of shrift of anybody at all.

Fulwar swilled his wine glass. 'Back before we notice you have gone.'

'Perhaps we might agree now to, if possible, hold the baptism until Tom can be there for it?' offered Eliza. 'And Tom! We would love you to stand as godfather, if you would be so kind?'

'I would be honoured,' Tom replied warmly. 'And that gives me something to aim for: I need to be home before he is walking.'

'And definitely in time to teach him to fish,' chimed in Mr Fowle. Cassy was touched to see the father try so hard to be cheerful. It was game of him. He was not naturally at home on the bright side, even at the happiest of times. 'No one can cast like our Tom. One more good reason to come back to us!'

'I do have another,' said Tom gently from the other end of the table, glancing over at Cassy and smiling.

Eliza beamed round at them all, pleased with this familiar coze. 'What luck for my children to have such a fine uncle.' She squeezed Cassy's hand under the table. 'And soon, of course, aunt.'

Just before dawn, Cassy went down to say her farewell to Tom for the last possible time. The air was sharp and freezing, the trap being loaded by the light of the moon. Mrs Fowle was, of course, down before her. They cut three miserable figures: fraught with the tensions inherent in the occasion. This time, it seemed to be Cassy's place to say goodbye in the hall. Mrs Fowle stood with them, waiting patiently for the lovers to finish, which, in the circumstances, did not take them long.

'I will write,' whispered Tom.

'As will I. And you know I will be following your progress. Be safe.'

'You can rely on it. Look after Eliza, as only you can.'

His lips glanced her hand, then he turned and he left.

Cassy stood for a moment, watching the shapes of mother and son embrace by the trap until she felt as if *she* were intruding, then dragged herself back up the stairs. She waited for that old sense of optimism, that positive instinct, but could only identify heaviness, misery. Grief.

Worse was to come.

A maid met her when she got to the landing and told her that Eliza was in agonies and calling her name. She rushed to the bedside and upon a scene of pure horror.

'I am losing it!' Eliza lay contorted, and sobbing. 'The baby! It is too early. It is coming too early.'

At once, Cassy started her ministry. She had already attended other births, albeit easier ones, and immediately knew what to do. The next hours were terrible, a sequence of rags and hot water; laudanum and fear. The baby – a boy, as so fervently hoped for – came into this world with the distracted air of one who had not yet decided how long he might stay.

It was Cassy's lot to go out on to the landing where Fulwar was desperately pacing, and impart the news. His terror and tender, loving concern for his wife overpowered him and were quite humbling to witness. She understood then that – however they chose to present to the outside – men, too, were all feelings beneath.

For the remainder of the day, Cassy hardly stopped nursing and comforting and working. But at some point, around four in the afternoon, Eliza slept and she was alone in the nursing chair, the baby, swaddled, in her arms. She held tight and rocked him, desperately willing him to survival. For this small, sad scrap of a being was the baby whom Tom was to come home to. He must live. He *had* to. Or what sort of omen would that otherwise be?

CHAPTER 5

Kintbury, March 1840

Cassandra woke early, aching all over, having fallen asleep propped up on her bolster with the letters still on her lap. What had she dreamed of? It was just out of reach, but she knew it to be dark and uncomfortable. She rose, dressed and, unable to shake the mood, indeed somehow keen to indulge it, she crossed the landing and opened the door to Tom's room.

With sudden force, she was returned to the turmoil she had felt there that Christmas so long ago, when she had stood on this very spot and quailed at the prospect of marriage, railed at the thought of leaving her family. That moment was a stain on her personal history. Her sense of guilt over it was, even now, enormous, overwhelming; it could still quite crush the air out of her. Though – for once trying to be kind, as if she were talking to a niece and not just herself – had she not, all her life, been but the victim of events?

For had they taken the other turn, those dark thoughts she had harboured could have been classified as doubts, pure and simple: the doubts that any soon-to-be-married young woman might respectably have. She would have been able to tell herself then, in that life, that it was perfectly natural. We women worry, all of us, about everything – especially marriage. After all, what was there more important than that? She could have looked back – from the comfort of their fireside with her husband beside her, from a nursery filled by their own, dear children – and seen that moment as a nothing. As one small, private stumble on the rosy path to conjugal felicity.

But life had not done that. It had robbed her and, in so doing, snatched away any presumption of innocence. And whenever she thought of that morning – which was not often; she tried to suppress it – she saw only her own apostasy, could only believe that her doubts had been heard and taken as curses. And was covered in shame.

She walked into the plain, simple bedroom. It had been home to so many Fowle boys since that one; a whole generation had grown there, then flown. There was no trace of Tom now. Although – she moved past the heavy oak bedstead and peered up – yes! The very same indifferent hunting print. Perhaps he never would have brought it with him to their vicarage near Ludlow. She should not, after all, have worried about living with that.

The cheval glass in the alcove by the fireplace was a later addition: a testament to the vanity of the younger generation. Her Tom would certainly never have had need of it. She peered in. Her old face was reflected back at her. And there, over her shoulder, were Dinah's narrowed, knowing eyes.

Cassandra jumped. 'Dinah! Goodness.' She turned round, faced the maid. 'You took me quite by surprise!'

'Miss Austen.' The negligible bob, a curt sniff. 'Is there something I can do for you, m'm? Lost your bearings again, is it?'

Another suggestion of her incipient senility. 'Not at all. I . . .' It was simply easier to pretend it was so. 'Yes. I am sorry. I cannot remember why it was I came in here.'

Dinah looked satisfied. 'Been looking for you, m'm. Was quite worried when you weren't in your room.' Her room! The letters – unhidden! 'So I cannot help you at all?'

'No. Thank you, Dinah. I am quite well. In fact, I think I may have a walk before breakfast.'

'As you wish, m'm.' Dinah creaked a knee before vanishing down the back stairs.

Cassandra retreated back to her chamber and, though she feared that particular horse had already bolted, collected the papers and hid them under the mattress. And she realised it was true: some fresh air was just what she needed. A good walk would always buck one up.

An encouraging smell drifted across from the bakehouse, but otherwise the household was quiet. Isabella, no doubt, still languished in bed. Cassandra met no one on the landing, took the stairs as quietly as possible and stepped around Pyramus who was stretched, luxuriously, out on the rug. The dog struggled to his feet. She did not greet him, certainly did not invite him, and yet, it seemed, he would be coming. They carefully negotiated the chaos of the hall and together set off into the morning.

To the right, past the church was the village, which would, of course, already be busy. There would be plenty of dear, familiar faces up there who would be more than happy to stop what they were doing and talk. But, huddling into her shawl, Cassandra at once turned left, her companion padding beside her, over the bridge and down on to the tow path beside the canal. She had villagers aplenty of her own back in Chawton. What there was not at home – the duck pond, though charming, could not help its own limitations – was the joy of a waterside walk.

How things had changed since that first Christmas when she was staying with Tom. Back then, there had been only a humble little river. This canal, now all boats and business, was but a plan and a controversy. She remembered the debates about it while sewing with Eliza in the drawing room every evening. Fulwar was, of course, loudly in favour. He strode around, declaiming: The March of Progress! The Wonders of Communication! The new varieties of employment! While old Mr Fowle sat in his chair and worried about the crime and corruption it would bring. And Tom?

Tom was greatly interested in the engineering of it, but otherwise unengaged. Though he liked to imagine their future together, he did not talk much of the future in general. Now that Cassandra thought about it, he never once showed any interest in the new century that was upon them or the changes, the revolutions, it might bring. How queer she had not noticed that before. A filthy, thin little lad rushed past her, jumped on to a coal boat and got his ear clipped. She stopped and stood, watched the sunlight dapple the water and looked over to the island, where a duck sat on eggs and her drake busied around with a beak full of twigs. A large sigh escaped her and hearing herself – where did that come from? – she was suddenly reminded that she was now an old lady. With all this reminiscing, she had quite forgotten the fact. How foolish to hang about in the damp at this hour of the morning. If she did not keep moving she would doubtless catch a chill, and then where would she be? She pressed on towards the wharf but that looked far too crowded at this time in the morning. Perhaps she would turn and go into the village, after all.

She looked up at the bridge before her, and noticed a little black figure. Why, Isabella was out even before her! So not languishing in her room at all.

'Miss Fowle!' They could walk back home together, Cassandra thought. 'Miss Fowle!'

Her thin voice could not carry above the canal

noise. She tried waving, but Isabella did not seem to notice.

'Miss Fowle!' Pyramus barked, trying to be helpful.

Isabella ducked away as a gentleman approached her. Cassandra was closer now and could see them more clearly. This was not a person she immediately recognised. Indeed, was he even a gentleman? She could not quite tell. He was not a tall man, quite stocky. He and Isabella had fallen into what looked like deep conversation. Cassandra left the towpath and hurried up to the lane. Did Isabella need rescuing? If only her legs would move a bit faster.

'Miss Fowle!' She reached the bridge. 'Isabella! I am here!'

But . . . how very odd: Isabella – and the mysterious 'gentleman' – were no longer there.

Breakfast was silent. Isabella, forbearing to mention either meetings or gentlemen, seemed mournful and subdued. Her eyes were swollen; her complexion was mottled: she had clearly been crying. She must miss her father – and, lately, her oppressor? – more than anyone could understand. Dinah, unnaturally attentive that morning, fussed about. Isabella sipped the tea that was poured for her, but did not touch any food, and when the clock chimed the hour, made her excuses and left. Cassandra wondered that the early-morning outing had not inspired an appetite in Isabella. She herself was quite hungry, and ate well, though alone. When finished, she went out into the hall.

The door was shut on Fulwar's study, but the sound of voices came through it. That was odd. She had not heard any arrivals. Intrigued, Cassandra moved over and loitered a little.

'Six times seven is forty-two,' a small boy was chanting.

'And rise and shine?' Isabella seemed to have pulled herself together.

'Seven times seven is forty-nine!'

'Well done, Arthur. You have practised well this week. I am pleased with you.'

Of course, Isabella took in pupils. She had been raised by her mother to be a good daughter of the parsonage, and a good daughter of the parsonage she had turned out to be.

How the village would miss having this family at its centre. To lose a much loved vicar was one blow; to lose his womenfolk quite another. Fulwar was a popular preacher, an active and, on the whole, fair politician, but he had spent much of his week riding to hounds. It was the women who provided the vital care the parishioners needed: the broth for the sick, the clothes for the poor, the basic education. Cassandra smiled with satisfaction and thought again how the Fowles were like the Austens, in so many ways.

As it seemed the household would make no sort of claim on her this morning, Cassandra went once again back to her room. A maid had been in: her pot was emptied; there was fresh water in her washstand. She rushed to the mattress and lifted it: yes, the letters were still there, undisturbed. The one great indulgence that had been afforded Miss Murden was a rather threadbare armchair beneath the little window – perhaps the poor woman herself had worn it so thin? Cassandra settled herself down to return to her labours.

CHAPTER 6

Steventon Rectory
October 4th, 1796

My dear Eliza,

I am so pleased to hear that you are much stronger in body – and sorry, but not surprised, that your spirits remain low. Of course, I have no experience of the sorrow you feel, but I do have deep sympathy and a rich imagination. And thus armed, I cannot agree with the rest of your family. You have suffered a loss as profound as any death, and have had not yet a year to recover. That your poor baby only lived for a day is quite immaterial. We do not calculate love by the hours spent with the loved one. Please know that you are in our thoughts and our prayers.

All that said, it seems I simply do not have it in me to write a letter that is all on one shady note of sadness and condolence. With my pen in my hand, I find there is nothing for it but to at least <u>try</u> and amuse you, and bring in a glimmer of light, if just for a moment. I am sorry. Forgive me. It is a failing I have. And there is so much going on here that I think will amuse you – it is all too hard to resist.

For lately our quiet little home has been transformed into the most industrious marriage market! For a connoisseur of domestic drama – such as myself – it is almost impossibly diverting. My eyes have quite left my head and now sit permanently on stalks. I need not tell you that I play no part in it at all, other than that of delighted observer. It is all the doing of my mother and sister, and each is enjoying herself hugely. That Mrs Austen is up to her tricks will not surprise you – she prefers matching over any other form of employment. Cassy's part in it all, though, is more unexpected. I can only put it down to her own elevated status as an engaged woman. She has a future husband, so everyone must have one – as when one is suffering from the coughs or the sneezes, it is a great comfort if others are similarly afflicted.

I must add that no attempts are being made to match <u>me</u> – or none of which I am aware. Perhaps I shall wake up one day and find myself ushered before an altar, but I rather suspect not. It pleases me to report that my own fortunes are being quite over-looked. In fact, dear Eliza, it is your two sisters who form the objects of all this activity. Now, please admit it – you <u>do</u> find this amusing! I knew that you would.

Let me start with the eldest. It has been decreed, by the Austen ladies, that your dear sister Martha shall marry my dear brother Frank. Yes, I know as well as you do that there are problems inherent in this arrangement. He is much Martha's junior, far away at sea and years off being wed – all mere inconveniences, according to the plotters. There is also the small matter that Frank has never, as far as I am aware, expressed any opinion on Martha. That bothers me less, as who could fail to love such a kind and intelligent woman? I should marry her myself if I could. But putting all that aside, the marriage will happen, or so I have been firmly informed. And on Frank's next shore leave – poor lamb, he cannot know what is about to hit him! – he too will be apprised of his own situation. I do hope he has the sense to comply.

But more immediately, the scheme to attach your sister Mary to my brother James is progressing at full pelt. Mary has been staying with us for a week, at my mother's instigation, so that James cannot avoid her when he comes here. And, whether by coincidence or design, he happens to visit us every day! Mrs Austen is in paroxysms of excitement and, for once, I do not think it is a case of her imagination getting the better of her. For all the time that James is conversing with <u>us</u>, he is studying <u>Mary</u> discreetly. His eyes follow her about; when she leaves, his gaze lingers on the door. It is not yet love, as far as I can gauge it – do not hope for that – but it is a profound interest. He is assessing her, considering her, in that slow and serious way of his.

I must warn you that there are other young ladies in the county who have their sights on him. Is it not interesting that a widower in indifferent humour should have so much choice, when your cheerful sisters have so little? But do not worry. My mother has decided that your Mary shall triumph and, as we well know, when Mrs Austen has decided then the fates must abandon their designs and bend to her shape. And for all our sakes – not least that poor motherless child of his – James must marry again soon.

Tomorrow night, we are all to go to the Basingstoke Assembly – Martha is joining us! – and I have a feeling that, there, the situation may reach its conclusion. And if so, I shall be as delighted as my whole family. For I shall have had my revenge on you then, Eliza: you will have my own darling sister, but I shall have one of yours!

As ever,
J. Austen.

The Assembly Rooms were humming, the dance floor was filling and, over by the wall, the four ladies – Cassy and Jane, Martha and Mary Lloyd – stood alone in a cloud of anxiety.

'There. I knew it. I feared this would happen.' Mary Lloyd dropped, with a dejected thump, on to a chair. With a little more grace, the other three took their seats beside her. 'He has not looked at me, not once, since the moment of our arrival.'

All relevant feminine eyes searched the crowds to find the figure of James Austen. He was over on the far side with his back to them, in animated conversation with friends – as if they alone were the party; as if there were no others at all in the room.

'I am sure he is merely greeting the Terrys,' Cassy was swift to reassure her.

'It is not entirely unreasonable of James to be sociable', Jane cut in briskly, 'at what is, after all, a social event.' She flicked open her fan. The evening was only beginning, but Cassy could see that Jane's patience had already worn dangerously thin.

Martha patted Mary's knee – the pat of a kindly, consoling, concerned elder sister.

Mary remained unconsoled. 'I should never have got my hopes up,' she moaned. 'Why would a man like James look at me? Oh, Cassy,' she sighed dramatically. 'Would that I were as handsome and elegant as you.'

Martha looked down at her hands. Jane raised an eyebrow.

'I have never seen you look as elegant as you look this evening,' said Cassy warmly. The ladies had spent hours on Mary's preparations. A new paste had been purchased from the apothecary, the very latest method for concealing the smallpox scars with which she was so horribly afflicted. Its application had proved a little trying. 'I would go so far as to say that you are glowing.' In fact, the paste was now starting to flake in a manner that was rather alarming. Cassy worried that the heat of the room might be having an adverse effect.

'And that pale blue does become you so,' Martha added. 'I wish I could alight on a colour that served my complexion so well. I fear this pink might be a mistake.'

Mary, encouraged, smoothed her own muslin with quiet satisfaction, but issued no compliment in return.

The band struck up a cotillion and the dancers arranged themselves. Jane stood up. 'Well, I, for one, do not intend to spend the whole evening staring at the back of my brother. Come, let us take to the floor.'

Cassy longed to dance, but was torn. Mary was clearly not quite in the mood, and she felt more than a little responsible. But before there was time to decide, the door opened. A new party blew from the night into the brightly lit hall. And she turned and saw there, on the threshold, a new – much discussed, deeply dreaded – threat to the evening. Cassy's heart fell with a thud.

She leaped up and blocked Mary's vision. 'Instead, why do we not take a turn about the room?'

But it was too late. 'No! *She* has come!' Mary wailed, her neck flushed and mottled. 'Cassy, you said she was out of the country! That is it. I am sunk.'

'Nonsense,' Cassy retorted firmly. She pulled Mary out of her chair, and signalled to the others that they too must help her. 'There is no evidence whatsoever that James has even noticed Miss Harrison. He has never before mentioned her to me.'

The ladies began what was hoped to be a dignified parade through the hall, the Lloyd sisters in front, the Austens, arms linked, following behind. Cassy sighed heavily.

Jane leaned in and dropped her voice to a whisper. 'This scheme of yours, Cassy, to bring Mary into our family . . . You are *quite* convinced it is sound?'

'Why, of course!' Cassy replied. 'Mama believes—'

'Oh, *Mama*!' Jane interrupted. 'Do not talk of Mama. She merely favours marriage in general. She cannot help herself. But what of you, Cass? What of *us*, indeed? Do we truly want Mary as our future sister?'

'Jane!' Cassy laughed. 'The Lloyds are our

greatest friends, are they not? And the sisters of Eliza. We will be all of one clan. There never was a more perfect arrangement.'

They sidestepped the dancers, and were forced back into the wall.

'I would say that Martha is our great friend, certainly,' said Jane. 'And Eliza, of course. But Mary . . . would you not say Mary is of a more difficult nature?'

'Oh, Jane. Why must you be always the pessimist? Any character flaws on display at the moment are due entirely, in my view, to the fragility of her confidence. Once settled, Mary will bloom. Mama and I are in one accord on it. My only concern now' – they had reached the top of the room, and Cassy looked about her – 'is that this evening is shaping into a perfect disaster. I must salvage it. Where is James?'

She studied the dance floor. James was on it, in partnership with Miss Harrison – now smiling, now laughing, his poor widower's spirits seemingly banished. She glanced over at Mary, and watched as a tear – ill advised and regrettable – cut a livid, red path down a white, pasty cheek.

'I have a new idea,' she called, brightly, over the noise. 'We should withdraw for a while. It is not long till supper. I hate to be last and deprived of a good seat.'

They were the first there by at least twenty minutes, which three of them spent in false animation, while Mary sat blowing her nose. At last,

James came through. Mercifully, he was alone. Cassy jumped up and took him to one side.

'Rather a good evening, much to my surprise.' He was quite uncommonly cheerful. 'I hope you are enjoying yourselves. I have not seen you since the coach!'

'It does seem a success,' she began, with some caution. 'Though I am surprised that you have not yet asked Mary to dance.'

'Mary?' The very fact of her existence seemed to have slipped James's mind.

'Miss Mary Lloyd.' Cassy smiled. 'It looks a little strange, Brother, when she is staying as our guest and you have spent so much time together lately. I think it would be in order for you to pay some attention to her now.' She paused, breath bated. It was not in her character – and had never before been necessary – to tell her eldest brother how to behave, and she was not sure quite how she would now be received.

Fortunately, his new good humour was robust and undentable. 'If you say so, dear Cass. Of course.' He took her arm and led her over to the small, feminine party. 'Is there space at this delicate table for one hungry man? Might I join you?'

In the moment it took for James to pull out a chair and be seated upon it, Mary's countenance altered. While he stood, she was the picture of Tragedy; when he sat, the embodiment of Joy. Only a man with no vanity could fail to notice the difference between the two Marys, or believe that difference was not down to him. And for all his many excellent qualities – he was intelligent, articulate, loyal and godly – James Austen was not a man without vanity. He did notice, and was visibly pleased.

'I hope you ladies are enjoying your soup. I am not sure that I can quite take any at the moment. I am warm enough from the dance floor and it is – as ever – too hot in here.'

Mary put down her cup and nodded earnestly. 'How right you are, Mr Austen, and how pleased am I to hear you say so. My sister was earlier remarking about the draught in here. Fancy! Draught? said I. What draught? And do you know what I said then? I said: It is – as ever – too hot in here! Is that not the most remarkable coincidence, Mr Austen? We both used the *very same phrase*.'

Jane's face lit up with amusement. Cassy – who had not witnessed any discussion of a draught – was surprised to see how gratified her brother was by this support. He followed it up with a discourse on the music that evening: 'I am quite sure it is an improvement on the last time I was here.'

'Why, how right you are again!' Mary seemed quite taken aback by the force of this insight. 'I do not believe I even noticed until you said so. I am quite staggered it did not strike me at once. But it is – to be sure – a vast improvement on the last assembly. I could not agree more.'

Jane gave a loud snort. James's mood expanded yet further. 'And how pleasant it is to be agreed with, Miss Lloyd. As soon as we arrived, I struck up a conversation with young Terry about this season's hunting. I merely said I hoped for better than last year, as to my mind last year was quite dull. So imagine my surprise when I found that we were in something of a dispute. Mr Terry has memories of a blistering campaign against the fauna of Hampshire that I simply cannot recognise. So forceful was he I began even to doubt myself!'

'Oh, but it is *your* memory that is the correct one, sir!' Mary insisted. 'Of course, I know nothing of hunting, but I have listened attentively to all your conversations on the subject. Well, all those I have been lucky enough to hear. And your reports were certainly of a general disappointment. I do hope,' she added earnestly, 'that you enjoy better sport this year.'

'Well, I must congratulate you, my dear sister,' Jane whispered to Cassy as they returned to the ballroom. 'Victory is yours.'

'Do you think so?' For some reason, Cassy was suffering from a momentary loss of faith in her own plan.

'Oh, very much so.' Jane chuckled. 'Mary played her best hand. We need no longer worry about her lack of a fortune, or flaking complexion. For a gentleman like our brother, there is no greater proof of superiority – in charm, wisdom and intelligence – than agreement with his every word.'

Dancing resumed, and this time James led Mary on to the floor, and at last the other ladies were free to enjoy themselves – while keeping their eyes on the situation, like anxious aunts over a debutante charge. As the couple danced again – and again – they began to relax, began even to feel something like confidence.

The crowd was thinning by the time Mary finally came back to them. She was flushed now: flushed with exertion; flushed with her own natural high colour since the paste had dropped and scattered all over the dance floor. And, on top of that, flushed with success.

'Well,' Martha cooed at her, patting her hair back. 'You have a conquest there, Mary. Of that there is no doubt.'

'Oh, Martha.' Mary flicked her hand away. 'I shall take wisdom from Cassy if I have to – *she* is betrothed. But you, my poor sister? What could you possibly know?'

CHAPTER 7

Kintbury, March 1840

Cassandra had chosen to forget, and did not enjoy being reminded, that she had once been so energetic in her promotion of Mary Lloyd's cause. Jane, of course, had foreseen the inherent problems right from the beginning: she could not – would not – trust a girl who was so dismissive of her sister, and never did share Cassy's trust in the wisdom of their mother's many plans. From the most tender age, she had a seer's talent for the analysis of character and the prediction of disasters. She was, indeed, something of the Cassandra of legend. It was their joke that the name should rightly be hers.

Jane's letter was unhelpful; Cassandra must remove it. For on becoming Mary Austen, Mary Lloyd had rewritten her own history. And in her version, it had always been a love match for James: unconquerable, inevitable. Were she to read this evidence of plotting and conniving, unpleasantness would surely follow.

Cassandra folded it up, rose, lifted the corner of

the mattress under which she would hide it, when there was a quick rap at the door.

'She's 'ere.' It was Dinah, flicking her head, rolling her eyes, and then remembering herself. 'Sorry.' She bobbed, adding: 'M'm.'

Cassandra looked up in horror. Caught red-handed in her room – surrounded by papers to which she had no right! She started to gather them all up, hurriedly, while Dinah stood there and watched her.

'Best leave all that for now, m'm. Miss Fowle needs you, most urgent, downstairs.'

She found herself being led away, feeling as befuddled as Dinah liked to imagine her. 'But who is here, Dinah?'

By now, they were on the main landing. There was some sort of commotion going on down in the hall.

'I was insistent that it could not be possible.' The shrill voice was quite unmistakeable.

They moved towards the stairs.

'That no member of my family would come *here* without first informing *me*. It was a slur on my reputation to suggest it. I had no choice but to mount the strongest defence.' The speaker was clearly aggrieved.

They reached the turn at the window.

'Mrs Bunbury and I had quite the falling-out on the matter. A falling-out that will not be easy to rectify. Things were said. There was a scene. It was really most unpleasant.'

They got to the foot, where the disturbance in the air was palpable.

'And not, with hindsight, *my* fault at all. Time will tell if *she* has the grace to apologise—'

Their presence was noticed.

'Ha! There. So it is true. You are here, Cassandra. Well. This is a surprise. And – if I may make myself plain, which I feel perfectly at liberty to do under the circumstances – not entirely a pleasant one.'

'Dear Mary.' Cassandra approached and bent to embrace her short, broad sister-in-law. 'What a pleasure to see you. How good of you to come.'

Isabella, welcoming the protection, moved to her side. Pyramus stood with them and growled.

'And that dog is feral, as I have had cause to mention on many an occasion. Isabella, now your dear father is gone, it must hereon be banned from the house.'

Cassandra stroked Pyramus's head, rubbed his ear with a new-sprung affection, and suggested they all might move through.

It was not a comfortable visit for anyone. Mary Austen had come with a long list of grievances and an ungovernable impulse to air them forthwith.

'We are supposed to be *sisters*,' Mary chided Cassandra, 'though I do know you never considered me quite good enough. Fred! Where is Fred? Where does that man hide himself? This is the most miserable fire.'

Isabella called for coffee, which Cassandra regretted: more stimulation was not what their visitor needed.

'And to think that you drove past the bottom of my lane without even telling me! Whatever crimes you imagine I have committed against you, I surely could never deserve such an insult as that.'

Dinah came in bearing a tray and an amused expression.

'Is that the best china you have left here? Then I suppose it must do.'

'I am very, very sorry, Mary, for my thoughtless behaviour. I arrived only yesterday—' Cassandra began.

'According to Mrs Bunbury's coachman, who happened to speak to *your* man at the turnpike who, mindful of his duties, reported it to *her*, who then took too much delight in telling *me*, you have been here *two nights already*. Can that possibly be true? Are you now to deny it?' She paused and for the first time looked around her. 'Isabella, what *have* you been doing, dear? Why is this room not yet cleared?'

After a short luncheon, which did not at all agree with her – Dinah must know by now that she was never quite right after cheese – it at last seemed that Mary might be persuaded to leave.

'You must excuse me, Aunt Mary,' Isabella was saying, leading her guest back through to the hall.

'As you yourself have pointed out, I have much to be getting on with.'

'Well, that is certainly true,' Mary conceded. 'I had simply no idea how badly you were managing.' Dinah was already waiting with her outdoor clothes, and dressed her at speed.

'I shall be back, though,' she promised over her shoulder. The dog was herding her to the doorstep. 'In the morning. I shall bring Caroline with me.' She stopped there, turned and glared round at all of them. 'And – yes, I am of course horribly busy but I believe, with some effort, I can somehow effect it – we shall stay the whole day.'

In her wake, the household fell back exhausted, drained – like a body that had battled with fever. Dinah returned to the scullery, Isabella slumped off into a corner. Cassandra went back up the stairs. She could not count on her own privacy from the morrow onwards, and determined to make progress with this one free afternoon.

Steventon Rectory
13th February, 1797

My dear Eliza,

We see from the Register that Tom Fowle's ship has now left San Domingo and our house is returned to a pitch of excitement. I can hardly imagine the emotions in Kintbury. All those many, long months of Tom's absence! At last, we can start counting in weeks – or days, even – to the moment of his return. The relief – to be delivered of such a burden of worry! And now, because it is my wont to pick away at a thing while others embrace and enjoy it, I find myself wondering: what will he be like? After the voyage, the campaign, the experience, will we even know this new Tom Fowle? Oh, Eliza, I do hope so. He has always been quite the dearest of men. Of course, I pray that he comes back <u>unscathed</u> but, on top of that, also <u>unchanged</u>.

The weather stays sharp with us; the hail of the morning is now turning to snow. My sister and I do not mind it. It justifies us in doing that which annoys our household and brings us the most happiness: we stay in our dressing room and keep to ourselves. I amuse Cassy with words, and she attacks her trousseau with a new sense of urgency. Today, she is trimming a cap with lace that our brother Edward has given her, and very splendid it is, too – far too – fine for a humble Miss Austen; no doubt it will sit well upon the head of a proud Mrs Fowle.

With the approach of Tom's ship and, en suite, her own marriage, Cassy is all a jitter. For me – and I must stake my claim to be the person who loves her the most (apart, of course, from our Tom) – it is a delight to see her returned to high spirits. Though I will admit to some jitters of my own. It is finally here, the point at which she and I must separate and I take up my position of Solitary Daughter. I cannot welcome it, but I suppose I shall bear it.

And I do, of course, have my <u>new</u> sister, Mary, living close by me! That <u>will</u> be a comfort, no doubt. She and James seem all marital contentment – marital contentment being quite à la mode – and I can report that they call on us as often, if not more, than we could ever have hoped. That is in part due to my little niece, Anna – she still prefers to stay with us in the Rectory, but I think only because it is what she is used to. We have tried sending her back to Deane a few times, yet somehow she always seems to return. It cannot be long before she understands that Mary is her new mama, and <u>that</u> is her family. It will all work out well in the end, never fear.

I shall finish now, and return to our sisterly haven, while it is still mine to enjoy. No doubt, I can count on seeing you in person very soon, at some point during the nuptial celebrations. It will be a joyous event, and if I am seen to be crying, do make sure to tell the world that my tears are of pride. Not only will my Cassy be the most handsome of brides, but also the best possible wife.

Your dear friend,
J.A.

Cassandra was trembling. The letter fell from her hands. She was arrested – submerged – by a tide of self-pity that was quite overwhelming. The feeling was repulsive to her; one to which, ordinarily, she forbade entry. And yet now she could not even begin to control it. She read the date again. Yes. The very day, possibly – who could say? – the very moment. She surrendered the struggle; let the loathsome emotion wash over her. Oh! To reach across the years, and hold that poor little Cassy close in her arms.

By April, the season was turning. In the garden, around the small village, out in the rolling country of Hampshire, all was fresh, new and reborn; yet still, in the afternoons, the young Austen ladies did not venture out if it could be avoided. Through the dark winter months spent waiting, they had found joy here in their dressing room. The closeness that had existed between them since childhood was explored, developed – mined to a new depth that both found enriching. Each preferred the company of the other over anyone. A habit had been formed.

'You are writing at quite a pace today, Jane.' Cassy was kneeling and pinning the empty shape of a lilac gown that she, as Mrs Tom Fowle, would soon one day inhabit. 'Mind your hand. Are you sure you will be able to decipher it when you read to us this evening?'

'I am a novelist in haste, Cass.' Jane's pen ran

on; her voice was distracted. 'If I am to finish this before we are all weddings and departures . . .' She looked up and smiled at her sister. 'How I shall miss you, my dearest.'

'And I you.' Cassy swallowed hard, turning her eyes back to her needle. 'It will be strange for us at first, I do not doubt. But then, this is something that most sisters must go through, must they not? And they seem to survive, somehow.'

'*Most sisters?* Is that how you think of us?' Jane was all playful outrage. 'Then forgive me, Miss Austen, for my previous intimacies. I had mistakenly assumed myself of somewhat greater significance.'

'Oh, Jane!' Cassy looked up in horror. 'You do know—'

'Yes, I do.' Jane softened. 'Of course I do. And it is for love of you that I am rushing this composition. I am sparing you agonies of dismay and frustration. For how could you bear to be dragged off to wedlock without hearing *this* piece of perfection through to the end?' For a moment, she gazed out of the window; then she turned her eyes back to the page.

Cassy held up a needle. 'Dearest, you have brought me such ease in this difficult period. As have the Bennets, of course.' She spoke through the thread between her lips. 'It really has been most diverting.'

'And that is most gratifying to hear.' Jane bowed her head in acknowledgement. 'For what do I live *but* to divert?' She drew a firm line with a flourish and collected the paper. 'There. I have finished the chapter. Would you like to hear it now, or wait for the drawing room later? I shall not be offended. I know full well you cherish the invisible stitching on your own undergarments over anything my poor pen can produce.'

'Is it the ball? At last!' Cassy leaped up from the floor with a squeal. 'Now! Please! I could not possibly contain myself all throughout dinner.' She took the chair next to Jane, fixed her eyes upon her. 'Quickly, before we are disturbed.'

Now laughing, now gasping, Cassy listened in the warm, little dressing room with the blue and white striped wallpaper: utterly, transfixedly, consumed with delight. Though when Jane read, in her best Mr Bennet voice – '"*That will do extremely well, child. You have delighted us long enough*"' – she was moved to protest. She did not want any sort of interruption, yet interrupt here she must.

'Oh, Jane. Does she have to be called Mary? She is so perfectly dreadful. And *our* Mary believes she has a beautiful voice. We should go carefully. It will not go down well when she discovers it.'

'But how could she discover it? Our new sister has limited literary tastes: if it is not by her husband, then it cannot be good. A remarkably singular position to hold.'

They both giggled. The subject of James's poetic endeavours was one they could only laugh at in private. 'She certainly never sits still long enough to listen to anything I have written,' Jane went on. 'As soon as we begin, she is checking the weather and telling James they should leave. Or suddenly remembering some item of news or an enquiry she has for our mother.'

'Perhaps, well – it appears to me, and I do have some sympathy – she does not feel fully comfortable here when the family is in full flight. You do not appreciate, Jane, how blessed you are, being so clever with words and able to provoke laughter in any company. Your gift comes too easily.'

'But she has been coming here, and sitting with us, as our *friend*, for so many years! I have never noticed her terrible *discomfort* before.'

'But – could it be? – she feels a new need to shine in front of her husband and that is hard for anyone to do in a room full of Austens,' Cassy countered. 'Now she is *of* our family, she perhaps feels her disadvantage more keenly. Since her marriage—'

'Oh, marriage!' Jane retorted. '*Marriage!* Always the excuse for all failures of character. One does so long for it to bring some improvements, but more often it appears the root cause of all poor behaviour. My own explanation is a simpler one and you must agree with me, Cass, even you who has not a bad word for anyone: the thrill of being Mrs James Austen has quite gone to her head.'

'Well . . .' Cassy thought for a moment, and

found she could not disagree. 'I suppose she is very happy to be married to James. And, perhaps, for the moment, yes, a little . . . bumptious with it.'

Jane laughed. 'You see? My theory put there in a nutshell: even happiness in a bride is irksome to witness. And yet the happy *single* lady spreads universal delight!'

'Jane!' Cassy protested, while privately resolving never to behave so herself. 'You know you do not mean that.'

'Oh, very well.' Jane reached across and the sisters held hands. 'I know that you, my dear, will be the perfect combination of marital joy and nobility of spirit; you shall serve as a model to the rest of this poor world.' She returned to her pages. 'And I promise you: if things improve – should Mary ever recover from the thrills of her dazzling promotion – I will change it. Until then, please indulge me in this private joke with myself.' She turned back to her pages, and the glances of Darcy.

Cassy sat in her blue armchair, soothed, bathing in her own pure contentment and ludicrous good fortune: the afternoon sun fell through the window, warming her hair; her betrothed was sailing home on his ship. Soon, she would be married and to one of the best, the kindest, the sweetest men there was in existence.

Yes, of course, she would own that she was still more than a bit nervous. And yes, she did worry about Jane. All their brothers had moved out now and on to their own, no doubt, glorious paths. Once she left, Jane would be all alone with their parents: the last one to be picked in the party game. It was an ignominious position, and there would be long moments of loneliness . . .

She pulled herself together, shifted her dark thoughts back towards the light. Jane's destiny would make itself known, surely; Cassy was confident that her own marriage would be the best that marriage could possibly be: all would be well. And on top of all that to which they looked forward, the two sisters had for the past few months luxuriated in this period of perfect happiness. She could not, right then, understand how conjugal felicity could be any better than that which they enjoyed here in their dressing room. But it had to be done. And at least they had known bliss: ludicrous good fortune, indeed.

This new story of Jane's was quite captivating. What a privilege it was to be the first audience. She already looked forward to hearing it again this evening, with the added delight of her family's reaction. She loved knowing what was coming, anticipating their glee.

'. . . *and even Lydia was too much fatigued to utter more than the occasional exclamation of "Lord, how tired I am!" accompanied by a violent yawn . . .*'

But at that moment, there came a sharp knock on the door.

'No!' Cassy moaned. 'I *knew* that would happen.

Who is this come to ruin our fun? Dispatch them immediately. Say we are most terribly busy!'

Jane, laughing, jumped up and opened it.

Mary Austen was there on the threshold, four-square and determined. Behind her – wearing the grey, grave countenance of a reluctant executioner – lurked James.

CHAPTER 8

Kintbury, March 1840

Cassandra felt a little unwell the next morning – her limbs were heavy; she was shivery with cold – but she knew well enough to disregard it. She went down to breakfast and found she was alone: Isabella, too, she was told, was under the weather. Long experience taught her that – physically – each of them was perfectly well. There was no doubt of it. They were merely suffering the symptoms of a deeper malaise that was sadly incurable: Mary Austen would be here for the day.

With a sigh, Cassandra settled herself at table, with ham, eggs and only Dinah for company. Sipping her tea, she thought of all the things she must do and had not yet even tried to accomplish. There should be at least a few hours of freedom due to her before the visitors arrived.

'Thank you, Dinah.' She watched as the maid poured some more for her. 'I was thinking that I might call on Mrs Dexter after breakfast.'

'You're going there?' Dinah thumped down the

teapot. 'Well, if it pleases you.' She turned back to the sideboard, muttering audibly: 'Each to her own.'

'I am troubled, Dinah, by this issue of where Miss Isabella might now live. It surely makes sense that she should be with her sister. But there seems to be some sort of stalemate?'

'Is that what you call it? It may not be my business to say so—'

It was not, though Cassandra had early on established that Dinah's position in the household with just the one mistress was now something beyond that of the ordinary servant.

'—but Mrs Dexter has been no sort of friend to Miss Isabella lately. That I can tell you.'

Cassandra sighed once again. She and her siblings were, to one another, a source of constant love and cheerful support. It was such a sadness to find other families so differently arranged.

'But surely, if Miss Isabella and Mrs Dexter *were* to live together, spend more time with each other, they would find they had more in common than not?'

Dinah shot her a pitying look – not dissimilar to that which Jane might shoot when Cassandra was too optimistic about the redemption of others – gave a sniff of derision, and withdrew the jam.

'Thank you, yes, I am sure I had finished with it.' That was a little regrettable. She had been looking forward, keenly, to jam. 'And what about you, Dinah? Has a new position been found for you yet?'

'I'm staying with Miss Isabella,' she replied firmly. 'We've been together too long to change now.'

'Ah. And you can both go to Mrs Dexter's?'

'I'm not going *there.*'

'So you would prefer it if instead Miss Isabella and her other sister, Miss Elizabeth, took a place in the village?'

'No.' And then, grudgingly: 'But at least *she's* behaved a bit better than *her.*'

'Well.' Cassandra folded her napkin and rose from the table. 'It seems to me that those are the only two options.'

'If you say so.' Dinah removed everything tempting from the table – 'You know best, m'm' – and left the room.

Perhaps it was just Dinah – the over-mighty Dinah – who was obstructing all progress in this matter. But what- or whoever might be the impediment, it was imperative that the matter was now resolved. For Cassandra knew from experience that, for the spinster on a limited income – most spinsters, therefore, at least of her own acquaintance – these moments of transition were the moments of danger. They could arrive without warning, lift the roof from your head, remove the table at which you once sat every evening. And even, if you were careless or simply unlucky, pluck the food straight out of your mouth. This was the peril inherent in every single situation. It took quick thinking, courage, sometimes something as low and unseemly as cunning, in order to simply survive.

The trick was to find some pattern in the chaos, trace the path to your own destiny, grope your way forward. Cassandra had been forced to realise that early, although, looking back, she must admit that even she had taken her time, and the occasional wrong turn. But poor Isabella had been cossetted and protected by family life and the family home until now – and this was her forty-first year! Clearly she had never developed an idea of, or instinct for, her own comfort.

Yes, this needed resolving. Miss Austen would see to it today.

Mary-Jane Dexter's cottage – a long, low and ancient affair – sat beyond the flint wall on the other side of the church. It was one of the nearest houses to the vicarage and Cassandra marvelled that two sisters such as Isabella and Mary-Jane could be so physically close and yet so effectively distant. She went through the front garden gate, approached, knocked and – yet again – found herself waiting for entry.

At last, a deep voice came out through the doorframe: 'Who goes there?' Mary-Jane had spent much of her married life out in India. The experience had left her with a certain distrust.

'Mrs Dexter, dear, it is I, Miss Austen,' she called back, feeling a little absurd. 'Come to call on you.'

There was a pause. Bolts were drawn, locks were turned and with a loud creak – as if it had not done so for decades – the oak door yielded and Cassandra was in.

'Forgive me.' The two women embraced. Mary-Jane stuck her head out, scouted the churchyard and cottages for threats and insurgencies, then pushed Cassandra through to the hall. 'One cannot be too careful.' There was a great deal of rebolting, relocking. 'You should not have come alone, Cassandra. It can be dangerous around here, you do know.'

'Oh?' Cassandra was surprised. 'To my eyes, Kintbury seems peaceful enough.'

'With respect, you were not witness to the riots ten years ago.'

'No, I was not. And I gather they were most unsettling, but lasted only a day or two, I understand?'

'It seems longer when you live with unrest, I can tell you. I have seen some things in my day.' Mary-Jane, a short, wide woman with a square, ruddy face and no-nonsense hairstyle, was dressed – well, Cassandra was not qualified to assess it. Suffice to say, she was prepared for conditions and climate not previously known to West Berkshire. 'I sleep with my late husband's gun under my pillow now.' She tilted her chin with defiance. 'And – so help me – I will not hesitate to discharge it, if needs must.'

They moved into the parlour and, once her eyes

were accustomed to the gloom, Cassandra took in her surroundings. Miss Austen was not a well-travelled woman. She had never been further east than Kent – had certainly never been as far as Bengal. And standing in Mary-Jane's quaint Tudor dwelling, she was amused to discover that she now did not need to: much of Bengal having, conveniently, come here.

Tigers bared their teeth at her; elephants their tusks. Under glass, a menacing snake – she chose to presume stuffed – was coiled, ready to strike. On every surface were enough swords to sever the heads from a multitude of rural workers impudent enough to ask for fair pay. A curious fragrance filled the room, which brought to mind some recipe of Martha's. It must be her curry, though there was some other musk-like ingredient in play. She looked around to find somewhere to settle. 'What interesting things you have accumulated, dear.'

Mary-Jane picked up an animal skin and tossed it on the carpet. She watched, waited for the dust clouds to clear; then she indicated the bench: 'Sit yourself down here.'

The guest did as bid, while her hostess lowered herself to the floor – with some effort, her limbs were not long – crossed her legs and reached for her pipe.

Cassandra studied her for a moment. Again, like Isabella, Mary-Jane was not what one would expect to be the issue of Eliza. Her friend had been beautiful and gracious. These daughters must surely have come as something of a disappointment: none of them had been blessed with the mother's many charms. Of course, it could be a burden to a girl to be born of a perfect mother: to feel that she is making no contribution to humanity's progress. Perhaps that had affected them. In that regard, she and Jane had been lucky. Mrs George Austen was of course splendid, too, in so many ways, but not least in her casual disregard for the concealment of her flaws.

'I had heard you were here, Cassandra. Forgive me for not visiting you,' Mary-Jane was now saying. 'Dare not risk it at this time of year, when the days are so short. I could get trapped there! By darkness!' Her small, brown eyes flared at the thought.

'Oh, I quite understand. And Isabella has been looking after me quite impeccably.'

Mary-Jane tamped down her pipe. 'Brave little thing. Heart of an ox. No idea how she manages there alone.' She took a long draw. 'Still, she will be coming to live with me when the old house is cleared out. Safe here. Away from the natives.'

'Ah, is that settled then? She is to join you? I was not sure—'

'What else would she do?' Mary-Jane shot back, suddenly angry.

Cassandra was quite taken aback by her tone. 'Well—'

'Do not tell me there is a return to that nonsense!'

She was shouting. 'My parents would not tolerate it! *They would turn in their graves!*'

'Nonsense? What nonsense?' Cassandra was starting to feel nervous. It was as if Fulwar were miraculously resurrected and returned to them. 'I am not sure I quite follow—'

Mary-Jane calmed down. 'No? That is all right then.' She puffed on her pipe. 'No harm done.'

Cassandra stayed only as long as was courteous, and not a minute more. With enormous relief, she returned to the vicarage, more delighted than was usual to find the reassuring figure of her niece, Mary's daughter Caroline, waiting in the hall.

'Aunt Cass, how good—' When she was able, Caroline drew back from the unexpected, untypical warmth of the greeting. 'Heavens. Are you quite well? You seem not much yourself.'

Cassandra, who did not like to appear foolish, composed herself. 'Yes, thank you. Never robust, as you know, but doing quite well enough. What a pleasure to have you here for the day.'

'Not all pleasure, Aunt.' Caroline lowered her voice and tipped her head to one side. 'My mother is in there. We are come here to *work*.'

'Ah.' Cassandra shed cloak and bonnet, steeled herself and made for the drawing room. All brightness, she said: 'Mary. Good day.' Then: 'Oh, dear!'

Mary was laid out on the sofa, with one leg balanced on a high pile of pillows and a collection of medicines by her side. 'It is the most cursed

119

luck, Cassandra. I woke up this morning, all happy anticipation of a solid day's labour, only to find that while I slept my foot had become most horribly afflicted.'

'Your foot?' Cassandra moved to the patient, examined her, but could find no obvious external symptoms. 'How strange.'

'Well, indeed. As you know, I have always been unusually lucky in the foot department. Mrs Bunbury suffers with hers most particularly. Never stops moaning, to the extent that it is hard to find sympathy. One does value bravery in others, above all. And, of course, though I am no stranger to suffering, *my* feet are among the best parts of me. I had no idea of the *agony* they can cause one, till now.' She lifted a limb, gasped and fell back. 'The upshot of it – and this distresses me greatly – is that *I* cannot do anything but lie here today. Nevertheless, while suffering, I have come up with a table of tasks that the rest of you might accomplish, under my guidance.' She passed the paper to Cassandra, made herself yet more comfortable on the sofa, and added: 'Oh, and please tell Dinah we shall, after all, be staying for dinner. I know that none of you would want me to hurry home in this sorry state.'

The day did, at least, pass quickly. The house was moved further towards some sort of order. And Mary's mysterious condition kept her downstairs and away from the letters. It also forced her away from the dinner table. She took her meal on the sofa, while the three mild-mannered women dined contentedly alone.

It was with some reluctance that they rose and moved through to the drawing room. Caroline – the most hardened by battle with her mother – led the way; Cassandra brought up the rear. At the doorway, she thought to thank Dinah.

'Yes, m'm.' Dinah nodded, heaping plates on a tray. 'And how passed your morning? I 'ope you found a pleasant welcome from Mrs Dexter?'

'Very pleasant, yes, thank you,' Cassandra replied properly. 'I was interested to see her – er – fascinating house at last.'

Dinah put down her tray and came close to Miss Austen. 'You didn't say anything did you, m'm? Nothing to suggest we might think of going there?'

Cassandra had always been the kindest of employers. A certain warmth, a dash of intimacy between servant and mistress were, over time, unavoidable and also, managed correctly, promoted efficiency. However, insubordination at this level was not only outrageous – astonishing! – but bound to create difficulties. It must be stamped out at once.

'Thank you for your interest, Dinah. Naturally I could not disclose that which was said in a *private* conversation. We would like tea, now, please, by the fire.'

* * *

Cassandra watched the two cousins busy themselves with pouring and serving, and was struck – and touched – by the familial connection between them. Isabella and Caroline were close in age, and similar in build – trim enough figures, average sort of height. There was nothing in the appearance of either woman to which an onlooker could reasonably object.

And yet they shared the same destiny – or rather, the lack of one: a spinsterhood spent in long-suffering service to parent and siblings. Not that there was anything wrong with spinsterhood – far from it! But when the spinster herself was so reluctant about it, as these two women were: well, that was a shame.

Isabella, she suspected, was, in some measure, the victim of parental neglect. Fulwar and Eliza had put considerable energy into their eldest daughter Mary-Jane's match, and when the only candidate insisted on removing her to India, were conspicuously brave in containing their grief. By contrast, the prospects of their younger daughters, who had the virtue of being much easier characters, were not blessed with such keen attention.

With Caroline, she knew and had been its witness, the problem was one of maternal control. Though Mary herself had benefitted enormously from the institution of marriage, she held no similar ambitions for her offspring. She liked, at all times, to have Caroline beside her, and found no pleasures in wider society.

Still, Cassandra had often wondered that neither Isabella nor Caroline had found suitors of their own. After all, many a more unattractive woman was married; plenty of less sympathetic women had children. Yet somehow these two had failed to provoke Life into noticing them. It had simply just passed them by.

Were she to work on their likenesses – had anyone ever done so? Neither had the sort of personal power that inspired others to cause their likenesses to be taken – Cassandra would use only charcoal for Isabella. With the exception of those bright blue eyes, and the pale brown hair that had not yet any grey, she was otherwise a naturally monochrome creature. Caroline, though, would demand the use of her colours – the stronger, the redder, the better – for she flushed at the merest suggestion of attention. A casual 'Good morning' could provoke the deepest of hues.

Caroline was reddening now as she asked Isabella a question. Her voice was low but the room was all ears: 'So have you seen the good doctor since the funeral?'

'Doctor?' Mary's voice cut in from the sofa. 'Are you, too, unwell, Isabella?'

'Quite well, thank you, Aunt Mary. Other than the stress of my current situation.' Isabella rattled the cups as she passed round the tea.

'Ah. This must be the doctor Caroline speaks of, who attended your father?' Mary turned to Cassandra: 'You may not know that Caroline

123

offered an incalculable support to the family when Fulwar was dying. The poor girl was quite wrung out by it, here all the time.'

'I did not know,' Cassandra replied warmly. 'But am most pleased to hear that someone helped carry the burden.'

'Oh, but I only came for a few afternoons, Mama! It was Isabella, truly, who did everything. She never left my uncle's side.'

'Nonsense, my dear. It is my clear recollection that you were almost permanently absent over that trying period. Caroline is' – she addressed the room – 'like her mother, too prone to give.'

'Shall we read?' Isabella asked brightly. 'Cassandra and I have started your Aunt Jane's *Persuasion*. You will know it well, of course. I did not. It really is most entertaining!'

'If you happen to appreciate *novels*,' countered Mary. 'Poetry, to me, offers a more profound experience. Poetry and more *lyrical* prose. Caroline, pass my bag. It so happens that I have with me my husband's journal. While a great deal of fuss is made of your Aunt Jane, it is most useful to remind ourselves that she was not the only writer in the family. Indeed, nor the best, I have heard some people say. And I do believe my James-Edward to be the greatest of all. He has his father's talent and then some. Mark my words: he will write something some day and astonish the world with it. *Then* the Austen name shall be made.'

Cassandra felt a dull ache – first in her back,

then creeping round to her groin – which she ascribed to nothing beyond deep irritation. Why must she refer to it as a 'journal' when quite clearly it was nothing of the sort? This red leather album that Mary was now opening with reverence was no more than a scrapbook, filled with fragments of James's writing. The woman's ignorance in all matters of literature was so profound and far-reaching that she did not know enough even to know she was wrong.

'I think we should hear his Kintbury poem now. Do not you agree? I presume you know it already, Isabella? No doubt you, like me, can recite it almost word for word. No? You do *not* know it? What were my sister and brother-in-law doing with their time and their children, I often wonder? It is not every family that has such words, such exceptional *poetry*, written for and about them! Why, if such a thing had been composed in honour of *me* and *my* kin I should make sure to celebrate it! Well, thank goodness I brought it – that is all I can say. This may, after all, be the last time we ever sit together in this very drawing room, and this very drawing room is above all the best place in which to hear it. But prepare yourself, Isabella dear. Do prepare yourself. I warn you, it is moving' – she dabbed her nose with her handkerchief – 'so very, very, quite exceptionally moving. I do not believe there has ever been a writer like my Austen for *moving* a person.' She cleared her throat, and began in her flat, lacklustre tones:

> '*Amid the temperate hours of evening grave*
> *Oft was I wont in thoughtful mood to stray*
> *Where Kennet's crystal stream with limpid*
>   *wave*
> *Through Kintbury's meadows takes its*
>   *winding way . . .*'

Mary was forced to stop for a moment, over-come. '*Limpid wave* – is that not wondrous? *Limpid wave.*' She looked around her, shook her head. 'Only Austen. Only my dearest Austen.' She collected herself and went on:

> '*And still in my mind's eye, methinks, I see*
> *The village pastor's cheerful family . . .*

'So that's the Fowles, dear! Yes. Your family! In *a poem*!

> '*The father grave, yet oft with humour dry*
> *Producing the quaint jest or shrewd reply;*
> *The busy bustling mother who like Eve*
> *Would ever and anon the circle leave,*
> *Her mind on hospitable thought intent,*
> *Careful domestic blunders to prevent.*'

She stopped again. 'Oh, that is so like your grandmother, Isabella! *Careful domestic blunders to prevent*! So like her! So brilliantly put! So like all we *married* women, of course.' She looked around the room, took in, one by one, the single women gathered about her and gazed at them with sympathy, then shrugged and went on: '*While yet a gayer group, four manly boys*— He is writing of your father and his brothers, now. Where was I? Yes:

> '*While yet a gayer group, four manly boys,*
> *Heightened with relish of domestic joys,*
> *Of future happiness gave promise fair,*
> *And eased with pleasing hopes a parent's*
> *care . . .'*

Caroline and Isabella both glanced over at Cassandra with fear in their eyes. The younger generation of her family took great care never to mention Tom in Cassandra's presence. Until that moment, she had never been quite sure whether this was a policy that they had agreed upon together, or whether it was merely because they had never known him and so he did not often come to their minds. She now understood – it was written on the younger women's faces – that they were gripped by terror at the thought of her reaction.

This revelation quite bemused her. Surely, if they knew anything at all, they must know that her own stoicism on the subject was quite celebrated. Yet now here they were, looking for all the world as if she were on the brink of A Scene! It was preposterous. She arranged her features into a study of calm, and focused, with dignity, upon Mary.

'And one sleeps where Ocean ceaseless pours
His restless waves 'gainst West India's shores:
Friend of my Soul and Brother of my heart!'

But – and it was most odd – this verse appeared to be new to Cassandra. Had she simply forgotten it? Or never before been made aware of it? Either way, she did fear that Mary was here straying into the region of tactlessness.

'For I had many a scene of pleasure planned
When safe returned to this dear native land . . .'

Of course, the region of tactlessness was to Mary something like her natural habitat. But Isabella and Caroline, she could not but notice, were becoming most discomfited.

'Much did I hope (it was a vision fair
And pity it should melt into thin air)
Our friendship soon had known a dearer tie
Than friendship's self could ever yet supply.'

Cassandra had now to own that she too was feeling discomfited – from the atmosphere in the room, of course. But also – she simply had to admit it if only ever to herself – by the quite execrable standard of this verse.

'And I had lived with confidence to join
A much loved Sister's trembling hand in—'

She rose to her feet to bring this nonsense to a close. Really, this was her brother's writing at its worst. It was not worthy of being read aloud in a family circle; not worthy even of the paper upon which it was written. 'Forgive me, all. I am really quite tired from our busy day. Do excuse me, my dears, if I go up a little before you.' To think that they might have enjoyed a few chapters of *Persuasion*! What a dead weight Mary was on an evening.

She bade them goodnight, and withdrew.

Cassandra fell with relief into the pure solitude of her room, but it took a few minutes of pacing and general, restless physical activity before she could restore her calm spirits. She retrieved the bundle of letters from under the mattress. She opened her valise, removed her patchwork pieces, checked the papers beneath them, closed it again. She brushed her hair, washed her face, gazed for a moment through the window at the grey, starless night. At last, her heart returned to its old pattern; her limbs stopped their shaking. Closing the curtains, she settled into the armchair, reached for the letters and thought how to best use this precious, short time.

She could certainly spare herself from reading the next one. Permitting herself just a glance at the date – 18 April 1797 – she then, carefully, put it aside.

But what was this? Next, in *Jane's* pile, in Eliza's

compilation of *Jane's* private correspondence, was a page in a quite different hand. She recognised it at once: this was from *Mary*. Cassandra was startled. What could it mean? Of course, it had been filed in error . . . It would be criminal to read it . . . Her head and her heart told her to return it, immediately . . . But her eyes – her poor, old, disobedient eyes – saw that same date. And read on:

Deane Rectory
18th April, 1797

My dear Eliza,

I write to tell you that I have fulfilled my sad duties on behalf of the Kintbury family and must report that the afternoon has left me quite depleted in energies and spirit. You will be relieved to know that my dear Austen has been most solicitous to me, so that I now feel sufficiently restored to give my account, as per your request.

We left for Steventon as soon as your letter arrived. While my husband – shocked and fearful of the effect that the news would have upon his sister – was all for waiting and prevarication, I was insistent. Cass. must know as soon as possible. The deed could not be put off. We found the ladies where they are always to be found, alone in their sitting room with the door shut to the world – I must confess to finding this closeness of theirs most unnatural and very excluding of others. No good will come of it. But Austen forbids me from saying so to either parent. There we are. I am forced to keep my wise words to myself. That is what it is like here, I am sorry to tell you. There will be no criticism of The Girls. And I dare say that will be more so after the events of today.

As we mounted the stairs, I could hear their laughter – they do laugh an unusual amount, in my opinion. I used not to mind, but lately have found it a source of great irritation. My poor heart sank further at the prospect of that which lay before me but my courage did not falter. They were both at work of some sort – I got the impression it was an item for her trousseau that Cass. had about her as we entered – so it was as well that we came quickly and spared her more labours. For what use is a trousseau to the poor woman now?

I believe that as soon as C. saw my face, she knew the purpose of my visit – I was and still am quite pale with the shock of it – and when I asked that Jane leave, her air darkened considerably. I came to the point at once. Austen had thought that he might speak first but I feared he would only prolong the misery. When bad things must happen they must happen at once and we women – married women in particular – are so much more sensitive to that which is required in a difficult situation. As when Anna is up to her bad tricks – the child's terrible behaviour shows no signs of abating – why wait for her father to deliver one of his long sermons? I give her a good, short, sharp slap on the back of her legs and there is the end.

So as soon as the door closed upon Jane – and <u>she</u> was reluctant to leave us in privacy – I delivered my message, simply and directly – Tom was dead, of Yellow Fever, and these past two months had lain buried at sea. I regret to say that the ensuing scene was quite desperate. Cassandra fell to the floor and was beset with such a fit of grief that it was quite an agony to witness. In the midst of such a distressing situation, you must know that I did not miss a detail and conducted <u>myself</u> with aplomb. I passed on Lord Craven's condolences, but even that did not seem to console her. And I remembered to add that his lordship had no knowledge that there <u>was</u> such an engagement: he would never have taken a betrothed man aboard, but Tom had not thought to mention it. Well, Eliza! One might have hoped for an expression of sympathy for poor Lord Craven's position. In its place, we had the hysterics.

I am so grateful to have had my own husband there to comfort me. He has been most solicitous ever since. He is conscious that it was the most terrible ordeal for me – especially now, in what should be my honeymoon period, when I have all the excitement and happiness of having become so lately Mrs James Austen – it does still bring a small thrill to write those words – it is quite tragic that I of all people should have been the one to have to perform such an onerous task. Is it always to be my lot to have to deal with the dramas of my new sisters?

But, dear Eliza, there, 'tis done. You will be comforted to hear that I am now before a good fire with a tisane beside me and that James has had the sensitivity to send Anna to the Austens until I should begin to recover – she will cling to her father so even when I am there in the room – it is most seriously vexing and should be more than my nerves could stand to have to deal with the child now. It was also in my thinking that it may benefit all in the household to have to look after her – a welcome distraction from that dull business of grief. He will soon read to me from his own poetry. I think his Sonnets would be appropriate this evening. They always soothe me and heaven knows I need soothing tonight.

Ever your loving sister,
Mary Austen.

133

Cassandra's immediate reaction to the letter was simple astonishment. This could not possibly be genuine. It must be a parody: Mrs James Austen through the medium of satire. Perhaps – it went through her mind in the very first minute – this was by Jane? She was, after all, quite brilliant at capturing their sister-in-law for their private amusement. Only the other day, back in Chawton, Cassandra had come across a comedic letter of complaint her sister had written years before, in Mary's voice to the portrait painter: *You claimed that you had captured me perfectly, and yet my family points out that your picture is of a woman most plain and, moreover, sour* . . . She had enjoyed it anew and then burned it at once.

Her eyes moved back to the top of the page. She began it again. And this time her emotions were quite other and completely beyond her control. She felt tears course down her cheeks, her neck, over her hands on to the paper and did nothing to stop them. She could hear her sobs – choking, gulping sobs – pierce the air but did not try to arrest them. Instead, she let her misery take flight, swell, fill, press into the walls of this mean little chamber they had thought good enough to put her in.

'How dare she?' she cried.

Now she felt none of that passive self-pity.

'How *dare she*?'

She was not revisiting her grief.

'HOW DARE SHE?'

This was outrage, pure outrage that consumed and possessed her. How dare Mary peddle this hideous calumny? How could she – even *she* – write something so vile?

From the moment that the news had been broken to her – badly, insensitively, not as she would have liked or deserved, but no matter – Cassandra had identified that as the occasion to which she must rise. She could remember it – clear as a bell – all these years later. Listening to Mr and Mrs James Austen, asking for details, accepting their sympathies – her back ramrod straight, her voice calm and quiet – and thinking that this was the thing by which she would be defined from here on. She would have no other opportunity. Her future was to be denied her. She would have no marriage to succeed in, no vicarage to run, no children to raise. This was to be the test of Miss – forever, eternally Miss – Cassandra Austen. And by *God* – that God who had in His wisdom chosen to try and destroy her – she would pass it.

And pass it she had. Cassandra's grief had been noble; her countenance quite simply remarkable. She had borne it with a fortitude that had astonished them all. They had talked of it, written about it, discussed their admiration of her openly and incessantly: in the face of the most appalling tragedy, she had shown a strength that placed her squarely in the upper echelons of strong women. *That was her truth.*

Yet Mary – who was with her then, who was

there throughout all that misery – had somehow concocted another truth entirely. How wide had she spread it? How far had it reached? And Cassandra saw now, understood for the first time, the immensity of the task she had lately set herself: how impossible it was to control the narrative of one family's history.

Well, there was at least one small thing she could do. She picked up the letter again, and – with as much violence as one old lady could bring to bear upon one old piece of paper – ripped it to shreds.

CHAPTER 9

Steventon, May 1797

The next few weeks were, presumably, clement – it was that time of year when the mornings were bright and the evenings lengthening – but, in truth, Cassy had no sense of the weather. She lived under an immoveable shroud of her own darkness. Oh, she carried on. Of course she carried on! Not once did she falter in that immediate resolution to remain dignified for everybody, to always appear strong.

In the mornings, she worked in the house with a frenzied determination; she sat with her embroidery in the circle around the fireside in the evenings. She and Jane still spent the afternoons in their dressing room. Work on her trousseau was abandoned, those lovingly sewn items packed away, carefully: another, luckier bride might, perhaps, one day have use for them. For Cassy, there would be nothing but black from hereon.

All her free time was now spent on letters of condolence. Her post was quite overwhelming, more even than when she was newly engaged.

Conscientious as ever, she committed to reply promptly to every one. Meanwhile, Jane still wrote. She was finishing *First Impressions*, and reviewing an earlier composition, *Elinor and Marianne* – all for Cassy's own entertainment. She listened, even smiled, sometimes. But she could no longer laugh.

One such afternoon, perhaps a month after the collapse of her world, Cassy opened a letter and let out a gasp.

'What is it, dearest?' Jane jumped and ran to her. Her nerves, too, had been shattered to pieces by the news of Tom's death. It would be a long time before either sister – so recently cheerful, untouched by tragedy – could find it within her to trust fortune again.

'This, from Eliza.' Cassy's hand shook as she passed Jane the paper. 'Tom's will has been read.'

Jane took in the message and then looked at her sister. A young lady did not need a strong grasp of arithmetic to interpret the figure there on the page, and these two intelligent daughters of the parsonage understood it at once.

'One thousand pounds!'

'One thousand pounds.'

'Oh, how he loved you.'

'What a good and kind man.'

'Then good Lord Craven did pay Tom most handsomely for his short service. That must be on your account, dearest. Because he was soon to be married.'

'I think not,' said Cassy quietly. 'It appears that

Tom did not mention me to his patron.' Her throat tightened. 'Or so I have been told.'

'Told by whom?' Jane demanded.

Cassy looked to her lap.

'*Mary!*' Jane set off on a furious pace about the room. 'Well. She was most *conscientious* in her duties indeed, that she felt she must include even that manner of detail.'

'Please.' Cassy raised her hand to put a halt to Jane's raging. 'Let us not pick over it. It is not helpful.' Tom's omission was certainly hurtful. But in the great scheme of her agonies, she found it provoked but a moderate pain.

Jane quietened and sat again. 'So. One thousand pounds. It is still not very much – is it? – for a gentleman of nine-and-twenty and a sound education.'

'I fear life treated him ill.' Cassy winced as that hideous vision revisited her: Tom sick and dying; his young body slipping below the surface of the water; falling, alone, unheard and unwitnessed, to that foreign seabed. She hid her hands under her skirts to conceal their shaking and looked out of the window. 'But I shall be sure to always be grateful. I am now covered, at least, for any emergency that might strike.'

'Indeed. And yet—'

They sat, each in silent computation, both achieving the same, irrefutable, result. One thousand pounds, over a long life, used carefully, keeping enough in reserve to ward against calamity, came to this: Cassy could put her own pennies in the poor box, and trim her own caps.

Jane saw that she was shivering, wrapped a shawl round her shoulders and tucked it tight. It was not, though, the cold that affected her, nor, just at that moment, the loss of her Tom. Rather, it was the knowledge of her own vulnerability: the years she faced alone with minimal protection.

Of course, Jane understood that. 'Oh, Cass. What is to become of us? How do you think we will make it through, when Papa is gone and we have to leave Steventon?'

Cassy fixed on her brave face. 'You will be established long before then, dearest.'

'I will not.' Jane's voice was low. 'I know that is not going to happen.'

'What about this Mr Blackall, who is soon to be delivered to the county for your delectation? Everyone has high hopes of the match. He may well turn out to be perfect.'

'I very much doubt it. I could never, anyway, think of leaving you now.'

'That is silly. It is time for you to start m aking an effort, and not discount every man at first sight. And I shall survive – in great style, thanks to my one thousand pounds! Please look to your own future. There is no need to worry about me.'

Cassy wanted to scream, rage at the Furies who had conspired against her, but did not. She simply reminded herself to be grateful, and returned to her tasks. It would be wise to reply to Eliza later: the matter was too delicate to rush at. She moved on to the next in her pile.

'Ah! This is from Edward. He invites me to Kent. Henry can deliver me . . .' She read on.

'Yes, well, do remember that Elizabeth is approaching her confinement.' Jane sounded caution. 'I am quite sure they would welcome you, but truly, Cass, you are not currently strong enough to take on all that work.'

'Strong!' The word flashed through her. 'I am *perfectly* strong, Jane. And, anyway, they cannot be expecting to use me at this sort of notice. Elizabeth is bound to have her arrangements in place. After all, they knew that I could not be avail—' She stopped. She had not been asked to help with this baby, because this was the month in which she was expected to wed. 'I think you are being too cynical, Jane. Listen. He writes: *I think of you often, dear Sister, and would do anything to be with you there, to offer you comfort. You must understand that this is not the right moment to leave my family. But if it would help <u>you</u> to come to us <u>here</u> . . .* You see?' Edward is simply being kind.'

Jane, though unconvinced, did not argue further but returned to her writing; Cassy sat and thought for a while. The fact was that she was finding her position at home in the rectory difficult. She had long ago become used to pleasing; she liked to look at her parents and see contentment, pride, a sense of satisfaction reflected back in their eyes. This new identity – the black-clad Tragedy Queen – compounded her misery. Her father looked across the silent dinner table and sighed; her mother burst into tears whenever she walked into a room. She was reduced now, subsumed: the symbol of loss.

There was even, for the first time in their lives, a new awkwardness with her sister. On that first afternoon after Mary and James had broken the news, Jane had been horribly shaken by the one, short, private outburst of grief that could not be contained. Since then, Cassy had resolved never to expose her to it again, with the result that her nights were yet more uncomfortable. In their snug little bedroom, she had to feign sleep until Jane herself slept. Only then could she turn on her side, gag her mouth with a handkerchief and weep silently until she was spent.

They were, the four of them, now locked into this unhappy situation. All needed to break free of it. To Kent, Cassy decided, she must go.

'My dear sister!' Edward Austen stood in the elegant porch of his gracious home, sleek with contentment and acting for all the world as if nothing had changed since the last time they met. 'I hope your journey was pleasant? You picked a fine day for it.' He guided her through to the ample hall. 'I know you will want to gather yourself' – the footman saw to her luggage, a maid

142

vanished her cloak away – 'but, I must tell you, the children are quite wild with excitement. If you do not soon go to the nursery, they may be in danger of bursting!'

Cassy was on the stairs before she noticed that her brother had made no mention of her bereavement or her pallor or her now skeletal frame. Of course, Edward had already dealt with the matter in their earlier correspondence. He would feel no need to raise it again. With a sense of relief, she followed the maid down the long corridor, past a sequence of doors opening on to to sunny, south-facing bedrooms: there was space enough here to contain any number of heartbroken young ladies, where they could weep undisturbed. She was shown into her own room, tested the mattress on the pretty bed with its muslin hangings and found it to her liking.

A wisteria bloom peeked through the window. She lifted the sash, drank in the scent, surveyed the Kentish countryside arranging itself fetchingly into the distance, and then looked down to the lawn, where her two brothers walked side by side. Resting her forehead on the cool glass, she watched and wondered if they – as everyone at Steventon did, constantly – were talking about her? But studying the set of their heads, catching the occasional outburst of carefree laughter, she deduced they were not. These men had more cheerful matters to concern them; neither was minded to dwell on misfortune for long. And she thought:

All this is just what I needed. Here, for a while, I might find some relief.

Edward lived in a whole other world from the rest of the Austens. Though not the most intelligent or talented member of the family – indeed, far from it – he was the luckiest by some considerable measure. Through the simple virtues of his charm and easy good nature, he had been adopted at the age of fourteen by their distant relations, the childless and wealthy Mr and Mrs Knight. His current home, Rowling – far beyond anything his siblings could dream of – was but a resting post on the route to his eventual destination: he would one day inherit three extensive estates – Steventon, Godmersham and Chawton – and live the enviable life of the well-landed gentleman. In the meantime, Rowling would do.

To the blessings of a generous income and plenty of acres to manage, he could add three charming children and a beautiful wife who had wealth of her own. Why must money marry money, when the world would be so much happier were that not so?

Edward's wife, Elizabeth, a woman of exquisite manners and breeding, was always unfailingly polite to her Austen relations – actual affection she reserved for the much richer Knights – but, Cassy well knew, she did not quite approve of them all. Jane she clearly found too clever and eccentric – somewhat satirical, always reading, and at Rowling that was thought to be a little bit *odd*. Mrs George Austen: well, Mrs George Austen . . . Well meaning and so good and kind but, of course, she too was cleverer, and more outspoken, than good society required. But Cassy? Cassy had the great virtue of being unfailingly useful, and the comfort of knowing that – if Elizabeth must have a feminine in-law under her roof – then she was the one always preferred.

On this visit, Cassy found in Elizabeth the perfect companion. Elizabeth cared little for much save her husband – whom she adored – her children – each, individually, a marvel – and her charming, well-appointed home. So all this fresh, raw grief did not seem to trouble her unduly. Cassy could sense it, and for that, she was grateful.

One afternoon in late May, the two women sat alone in the sunny dressing room upstairs: Elizabeth gazing out at the park; Cassy knitting a shawl for the new baby.

'Oh, Cass, do look! Do look at Fanny out on her pony. There she goes. Oh, the cherub! I must say – do you not agree? – she is already developing the most exquisite seat.'

Cassy looked too, and complied: 'She is an exquisite child in every respect. Already a lady, and only four years old.'

Elizabeth sighed with satisfaction, and patted the baby inside her. 'Perhaps this one will be a sister for her to play with. I think I should like that, after two little boys. Although husbands are – are they not? – always so delighted when one presents them with sons. Hmm.' She thought deeply. 'No. I do not think I mind whatever it is, this time.' She shifted uncomfortably. 'But I do dearly wish it would come.'

Cassy cast off and started another row: knit one, then purl one. 'It cannot be much longer now.'

'Oh, indeed. And I am so grateful to have you here, after all. To think I was going to have to manage without you! I confess I had not come up with another arrangement to suit me.' She smiled, complacent. 'It *has* worked out well.' Then had the grace to look, momentarily, ruffled. 'Oh, forgive me – I did not mean—'

'But of course,' Cassy assured her, and loosened a stitch.

Little Henry arrived safely, his father was suitably delighted and Cassy's days were full from then on. It fell to her to keep the nursery happy while Elizabeth was confined. She oversaw Nanny and Nurse, played spillikins, taught cup and ball with an expert precision; consoled, controlled and amused. There was the occasional skirmish with Fanny, who was deeply attached to her devoted mama and developing a rather strong character, but even that Cassy welcomed: balm could be applied to those childish miseries; there was no sort of balm for herself. The danger times came when the children napped or took air. Cassy dared not sit idle, for then dark thoughts and grief might rear up and consume her. So she would relieve Nurse, and compulsively dry, press and fold pile upon pile of muslin squares.

The great blessing of this interlude was that her evenings were easy. She and Edward dined alone, and in harmony; his company was never less than pleasing. This brother was not one for deep reflection or spiritual discourse or books, even: there was no reading here round the fire. Instead, they enjoyed an excellent dinner, very good wine and an uncomplicated, contented conversation that followed the same pattern night after night:

'I spoke to Spike today. He predicts the year's crop will be excellent.' This over a dish rich and substantial: say, a large slab of venison pie.

'There is talk of a good young filly coming up at the next auction. Though my stables are already crowded, she may be hard to resist.' Here, he might add a good slice of ham.

'So another fine son, and Elizabeth safe and getting stronger by the minute.' Edward generally enjoyed two servings of syllabub. And once his glass had been filled to the brim with his very good port, would always thus sum up his thoughts for the evening: 'Yes. All would be splendid in every direction, were I not plagued with this insufferable digestion. It makes one quite bilious.'

Then, with an affectionate 'Goodnight', they would part good and early. Cassandra could return to her room at the end of the corridor, and weep undisturbed.

At last, one month into Cassy's stay there, Elizabeth was able to return downstairs for a much discussed, highly anticipated Family Dinner. In a triumphal progress worthy of the Queen of Sheba, she returned to the drawing room, leaning on Cassy's arm.

'How more than pleasant to be back!' she exclaimed in response to the warm welcome. 'I must own that I have been looking forward to this moment with mounting excitement.'

Cassy settled her into her favourite armchair and tucked a rug around her knees.

'All of us together again. How blessed we are, husband. Mrs Knight, my mother and my sisters must be arriving shortly.'

Satisfied that her charge was comfortable, Cassy turned to leave.

'Although how I shall struggle through the evening without once gazing upon the beauty of my dear little Henry, I am not at all sure.'

There was not long now until dinner and Cassy needed to wash the nursery off her person and make herself presentable.

'His eyelashes, Edward, are really quite astonishing! I am convinced they grow as one watches. Oh, how I shall miss him tonight.'

'Do not worry yourself, my love,' Edward reassured her. 'He will be safe with Nurse.'

The drawing room was so very long that Cassy was only at the door, and therefore still able to hear Elizabeth's insistence: 'Oh, he cannot be left with just Nurse, Edward. He is far too precious! Cassy can sit with him while I am here. We must not forget that she is still in mourning. It would not be appropriate for her to join our happy party. The servants can send something up on a tray.'

'But, my dear,' she caught Edward's reply, 'I thought this was a *Family Dinner*?'

'Indeed,' agreed Elizabeth. 'Now where is my family? I did think they would be with us by now.'

Biting her lip, nails pressed into palms, Cassy moved swiftly through the hall, up the stairs, along the long corridor into her room and shut the door behind her. Henry's lashes could go unmeasured, just for two minutes. She needed to think.

In fact, this was a moment of sharp revelation. Since her youth, she had held a strong sense of her own purpose. She had been put on this earth, blessed – though it sometimes seemed more of a curse – with a sharp intelligence, and great appetite for employment, for a very good reason. It had seemed safe to assume that ordained destiny had been marriage to Tom. But there, she had been sadly mistaken.

So what now? The day would come, sooner or later but would come for sure, when her parents were gone and Jane would be married. (Her mind always snagged on the words, but one must believe they were true.) Yet her own future appeared murky and unfathomable – like a pond after rain-fall. She looked and she looked but could not see her way through. Suddenly, courtesy of Elizabeth, all was made visible.

Cassy might not have much money, but she knew herself to be rich in one other sound currency: usefulness. And on that she could get an excellent exchange. Elizabeth had four infants already and was still young; there could be plenty more yet. Kent was the place – the only place – in which Miss Austen could live well and work hard, keep herself to herself and not be a nuisance. Here, she could become a near priceless com-modity: the single sister. The spinster aunt. The invaluable treasure. This, after all, must be her purpose; this, God's design all along. She would prove indispensable.

A new and cold sense of calm came over Cassy as she splashed her face with water, adjusted her cap and returned to her duties.

CHAPTER 10

Kintbury, March 1840

'*From this time Captain Wentworth and Anne Elliot were repeatedly in the same circle.*'

It was Caroline who was reading this evening. Determined not to be ill, Cassandra had still to admit to being not quite well enough. Though she had made plans – to help in the house; to visit Elizabeth Fowle and insist she commit to a new house with poor Isabella – she had, in fact, been unable to be useful all day.

'*Whether former feelings were to be renewed must be brought to the proof; former times must undoubtedly be brought to the recollection of each . . .*'

Isabella and Caroline had been working together clearing the bedrooms, and Cassandra had deemed it unsafe to read through the letters: anyone could walk in at any time. The afternoon she had passed on the sofa, in an unfamiliar idleness. She had not even made progress with her patchwork; her fingers were too stiff and swollen to sew.

'*They had no conversation together, no intercourse*'

but what the commonest civility required. Once so much to each other! Now nothing!'

The one blessing was that Mary had been unable to join them, foiled by the twin curses of her mysterious foot and her legendary busyness. So at least the household had been perfectly peaceful.

'Now they were as strangers; nay, worse than strangers, for they could never become acquainted. It was a perpetual estrangement.'

'Oh!' Isabella burst out. 'Poor Anne! I do feel for her most awfully.'

Caroline stopped, for the tenth time that evening. A newcomer to listening, or certainly a newcomer to listening with any sort of enjoyment, Isabella was a most participatory audience. It was as if she were at the circus rather than listening to a novel. She was unable to sit still: one moment half out of her seat with excitement, the next slumping back in despair. Every few lines she exclaimed at what had just happened and wondered out loud what might come next.

'Will they ever be united? I think they will soon be united. Oh, *will* they be united? What will become of Anne if they are not?'

Caroline demurred and continued: *'When he talked, she heard the same voice and discerned the same mind—'*

'I must say', cut in Isabella, 'that your sister understood affairs of the heart better than anyone else I ever heard. Do tell me, Cassandra. Did she <u>know</u> love herself?'

'No, my dear, I fear not. Though it was never a matter of particular sadness to her.' Cassandra smiled. How she loved the chance to talk of her Jane. 'She could always enjoy the company of the heroes of her novels, but in life she never had the good fortune to meet a man who was worthy—'

'Forgive me, Aunt Cass, but I think you are mistaken!' exclaimed Caroline. 'Surely, there *was* once a gentleman!'

Cassandra felt suddenly uneasy. What was this new, alternative history? She issued the line she had perfected and honed: 'I can assure you, my sister never once formed any sort of attachment of the strength to disturb the surface of her contented existence.'

'But', Caroline went on, with mounting excitement, 'I am talking of the gentleman you both met at the seaside. You told me the story yourself, Aunt.' She turned to Isabella: 'It truly is the stuff of romance,' then back to Cassandra: 'I recounted this all to my brother James-Edward, only recently. Do you not remember? Oh, dear Aunt Cass, I do believe I have never before seen you quite so confused.'

'And pale!' added Isabella, coming over to her side. 'Perhaps you should go up and rest? You have not been yourself these past two days.'

Cassandra's head was spinning. She felt weak. She had no recollection of saying any such thing, ever, to any— And at once her mind flooded with the recollection of the whole sorry scene: the one moment of weakness and deceit in a lifetime of honesty and iron self-control. For the sake of her dignity she had simply chosen to forget. 'I must say I do not know what on earth you are talking about, Caroline. What is this fancy you have got in your head?'

'Only one *you* put in there! Well, if you really do not remember' – Caroline glanced sideways at her aunt – 'then let me tell the story.'

'Indeed,' Cassandra replied, outwardly calm, all turmoil within. 'Please do.'

'So,' Caroline began. 'This is the sum of it and all that I know. It came out – when was it? About '28 I think it must have been. You were staying with us near here, at Newtown. Or perhaps you do not recall Newtown, even? Where we lived with my brother?'

'Thank you, Caroline,' Cassandra replied, tartly. 'My memories of Newtown are perfectly clear.'

Caroline turned back to Isabella. 'My brother had a friend, a Mr Henry Edridge – a quite unusually good-looking and charming gentleman.'

Isabella sat up; this piqued her feminine interest.

'At that time he was with the Engineers.'

'Ah, the Engineers.' Isabella sighed.

'And he happened to call on us when my Aunt Cassandra was staying. Well, *she* was very much struck with him. Could not take her eyes away! And really quite altered in the young gentleman's presence. Almost kittenish, I am inclined to describe it.'

154

The cousins laughed; Cassandra squirmed.

'And *I* was very much struck by her admiration of him. For Aunt Cass rarely admires anyone, as you well know.'

Why, Cassandra wondered and not for the first time, did Caroline find it so hard to like her? The issue had long puzzled her, for she had always endeavoured to be the kindest of aunts.

'It was quite soon after that visit that we heard Mr Edridge had died.'

'No!' Isabella gasped. 'Poor Mr Edridge!'

'And when I related this fact to my aunt here she behaved in the most astonishing manner. She jumped up at once, then – legs too weak to hold her – sank back in her chair.' Caroline acted this out to add to the drama. In fact, there was more of the melodrama in her performance. If only she, too, had chosen forgetfulness. 'Her hands flew to her heart. She was completely beside herself, quite close to tears. And as you know no one has ever witnessed *her* crying – save my mother, of course.'

'Well, indeed.'

'And then the words just poured out of her: Mr Edridge had struck her as one unusually gifted with all that was agreeable.'

'Dear Mr Edridge.'

'*And* that he reminded her strongly of another gentleman from the past, whom they had met one summer when they were by the sea. I think, Aunt Cass, you indicated this was in Devonshire?'

Had she indeed? That was unfortunate. 'As this

did not happen,' Cassandra found the presence to reply, 'I strongly doubt that I indicated any such thing.'

'You did not name the place, that I do know,' Caroline persisted. 'Though I am sure you did not say Lyme, for that I should have remembered.'

'Nothing ever happened in Lyme, to that I shall testify.' Cassandra cleared her throat. 'Though there was that fire when my family was staying—'

'Yes, yes.' With a flick of her hand, Caroline extinguished that tired anecdote before it could find life, and resumed. 'And this gentleman seemed greatly attracted to my dearest Aunt Jane. Imagine, Isabella, meeting a gentleman by the seaside. And falling in love.'

'Oh, *imagine*.'

'I gathered that this was an intercourse of a few weeks. And then it came to that point that all lovers dread: the moment of parting.'

'The worst, the very worst moment of all,' Isabella said, with some feeling.

'And he was urgent to know where the family might be next summer, implying – *I* think – that he should be there also, wherever it might be.'

'Yes?'

'And soon after they heard of his death!'

On that tragic note, Isabella was struck dumb, as was Cassandra, for quite different reasons. Half of Caroline's story was plainly ridiculous. The girl had always had a strong imagination, as well as a talent for embroidery, and was employing both quite liberally here. But how now to proceed? It was not easy to dismiss as complete fabrication that which held the kernel of truth. She paused. It was vital to choose her words carefully.

'Well, what a lovely confection of nothing at all that was, my dear,' she began, sounding, she hoped, characteristically firm. 'Most charming, indeed; so charming I almost wish it had happened. How amused your Aunt Jane would be to hear of herself as its heroine.' With some effort, she drew herself to her feet. 'I remember your Mr Edridge quite clearly, now you remind me, and I do agree I was most moved by the news of his death.' She reached down for her valise. 'As one is when any young person of promise is taken too early.' She went to leave the room. 'I can only think that the sadness of it all promoted some strange episode within me.' The very act of walking was increasingly difficult. She clutched at the door-frame for support. 'Such confusion can strike sometimes, when one is old. It may happen to you when you are my age. And so now you know that, these days, you can no longer count on me as any sort of reliable witness. The past is becoming increasingly blurred.' She felt for the doorknob and turned on the threshold. 'I should not repeat that story if I were you, Caroline. When your Aunt Jane was still with us and enjoying her little burst of success, there came a few vultures who liked to feed on any scraps of her life. The stories were not enough for them. They wanted the facts about her, and she was not minded to share them. As her novels live on – and I hope and believe they will do – there may well be more in the future. We must be very mindful of what we leave out for them to pick on. Very mindful indeed.'

Cassandra opened the door, stepped into the dimly lit hall and, as she did so, caught an indistinct figure shrink suddenly into the shadows. 'Oh!' she cried out in alarm.

'Excuse me, m'm.' The figure stepped forward and bobbed. 'Only me, m'm.'

'Good heavens, Dinah! You gave me quite a turn.'

'Just at m' dusting, m'm. No rest for the wicked.'

Dusting the keyhole? '*Most* conscientious,' she said, smiling. Was it a trick of the lamp or did the maid, for once, look almost abashed? 'But please, do not work *too* hard. Goodnight, Dinah.'

''Night, m'm.'

Cassandra turned away. She felt thoroughly weary and the vicarage stairs now loomed before her, steep as an Alpine peak. Slowly, carefully, she scaled them. By the time she got to her room, she was almost breathless. Shutting the door firmly on the horrors of the evening, she fell on to her bed.

Thoughts of such mundanities as changing into her nightclothes or attending to her toilet were stillborn. Cassandra's mind was full. Her brain was pounding. Her whole being was consumed with involuntary, recovered sensation: the sea air on her cheeks; the pretty tinkle that shop doorbell made when one opened it; the shock – that piercing, scorching, quicksilver flash – when her gloved hand chanced to touch that of a stranger. And that warm melting sense of homecoming when she looked up and into his eyes.

'Miss Austen? Miss Austen!' Dinah's voice came as though from the end of a very long tunnel. 'Oh God save us, don't tell me she's gone and died on us. That's all we need.' In a moment of blessed relief, a cool hand touched her forehead before it was whipped away again, sharply. 'She's on fire! Can you hear me, Miss Austen? You stay there, now. I'll get help. Miss Isabella?' The dark room fell silent once more.

Now roused to something like consciousness, Cassandra felt agony all over her person: head, throat, limbs all throbbed and burned; her mouth had, unaccountably, been filled with sharp objects; lungs were in combat with air. And yet that was as nothing to the pain in her psyche. Was this it: the thing she dreaded above all? Oh, she had never feared death – indeed, had often felt impatient for its protracted arrival. What, she might ask it, took you so long? – but when it came, it must come to her in her own bed. To die when away visiting – inflicting such inconvenience, suffering those final indignities in a foreign house; denied a last gaze upon her own bedroom walls, or a silent farewell to her beloved home soil – that was the worst fate of all.

As she struggled to sit up, another thought struck with a force that sent her back deep into the pillow: she could not, she must not go now. *Her work was not done.*

'Cassandra? My dear, can you speak to me? Tell me, what are your symptoms?'

She thought she replied – 'I must confess to feeling a little under the weather, Isabella' – but they did not seem to hear.

'It's a fever, madam. Feel her. A raging fever. I'll call the doctor at once.'

'No, Dinah!' Isabella was sharp. 'We will *not* have the doctor.'

Cassandra tried to speak. 'But I have plenty of money. Do not worry about that, Isabella. Oddly enough, I have ended up rather well off in my old age. That is the unexpected benefit of outliving one's loved ones. I have profited most shamefully by my longevity. So please, do not consider the cost of it. I insist I will pay.'

'Listen to her. She's got the deliriums. She must be in terrible danger. She's as old as them hills. Please, Miss Isabella. I'll run and get him now. We don't want her pegging out here.'

Cassandra tried again – 'I am only sorry that I may not be much help in the house, just today' – but no one acknowledged her.

'No,' Isabella talked over her. 'We cannot and we will not have the doctor and that is the end of it. It is simply unthinkable! I shall nurse her myself. Let us not waste any more time in discussion.

Fetch the laudanum, Dinah, the Tartar, cold water and flannels. Then go up to the big house and beg for some ice. They should have plenty at this time of year.'

Though the voice was unmistakeably that of Isabella, the commanding tone and active efficiency were quite unexpected, as was the hostility to professional medicine. Had not she been most complimentary about their doctor before? Cassandra wanted to open her eyes just to confirm the identity of this confident individual but that did not seem to be possible, right at that moment.

'Do accept my apologies for causing all this inconvenience. I am sure I will be perfectly restored after a few hours' sleep.'

'Try and hush now, Cassandra. You will hurt your throat with that moaning. Now, I am going to undress you and get you under the covers.'

The first of the many indignities!

'Do not struggle, dear. You will exhaust yourself further. It is only me, Isabella. There we are. That must feel better now, does it not? I am just going to slip your nightgown over your head.'

The arms that pulled back the bedding, plumped up the pillows and were now tenderly laying her upon them were careful, expert and strong. Cassandra wanted to think more about this, to reassess her hostess in the light of this revelation. But then her mouth was opened, laudanum dropped on her tongue and all thoughts were lost.

★   ★   ★

161

Like a tempest, the illness raged through her. For several days, Cassandra battled and raved at it. This would not take her. She must prevail. All sense of time was lost as she took on each symptom and summoned some sort of strength to beat it away.

There was the odd false release, when the illness lulled and her body could rally. Then, she might see Dinah in the doorway – gimlet eyes set in a face hard with resentment – or Caroline wringing her hands, unsure what to do. And Pyramus, always Pyramus: standing guard at her bedside and willing her well.

The darkest hour came when her sister-in-law, Mary, appeared. Then Jane's voice came through to her, from another sickroom in another, more terrible time: '*She* is to attend *me*? I can admit now to having harboured faint hopes of recovery. But if Mary is coming, I must face it: Death cannot be far behind.'

'I pity you, Cassandra. I must say I *pity* you,' Mary was saying. 'It is a maxim of mine that one must mind never to fall ill when one is visiting – the height of bad manners – and I am proud to say that *I* have never once had the misfortune to break it.'

Cassandra decided that she was too frail to respond.

'Of course, there was the one occasion when I was staying with your brother in London and brought down with the face-ache. Oh, the pain.

162

One can know no true discomfort until one has suffered *that*. But *I* had taken my own maid and – how lucky I was, then – a dear, caring *husband*. But you, all *alone* . . .'

A weak sun filtered between the thin curtains. Cassandra had lost track of the days but could sense that, while she had lain there and done nothing, spring had been striding ahead.

'It must be *misery*, aware as you must be of the terrible impact you are having. The house was already at sixes and sevens. I must say . . .'

For the first time, she felt a confidence that she would be up and about soon, and able to drink up that brisk, fresh air.

'. . . I do feel for poor Isabella. As a vicarage wife myself, then – alas! – a vicarage widow, I know better than anyone what has to be done and the emotions entailed. I shall never, *never* forget your brother Henry's glee when it was *his* turn to take over Steventon. It is not pleasant to witness the elation of your successor in gaining what you have lost. Not a thought for us or our feelings! No respect for our home or possessions! Nought but a rapacious – *rapacious*! – desire to get all that he could.'

The pain had now eased, yet Cassandra still begged for a strong dose of laudanum. She felt an overwhelming desire for a very deep sleep.

There was, though, one positive aspect to this brush with her Maker and for that Cassandra was grateful. Even before the crisis, she had started to develop an affection for dear Isabella, that strange little romantic who had never felt a breath of romance. To that, she could now add respect.

She had already discounted Isabella's lack of domestic abilities. After all, Cassandra told herself, running a house – though important and someone did have to do it – was not the only indicator of personal depth. On her first full day here, she had hoped that the true talent of her hostess would be revealed. And now, thanks to this unfortunate business, it had.

Isabella was born to physic the sick: that much was clear. Her potions were equal to that of the highest apothecary; she applied them with wisdom as if properly trained. Her manner was all kind-ness but, on top of that, sensible – one might even call it professional. What a comfort she must have been to her ailing parents. What a comfort she was now to Cassandra.

'You know, my dear, I owe my life to you,' she proclaimed. This was, by her own standards, a rare outburst of the highest emotion, though her voice was so weak it took the force from her words.

'Nonsense.' Isabella lifted her, straightened the bed linen. 'Even at the crisis, I could feel that stubborn determination within you.' She smiled with approval. 'Your strength is extraordinary. It will take more than a fever to undo *you*, Cassandra.

That I can see.' She settled down in the armchair. 'Now, would you like me to read, or are you fit for conversing today?'

'Please, the latter. Tell me, how passed your morning? What goes on in the world of the well?'

'My best pupil was in with me earlier. Poor Winterbourne's boy. Such a good head for numbers.'

Cassandra was now in the calm, tedious process of convalescence. Not yet well enough for downstairs, she was at least less of a nuisance to the household. Dinah left her alone and a meek daily maid came in her place.

But each afternoon, Isabella sat with her and that was always the best part of her day. Through her life, Cassandra's happiest moments had been passed in the company of excellent women. They had all, of course, sadly departed. Oh, she missed and thought of them, constantly, and of one above all.

'His poor mother has never recovered herself, but *he*, I believe, could have a future. My scheme is to bring him on as well as I am able and then introduce him to my good friend at the Hungerford Apothecary. An apprenticeship like that will make all the difference to the unfortunate family . . .'

Now, here, in this vicarage, Cassandra had found another, most unexpected, excellent woman. She had quite forgotten the feeling, that deep, joyful and satisfying feeling brought by good feminine companionship. What a blessing to enjoy it once more.

Within days, Cassandra was well enough to rise from her bed, for just a few hours, and sit in the armchair with the sun on her face. Soon, she thought, she might have the strength to not only hold a novel but also to read it herself. Isabella rushed off to select something and was gone for some time.

'I do apologise. You must think us terribly wanting.' Isabella's mouth twisted with shame. 'I fear this is all I could find.'

'Ah. *Peveril of the Peak*.' Cassandra's arms drooped at the weight of it. 'Well, I have certainly not read this one and am slightly surprised that you, as my doctor, might think of suggesting it. Should you soon find me in horrible relapse, you know what to blame.'

Isabella, laughing, left her alone and Cassandra did, at least, try to start reading. But it seemed she was in no sort of mood for Sir Walter. That must be a positive sign. As she had never before known the mood required for that overblown nonsense, her old spirits were surely returning.

She dropped the book on to the table beside her. Perhaps, at last, she was well enough to return to her project? So much time had been lost; she could not impose on them here for much longer. Pulling herself up to her feet, she waited for the dizziness to pass and then moved over to the bed, slipped her hand under the mattress, felt about, felt again . . . And soon was searching most frantically through the length of the bedding. Under the pillows. Between the sheets. All over the room. There was nothing. She gasped, clutching at the bedpost to stop herself falling. Import coursed through her.

The letters were gone.

CHAPTER 11

Kintbury, April 1840

For three days, Cassandra was powerless. All she could do was stay in her bedroom and fret at the impossibility of her situation. It was unthinkable that she might ask for any sort of explanation. After all, the letters were not her property. She had no business keeping them. But was their removal simply a matter of innocent housekeeping, or was there a more sinister motive in play?

At last, the afternoon came when she felt almost well again. Isabella came in and exclaimed at the sight of her visitor, dressed.

'Well, you are better. Look at you! Quite back to life.' She placed a hand on a forehead and declared it temperate; she examined an eye and announced it was clear.

'Thank you, my dear Isabella. And may I apologise again for all the disruption I have caused you? I am very aware that maintaining my sickroom proved an onerous burden on your already stretched household.'

'Not at all.' Isabella looked around and assessed the state of the chamber. The process did not take her long. 'I wish now that we had given you more comfortable quarters. It is I who should say sorry, to you. It must not have been pleasant, spending so long in here. We thought – Well, we were wrong.' She ran a finger along the chest top. 'And I cannot pretend that much energy has been spent on cleaning while you were ailing. I fear the daily maid has never been known to perform above or beyond.'

Cassandra pondered. So that left her with two possible suspects: Mary, who certainly had been given the opportunity. Oh, why had she begged for that laudanum? It was pure self-indulgence! And Dinah. Difficult Dinah – who knew both *what* was hidden and *where*.

'There is no need to sit with me now, Isabella. Why not go off into the village? I am quite sure you have some good work or other to be getting on with.'

'Well, there is some calf's foot jelly I must take to the Winterbournes. You will not mind being deserted?'

Indeed, Cassandra would very much welcome it. She insisted. There were things she must do.

After a suitable hiatus, Cassandra rose and, for the first time in weeks, re-entered the world. She stood on the landing, and sensed the particular sort of silence that prevailed only in an empty household. How different it felt, sounded and smelled with its family away. The personality altered. It sank back into its shell. She wondered how it would behave when the Fowles had left and the new man in charge. It was pleasing that Steventon had stayed in her family and she had never to witness a stranger treating *their* rectory as *his* home.

Great progress – if progress was the word – had been made during Cassandra's absence. The Kintbury Vicarage, now half empty, was officially in interregnum. The Fowle paintings were gone and the blank walls stood, patient, awaiting those of another. There were no curtains on the window at the turn of the stairs. Tom's room was bare. She moved gingerly towards that of Eliza. Grooves on the floor were the last testament of the bed that stood there for nearly a century. Black marks bore the shape of those samplers. But the settle, that heavy oak settle, was still in its place.

Cassandra's one hope was that the letters had been put back where they belonged. That would be sensible and quite understandable; indeed, the only possible explanation. She chided herself – foolish old woman! – for thinking that there could possibly be any other. It was even more of a struggle to lift its lid now; the illness had sapped her strength. But she was determined, moreover confident, that effort would be rewarded. And, after some considerable struggle, at last the lid yielded. She was in.

All was exactly how she had left it. The Fowle children's letters on top, her mother's still beneath, with those of Martha. She rummaged through the next layers, where Jane's and her own should be, had they been replaced in a casual, innocent manner . . . They were not. Now she was worrying, leaning in further, hands delving deeper. Fulwar's script . . . Mary's . . . two Austen brothers . . . She threw them to one side. Nearing the bottom, she could see only the writing of strangers, upon paper that was now cracked and yellowing: old, meaningless missives, of no possible interest.

Cassandra surrendered all hope. With a creak of her joints, she sat back on her heels and took a moment to assess her situation. The letters had been removed from her room in an act of deliberate obstruction: that much was now clear. Her private correspondence, and that of Jane, was now in the hands of another. Their intimate thoughts and emotions, which she had sought to conceal, could be revealed to a stranger. Cassandra had come to Kintbury with but one, desperate objective: to protect her dear sister. And she had failed. Burying her face in her hands, she gave in to despair.

Tempting though it was to spend the afternoon moping, reasonable though it might be to wallow in misery – she was old, she had been ill, she was thoroughly spent – Cassandra did not have the luxury of time. The rest of the household could return at any moment. There were packets of letters all over the floor. She must cover her tracks. With a sigh, she struggled up and began to replace everything where it had been found. Now, how was it all arranged? Was James next to Mary, or was Mary under Martha? She cleared a small gap and there, to her astonishment, was a whole other bundle from Jane.

Cassandra seized it; she held it to her bosom. This was extraordinary! A gift beyond gold! And, as with all the best gifts, quite unexpected. She had had no idea that Jane and Eliza had corresponded so often. The two women were friends, of course, but not *so* very close. How did Jane have so much to say?

All thoughts of the missing papers forgotten, Cassandra shut the old settle and scurried back to her room.

Steventon Rectory
19th September, 1800

My dear Eliza,

We are delighted to hear that you are safely delivered of your recent encumbrance, and that the baby herself is thriving. It is a splendid name – an Isabella can only grow up to be a heroine – or a Spanish Queen, I suppose, but I think we will not wish that fate upon her. No. Isabella Fowle will be a heroine whose adventures are both magnificent and solely confined to the great county of Berkshire. I look forward to reading of them, sometime in the future, but in the meantime, please do assure her, mere thriving is all I expect and require.

All goes well here with us. I have nothing to report but the general health of all in the parish of Steventon and Deane. Of the more far-flung Austens, we have only good reports, and thank God for them. My sea-faring brothers continue to heap glory upon us – did you hear that Frank is now made Post-Captain? Of course you did. No doubt Kintbury has had so many letters on that matter that the Vicarage was buried and you have only this minute dug yourselves out from under. The act of writing the words brings such a thrill, that I cannot resist it. And now that he has a position, he can only want for a wife. I still harbour hopes of Martha for him. My family is greedy, Eliza – not content with taking just one of your sisters – we want all of them. And Martha is already a sister, in all but name. She is coming to us tomorrow. We have nothing ahead but a festival of books and chatting and walking – so much walking in this excellent weather. Quite desperate walkers, we three ladies are. It may not be everybody's idea of ultimate pleasure, but we are the oddest of creatures and will enjoy it enormously.

I hope the visit will distract Cassy from her

misery, for a few days at least. It is now three years since the death of poor Tom, and her spirits are nowhere near mending. Oh, I understand it, of course, I just wish it were not so. Her anxiety about her future is perfectly natural. After all, what <u>will</u> become of her? There is the question. And – this comes in deep confidence, dear Eliza – it leads us straight to another, which is: what, after all, will become of <u>me</u>, too?

Before we lost Tom, there was no reason to doubt that the Future was a happy thing and off far in the distance. Yet, suddenly, it seems it is upon us, and has a menacing air. One day, perhaps soon, we will have to leave Steventon. Oh, do not worry! My fine father is as hale as ever, but even he cannot be Rector in perpetuity. And we two poor, dependent daughters must then be turned out into a world which is unlikely to receive us with the warmest of welcomes. I cannot pretend that the prospect is pleasing.

Forgive me! This began as a letter of great celebration, and then without warning took a horrible turn. I am quite incorrigible. Present me with a clear blue sky and I will find you a cloud. Disregard all the above, and give our love to your little Isabella.

Yours ever,
J. Austen.

'Oh, no!' Jane's shriek pierced the air of the hills around Steventon. 'Please – Cassy! Martha! – stop now. I beg of you. Or I shall die laughing, as we used to say when we were at school. And you will have to carry my poor lifeless body back home.'

'I am sorry,' Cassy protested. 'It is true. She looked simply ridiculous.'

'She certainly did.' Jane giggled again. 'But have we not analysed the evening so very minutely as to destroy any memory of enjoyment? I thought it perfectly pleasant while I was there. Now, thanks to you two, all I can see is her thick neck and pink husband and in retrospect it appears to me perfectly horrid.'

'Very well,' Cassy conceded. 'And if you did enjoy it, then I am happy for you. These days, I find far more diversion in the analysis than the event.'

'Dear Cass.' Jane took her arm and became serious. 'You used to love dances and parties and going out in society.'

'Did I?' She found it hard to remember now. 'Then perhaps I am getting too old for it.'

'I am older,' their dear friend Martha put in. 'And I find everything amusing while I am with you.'

They crested the hill, stopped to catch a breath and gazed down upon Steventon.

'Home.' Jane sighed happily. 'Now is that not the sweetest of sights?'

'It is perfect,' Martha agreed. 'What is there

better than a small country village?' Bright autumn sunlight caught the edge of the steeple. 'There goes your father.' Mr Austen strode briskly down the lane in the direction of the parsonage. 'Such an excellent man. I do not know how he manages, both the church and the land, at his age.'

'Papa?' Jane scoffed, a little too violently. 'Fit as a flea! So fit as to put most fleas to shame.'

She led the march down the hill.

'And long may he remain so!' Martha plodded behind them. 'Still, he will be wanting James to take over ere too long, I dare say.'

Cassy caught something in her tone: as if Martha knew more than they did. 'He is not quite as agile as he was, that is true,' she said thoughtfully. 'And Mama's health is not all it should be. I wonder . . .'

'The weather is turning. We are in for some rain, girls.'

'What is rain to us, Martha?' Jane spun round, hands outstretched: her cloak dancing about her. 'Come on! We have at least a whole hour yet before we have to be home.'

But Cassy opted to return alone, and help her mother prepare for their dinner.

By the time she was through the back door, Cassy was wet through. She took off her cloak and her boots, put them to dry and made for her room to change. Passing the parlour, she heard the sounds of conversation within. Her brother James and his wife Mary were early – there was a surprise! She

176

reached for the doorknob, fully intending to go in and greet them. And then James's voice drifted through to her.

'So, Father, I am – we are – keen now to advance. As I enter my thirty-sixth year, it is an appropriate time for me to assume greater responsibility and perform to the full my role as a Man of the Church. I hope you agree that my talents are more than equal to the task ahead of me.'

'Oh, my dear boy,' Mr Austen proclaimed, 'I need not assure you of that. You are an exemplary curate to me and you will make an exemplary rector to the parish.'

'Exemplary,' Mary repeated with fervour, adding quietly but urgently: 'And then, Austen – the house. Remember: the house.'

'Ah, yes. The house. I – We that is – It seems, with our growing family—'

'We now have *a child*.' Mary could not resist any opportunity to mention her triumph in that regard.

'You have two children, my dear,' said Mrs Austen. 'Let us not forget Anna.'

'Yes, of course. I mean to say that we do now have *a son*.'

'And it occurs to us – it occurs to me, rather – that perhaps the space here may be proving too much for you both, with only the girls. Slightly smaller accommodation, less tiring for you, Mother, might be appropriate to the diminishing needs of your household as it is presently arranged.'

She heard her father stand up and start pacing.

'That you inherit the living has long been our agreement, and you have no need to doubt it. The question of timing that transfer, though . . . Perhaps I have caused some confusion by living too well and too long.'

'George, my dear! Please.'

"Tis but the fact of it, my love. We might have presumed that the Lord would take the matter into His own hands before now, but it seems He has other plans for us. Thank you for raising this, James. I have no desire to stand in the path of a good man's advancement. That cannot be God's intention. Allow me to discuss it in detail with your mother in private and, with His guidance, I have confidence we will be led swiftly and easily to a judgement of benefit to us all.'

Cassy pulled away and ran up soundlessly to their room. Heart thumping, she fell on to the bed and digested that which she should not have heard. It should come as no surprise. This was always meant to happen, sooner or later. It was simply that she had not been expecting it now. Where might they all go? She had no way of knowing, and did not expect to be consulted. This was their parents' decision, and theirs alone. By failing to marry, the daughters had forfeited any say in that matter. Cassy could accept it. This was her new life: to live helpfully, invisibly. She now viewed her own fate with the greatest indifference. But Jane?

For Jane, this would come as a terrible blow.

★   ★   ★

In the evening, at George Austen's request, Jane read from *Elinor and Marianne*. Her parents sat each side of the fireplace, each mirroring the position of the other – hands folded in laps, the light of pleasure on their creased, worn, old faces – like a sweet pair of book-ends. How they loved to listen to their Jane.

'Esteem him! Like him! Cold-hearted Elinor! Oh! Worse than cold-hearted! Ashamed to be otherwise. Use those words again and you will not hear back from me.'

From time to time, Mary leaned across to their mother, in an attempt to engage her in domestic conversation – 'Is the pig back from the butcher?'; 'Now, your chutney receipt . . .' – but Mrs Austen firmly rebuffed her.

'Excuse me, and be assured that I meant no offence to you, by writing, in so quiet a way, of my own feelings. Believe them to be stronger than I have declared; believe them, in short, to be such as his merit . . .'

Cassy sat with her sewing and felt soothed. As ever, Jane's words quelled her own troubled thoughts, and returned her to optimism. She might even have felt something approaching contentment, if only James would not fidget and smirk in that fashion. But jealousy in one – albeit a mild, silly jealousy that should not warrant notice – must always poison the mood of the whole company.

'. . . there would be many difficulties in his way, if he were to wish to marry a woman who had not either a great fortune or high rank.'

After half an hour, James could bear it no longer. He leaped to his feet, determined to make some interruption.

'Very clever, Jane. I must say. And so *brave* of you to even attempt that which has undone many a *good* writer: the epistolary form.'

'Indeed so!' Mary joined in, keen that the tedium be brought to an end. 'The epistolary form!' she repeated, obliging as a parrot, and with a parrot's comprehension of the words she repeated. 'Very challenging, I am sure.'

'There is an accolade.' Jane looked up and smiled. 'I appreciate it, coming from a writer such as yourself.'

'Quite so. I wonder if we should not return home now, my dear?' He strode about the room, retaking command of it. 'The weather and so on.'

'But we have only had reading, Austen. I do not feel as if we have yet had an *evening* here. Let us just talk among ourselves for a while. Or' – her eyes lit up – 'perhaps you, my love, might read to us now?' She spoke to the room. 'I know we would *all* enjoy that.'

'Oh, yes *please*, James.' Jane sat up, all enthusiasm. 'Do show us all how it is done.'

'Only if you insist.' Insistence was provided. 'Well then.' At once, the journey home lost its urgency. 'Perhaps my "Sonnet to Autumn" is most appropriate.' James settled down and began.

'Nymph of the straw-crowned hat, & kirtle
   pale,
Mild Autumn come, and cheer thy longing
   Swain;
Whether thou pleased survey'st the yellow plain
Bend in light currents to the Western gale . . .'

And Cassy's thoughts, so recently calmed, stirred again – rose up and overwhelmed her. What next? she asked herself as the sonnet trundled on. What came next in her tortuous journey? Where was life taking her now?

CHAPTER 12

Paragon, Bath
7th May, 1801

My dear Eliza,

My mother and I are arrived in Bath – you
no doubt want to congratulate us on that
towering achievement – and as for our failure
to stop off in Kintbury, there is no need to
chide us, for we chide ourselves quite enough.
Our excuse is that The Journey itself was
our master; The Journey decreed that it
should last but a day and we humble passen-
gers had no strength left to argue. Pleasant
though it would have been to be with the
beloved Fowle family, we too were keen to
get to our destination.

Thank you for your sympathies, but, having
begun life as a shock to which I should never
become accustomed, our departure from
Steventon came almost as relief. And for that,
as you so rightly predicted, I can thank your
sister. Though her overt elation did not ease
our moment of loss, Mary's keen delight to

get her feet through the door, propel ours out of it <u>and</u> rob us of all worldly possessions in the process, was such that the end could not come quick enough. We surrendered as soon as we could. I hope that they are all as happy there as she is expecting. There is no doubt my brother will prove a fine parson to the parish, and the house has already proved itself a good one for children. James-Edward will soon get his pony. And Anna does love the place so – the poor mite may there at last feel at home in her own family.

As for Bath – I cannot share my parents' high expectations, but then they are so very exalted I am not sure who could. Mr and Mrs G. A. are determined on a glorious retirement, with as much fine company and good health as a person can cope with, while we young ladies are promised to be met with splendid suitors in an endless array. We shall see. But should that all happen, I give you fair warning: I shall ignore all evidence of character or appearance or the good of our families and instead plump at once for the richest. I intend then to become so horribly spoiled and affected that you, poor humble Eliza, cannot hope ever to hear from me again.

In the meantime, we have been here three days and I have yet to meet a gentleman below the age of one hundred. And so far, even the city itself is toying with my affections. Its stone is refusing to glow in warm sunlight; instead it glowers darkly through a horrible fog. But I must give it time – not least because I have no choice in the matter. My future is here now, and I must make of it what I can.

There is at least the great distraction of getting settled to consume me. We are on the hunt for more permanent lodgings, which we hope to find soon. Perhaps then this loud city will feel more like a natural setting for us. And after that comes the first of our Great Summer Schemes, and we will, with Cowper's crowds 'impatient of dry land, agree, With one consent to rush into the sea'. Can you believe that these gay footloose creatures are in fact your old friends the Austens of Hampshire? Well then, nor yet can I.

You are kind to enquire so solicitously about my dear Cassy. While the world has moved on from her loss and on to other stories, it seems that you and I alone are left guarding her grief. I can offer the comfort that leaving our home has not caused her particular distress, but then I can remove it at once with my own reading: my sister's unhappiness is such that mere <u>place</u> no longer matters at all. My mother's hope that she will come out of it here and take to society are, I fear, unfounded. Yes, she still dresses in mourning, makes no more than the required effort with her appearance . . . You will have her ear, when she comes to visit with my father. Please, see if you can convince her; she does admire you so. Her current position is almost intolerable, and painful to this loving be-holder: all the conduct befitting a widow, without the past comforts of being a wife.

I am to tell you that she will be arriving on the 22nd and my father soon after. I trust that they find you both well and happy, and the nursery flourishing, and look forward to hearing all your news from them. As for us, please do try and get through to my sister, and give me your findings once they have left.

As ever,
J. Austen.

Cassandra was stupefied. This was not at all what she had expected. Perhaps the trauma of moving had loosened Jane's pen. She sat back to digest it: the confiding tone, the indiscretion even, were amazing to her. She had known of their friend-ship, but not of this depth of intimacy. And that Jane should write of herself in those terms? It was, she shifted uncomfortably, more than a little odd. She leafed through the next few. Each of these was peppered with references to Mary, and her treatment of Anna: *'she has now over-reached herself'* . . . *'please, can you talk to her'* . . . *'how much better it would be if she could stay with you in Kintbury'* . . . *'James' collusion causes us especial pain'* . . . *'The rare sight of a man taking the lead from his wife is ordinarily a matter for rejoicing, but in this instance . . .'*

This sorry story did not reflect well upon the family. Cassandra shuddered. Her fear was always that the Austens should be made into some sort of spectacle – albeit, she was well aware, but a minor one – and her present labours were devoted to the avoidance thereof. There was but one fact that was allowed to walk with the novels into posterity: that Jane had lived her short life as a stranger to drama; that few changes, no events, no crises broke the smooth current of its course. Anything beyond could be none of posterity's business.

She gathered them up – her valise was the only hiding place left to her – when her eye was distracted by the page that came after. What was this? No date, no place name and an un-characteristically hurried scrawl.

My dear Eliza,
    This comes to you with much thought and great urgency, so please forgive me if I move too swiftly to the Heart of the matter. You will know that I hope the Measles has passed now and all in Kintbury &c. &c. For I must share this with you, as I must share it with someone, though it is not my secret to tell. Even our parents do not as yet know the half of it and will not until we have some sign of an outcome. Oh, Eliza. My sister is deeply in love!

CHAPTER 13

Sidmouth, 1801

'What are we doing today, Aunt Cass?' Anna stood still on the doorstep, gazing wide-eyed at the bright vista before her. The year was 1801, and the Austens were in Sidmouth, on the first of their Great Summer Schemes. At Cassy's suggestion, her little niece had accompanied them.

'Well, first of all, we are putting on our bonnets properly.' Cassy leaned down and tied the ribbon under that sweet, pointed, eight-year-old chin. 'Today is going to be warm, and the sun is a fiercer creature here than in Hampshire. You do not want to get on the wrong side of it and end up in bed. There.' She straightened up again. 'What would *you* like to do, Anna? What is the top of your list?

'I cannot say.' Anna bit her lip and adopted the worried expression that bothered her aunts so. 'I have never been to the seaside before.' She had become so wary of giving a wrong answer to anything, she seemed these days too frightened

187

to say much at all. 'I am not sure – you decide for me, Aunt Cass.'

Cassy took her hand and together they walked down to the Mall. 'Let us start with the fish market; the earlier we get there, the better the choice, and your grandpapa's heart is set on mackerel for dinner.' She nodded and answered the good mornings from those out enjoying their promenade. 'Aunt Jane is already out in the sea somewhere, bathing.'

They scoured the machines, but one distant body looked much like another.

'Is bathing pleasant? It looks pleasant. Are children allowed?'

'You can paddle, my dear, later – if that is what you would like. Your aunt can show you. She loves the water. I cannot explain why, but I am no friend of the sea.' Cassy looked with distrust at the clear, still, blue bay: her mind could only see death and corpses. 'I shall stick to dry land. But the day is all yours to do as you please. Now, if I were still a little girl . . .' Anna looked up at her twenty-eight-year-old aunt with amazement. 'I was once, believe it or not. Though never one so grand as to be granted a summer in Sidmouth.' She squeezed the small hand that lay in hers. 'In your shoes, I should have liked to start some collection or other. There are so many shells we could find.'

'Shells!' The child's guard dropped at last.

'Yes!' Cassy felt excited herself. Anna was such

a bright little creature, full of natural enthusiasms that had not lately enjoyed outlet. 'And this is a very particular coastline. It is said you can find stones imprinted with shapes of strange, ancient animals.'

'Strange, ancient animals?'

They stopped then, and stared at the soft blue clay cliffs rearing up at the end of the beach – each finding it hard to believe in the legend.

'So 'tis said.' Cassy shrugged, and they resumed their progress. 'We shall have to investigate that for ourselves. But first, here we are.' They had passed the tearoom now, and arrived at the cottages, where nets hung on poles drying in the sunshine and boats were pulled up on to the beach. The catch of the day was laid out in baskets, and half of society was gathered around them.

'You see' – she bent down and whispered in Anna's ear – 'even the mundane matter of buying one's dinner becomes sport at the seaside. Hold tight, do not lose me. Let us go in.'

Cassy was so intent on her selection of mackerel that she was quite unaware of being an object of interest. But as the fisherman busied himself with paper and wrapping, she felt the prickle of unease that comes when someone is staring. She swung round, held Anna closer, and caught sight of a gentleman, out on the fringes, who was now walking swiftly away.

The heat was building as they made their way

back down the shingle. Cassy lifted her pale yellow muslin – here she, at last, had surrendered to popular pressure and given up all that hot, heavy black – to keep the hem dry. With deep concentration, and the odd outburst of joy, they hunted for shells and cleaned off the finest. Together, they made an affecting tableau: this tall, slim, handsome woman and sweet little girl, locked into their innocent pursuit. There were those on the Mall – and one in particular – who looked on it with pleasure, though they were themselves too busy to notice.

'This one is my favourite.' Anna stroked a small scallop inlaid with mother of pearl.

'It is a beauty,' Cassy agreed. 'But this is only your first morning. If we are to be serious about this, then there will be lots more to come. I have quite lost track of time. We ought to get back to your grandmother. But first' – oh, she did love a project! – 'let us go to the library on our way back, and buy a small notebook. Then you can keep a diary of your findings, and perhaps add sketches of the best ones? I can help with you that.'

This excellent plan was pleasing to both, though perhaps Cassy was the more pleased of the two. Chatting excitedly, they left the beach, crossed the Mall and made for the shop that stood next to the Reading Room. Its door was closed. Cassy's hand reached for the handle, her face turned away while she explained something to Anna. The bell gave its tinkle, her hand chanced to touch that of another . . . She flinched at the shock of it, turned and looked up. She felt the world change.

How long did they stand there? It could be a lifetime but was more likely a moment. Cassy dropped her eyes, caught sight of a book beneath his arm, focused on its spine, the words – *Elements of Conchology* – written thereon, and felt a fleeting disappointment it was not a good novel.

Then: 'Do excuse me.' He was bowing and tipping his hat. 'Good day to you, madam.'

She somehow effected a curtsey.

He smiled down at the girl – 'Miss' – and gestured to her hand. 'Forgive my impertinence, but I must say that is the most excellent shell.'

And with that, he was off into the morning, swallowed up by the fashionable crowd.

'How magnificent!' Jane blew in, untying her bonnet to reveal untidy hair and a glowing complexion. 'The water is at its finest this morning. Oh, but I do like it here. So much better than insufferable Bath. Now what have my darlings been up to? Well, you certainly look better, Cass – radiant, even. I hate to have to tell you that, despite your very best efforts, you seem to be recovering your bloom.' She took Anna's shoulders and peered into her face. 'And you, my child? Has the sea worked its magic yet? I think not! Now confess all, Anna. Where have you spent these past months – down a cave, up a chimney? Come now, spill out your wicked secrets.'

Anna giggled for the first time since her arrival. 'In Steventon, Aunt Jane, I promise!'

'Then there is no accounting for your pallor.' She laid down her hat. 'When your Aunt Cass and I lived in the rectory, we were careful to bloom every day. Quite rigorous we were with our blooming. Back then, it was thought quite rude not to. No doubt you young people have other ideas.'

Cassy laughed with them, quite distracted now from the unsettling events of her morning. Instead, she felt her heart twisting with pity for the poor child. There had been many regrets on leaving Hampshire, but the deepest was their withdrawal of daily contact with Anna. They had removed the one refuge from her troubles with Mary, which had always been difficult and, since the arrival of the blessed boy child, were now possibly intolerable. It had been a triumph to get her here for the summer. They would restore her: Cassy was sure of it. While the rest of the family besported themselves, she would bring this dear girl back to life.

'I will just go up and check on our mother,' Cassy announced, 'and then we can make plans for the rest of the day.'

'Is Grandmama very poorly?' asked Anna anxiously.

'No, my dear.' Jane gathered her up. 'There is no cause for concern. Your grandmother likes to take to her bed whenever we arrive somewhere new. It is her way of feeling at home. She can then test the mattress, meet the best doctors, sample the wares of the local apothecary and know just what to expect should real illness afflict her. Which it never does, incidentally. But perhaps that is her wisdom: prevention by good preparation. Like all the best invalids, she will outlive us all.'

'Jane, that is not quite fair. Our mother has suffered from biliousness since the journey. Travel affects her—'

'Or it does not' – Jane shrugged, smiling – 'and my thesis is true.'

By the time Cassy returned, her sister and niece were deep in a game – one was a pirate, the other a poor, castaway damsel; both were in fits of hilarity. The new notebook lay abandoned on the hearth rug. She retrieved it, picked up her embroidery and waited until they were done.

The following night, Mrs Austen declared herself quite well enough for a trip to the assembly. The illness had departed as swiftly as it had arrived, leaving no trace or effect, other than an urgent fancy for a few hands of Commerce. The whole family set off to indulge it at once.

It was six o'clock, and the red sun was dropping through a violet sky towards the line of the ocean. All of Sidmouth was out enjoying the cool. Jane and her father walked briskly together, and were soon quite ahead of the others. Cassy watched their backs, saw them laughing and stopping to exchange pleasantries with their new neighbours, while she listened to her mother with only one ear.

'My bowels feel much steadier now, thanks be to the Lord, after what was, as you of all people know, Cass, the most frightful evacuation. I think I shall like this apothecary. He has a good feel for my system.'

Cassy ran her eye over the promenaders coming towards them, with what she persuaded herself to be the most casual sort of interest. She was certainly not expecting to see anyone of any particular merit: oh, *no*. No one at all.

'I think I may visit him tomorrow, to discuss them further. After all, I *say* they are steadier, but never steady enough for my liking. If I could just be rid of this turbulent wind—'

And out of nowhere, there he was – suddenly upon them: taller than she remembered, more amiable than she had previously noticed. This time he smiled, revealing teeth that were good, white and even. And again in his green eyes she saw that warm recognition, as if remembering a connection in some other life. His hat was lifted, her knee was folded, agreement was met on the beauty of the evening. And just as suddenly, there he was: gone.

'And who was that fine gentleman?' Mrs Austen stopped and stared behind her, though Cassy would rather she had not.

'I am sure I do not know.' She took her mother's arm again and drew her back to their walking.

'Yet he seemed to have some knowledge of *you*.' She felt a beady eye upon her. 'And an interest, too, if I am not mistaken. You know not much gets past me and my good sprack wit. Well, well. Well, well, well.' A new friskiness came into her step. 'This is the most welcome development. It is nearly four years, now, my dear. God would not want you in mourning for ever.' Cassy loathed this tired topic of conversation, though that loathing never got in its way. 'Nor would Tom, for that matter.' Still, she thought she preferred even this to bowels and their behaviour. 'It is our dearest wish to see you girls both settled before the Lord comes to call us. And with my poor old stomach, that could happen any day.' This was a new hell: a fusion of spinsterhood with the troubles of digestion. 'The next time I suffer an evacuation of that magnitude . . .'

Cassy bore it courageously until they arrived at the door of the London Inn.

CHAPTER 14

Sidmouth, July 1801

'Are we nearly there yet?'

Beneath the warm blanket of familial kindness, little Anna was improving in confidence. She now felt able to ask for outings and entertainments – each increasingly lavish and demanding upon adults – like any other happy, loved child. She had taken ice creams, patted the horses, watched the water-mill wheel turn, become almost bored by the beach. Sadly, their great Shell Project had come to nothing, but Cassy contained her disappointment and went along with the rest.

'The pebbles are not easy to walk on.'

The cliffs were that morning's preferred destination. At breakfast, Anna announced that she would like to explore them: she wanted to find some of those earlier talked of 'strange, ancient animals'. Mr Austen perked up at once. He offered to take the child there himself, and began a short, preparatory lecture on the mystery of fossils. Cassy did not listen closely: the subject seemed of no particular interest; she started to think about the things she might do with this sudden free time. They were expecting new muslin in at Potbury's; she and Jane could go together . . . Then her father spoke the words 'Elements' and 'Conchology'. And suddenly it occurred that she was interested after all. Perhaps she would join them. Fossils *might* hold some sort of fascination. It was certainly worth taking a look . . .

'Not long now, child. See, the cliffs are just there.' Her father's academic enthusiasm propelled him at a speed that defied the length of his years. His long white hair shone in the sun beneath his sensible hat. 'There is no need to climb them, I am told. We have every chance of finding some treasure in the rocks lying down here on the beach.'

Cassy and Anna were struggling to keep up with him, so he arrived first at the chosen spot. Their view was blocked, but they heard him give a cheery: 'And good morning to you, sir!'

Ah: so they would not then be hunting alone. They came round the rock and emerged into the clearing.

And there he was. 'Ladies.' He bowed, tipped his hat and addressed only Anna: 'And if it is not the proud owner of that excellent shell . . .'

'So you are already acquainted?' her father began.

'Not exactly.' He smiled. 'We have yet to introduce

ourselves. I am Mr Hobday. Mr Henry Hobday.'
He nodded again.

'Mr Austen. And I have brought my daughter
and granddaughter, the Misses Austen, here this
morning. We are in search of fossils.'

'The Misses Austen. Then you are in the right
place.' He waved a small hammer. 'I have found
some interesting specimens. Come with me, Miss
Austen. I shall show you.'

But his words were – again – directed to Anna.
The three of them clambered over the stones,
leaving Cassy alone. She chose not to follow them
– it would be unseemly to clamber – and instead
leaned on the big rock and studied the party. Mr
Hobday – Mr Henry Hobday, the name itself had
a smile in it – and Mr George Austen were at once
the firmest of friends. Her father was a highly
intelligent man who was no respecter of fools. So,
if she read their demeanour correctly, Mr Hobday,
too, was intelligent.

The time passed and, to her surprise, Anna was
still deeply engrossed. Mr Hobday took care to
include the young scientist in all aspects of their
exploration and her capacity for concentration,
which only yesterday was pathetically limited, had
expanded dramatically. Cassy leaned into the rock,
sighed, looked out to sea and began to feel a trifle
disgruntled by her own predicament. The sun was
hot, the gulls were noisome and fractious. She had
been right in the first place: fossils were dull. Or
they certainly caused dullness in others. Everyone

had forgotten she was standing there, waiting. She failed now to remember why had she come.

It had not been – could not be due to a desire to see Mr Hobday. Mr Henry Hobday. It was a very good name. Anyway, it was not for him: of that she was certain. He might be attractive – he was definitely attractive – he might have about him some winning ways. What of it? She was Miss Austen, forever Miss Austen. Attractive, winning men were no longer of use to her. The idea occurred: perhaps he might do for Jane?

Now there was a scheme. Her sister's firm repulsion of each hapless suitor had long ago ceased to be a subject of parental amusement and was now one of general irritation. Cassy was in the uncomfortable position of seeing both sides: on the one hand, no man had been anywhere good enough; on the other, Jane could not go on in this fashion much longer. Their parents were determined to travel as much as possible during the years that remained, but must have someone to look after them. Cassy was, if not happy exactly, then at least accepting that she would be that someone, and after that Kent would claim her. But Jane? She was not one of life's carers and, what was more, needed stability. This peripatetic lifestyle would soon start to affect her: the mood would descend; there would be trouble ahead. But if this Mr Hobday, Mr Henry Hobday, was really as clever and amusing as the morning suggested, then . . .

Sighing, Cassy reached down for the picnic

basket and took out her colours. Drawing would soothe her. It always did soothe her when she was miserable and, she was forced to admit, she did, unaccountably, feel a little miserable all of a sudden. She would capture the party. She outlined the cliffs with her pencil, and began to draw in their figures, although as models they were all most unsatisfactory. Anna kept giggling and leaping about; Mr Henry Hobday – she gave an involuntary smile – was not still for a moment. She would have to concentrate on her dear old papa.

She was colouring it in when the party returned to her.

'Look, Aunt Cass!' Anna squealed, and held out a rock to her.

'Well, now.' Cassy peered at it, not much impressed.

'It is the shape of a worm!'

'Yes. So I see.'

'Mr Hobday says it is thousands of years old.'

'Many thousands, even,' Mr Hobday put in. 'There is our evidence of a creature that lived on this earth, perhaps even before man.'

Cassy stared again, and felt rather sorry for it. She would hate to be dug up and pored over some time in the future.

'What have you been drawing, my dear?' Her father approached now and looked over. 'Oh, that is charming. My daughter' – he addressed Mr Hobday – 'is an artist of some considerable talent.'

'Papa!' Cassy blushed at his boasting.

'Forgive me, but it is true. Look, Mr Hobday, you are captured here brilliantly.'

'May I?' He approached and Cassy grew hot with discomfort. She was sure she had worked more on her father. But looking again – how peculiar! – the figure of Mr Hobday did seem to loom large.

'It is but a sketch.' She packed it away in a hurry. 'Nothing distinguished, I assure you. Now, young lady, we must get you home and out of this sun.'

Cassy took her father's arm this time: all these exertions must have drained him. He would need her support on the return. Mr Hobday was of a more vigorous age. She walked slowly, holding the older man back a little, so that, with Anna skipping beside him, the younger might go on ahead.

Once at the Mall, they all parted cordially and to Cassy's relief made no plans for a subsequent meeting. He was soon swallowed up by the crowd.

'What a fine young man,' her father remarked as they walked up the terrace. 'He struck me as one unusually gifted with all that is agreeable.'

'Is he? I am sure I did not notice.'

Her father chuckled. 'Well, Anna did, certainly. Mr Hobday was especially kind and amusing to her.'

'Please let us do something.' Cassy put down her sewing with a sense of impatience. She was finding it hard to settle this morning. 'Perhaps when our mother is down, we could join the promenade?'

'Hmmm.' Jane carried on writing. 'Later, Cass, later. Mr Thorpe is being particularly obnoxious just now. He is amusing me greatly. While I have him here in full flight, I must just work on.'

Cassy rose and looked out of the front window and down along the terrace. Her father and Anna were out there somewhere. She had been foolish to turn down the offer to go. What did it matter if she were to meet any unsettling gentlemen? They took no notice of her; they clearly preferred to unearth poor fossilised creatures, long buried in stone. And she herself was secure in a place beyond danger. Nothing could possibly happen. There was no need to hide away here.

She watched the parade of the fashionable off in the distance and a pleasure boat leave from the beach. The world looked so happy and occupied without her out in it. Sighing, she went back to her seat. Oh, when would her mother arise?

The brass knocker rapped upon the front door then, and she sat up with interest, turned an ear in case this might be a visitor. But she could tell from the exchange that it was only a servant. She sat back again and tried to stem her sense of despair.

'A note for you, Miss Austen.' The maid came in, bobbed and left again.

'A note?' Jane looked up at that and could not

help but notice her sister's hand was trembling. 'What is this then?'

'Nothing at all interesting,' Cassy said smoothly. 'Do go back to your obnoxious Mr Thorpe.'

'Who is it from?'

'Oh, nobody at all. Indeed, no one I know. A Mrs Hobday,' she said, reading. 'An invalid, I gather, who is staying on the Crescent. She asks that I might call on her this morning.'

Jane was out of her chair now, and reading over her shoulder. 'That is a little odd, is it not? If you have not made her acquaintance. Oh, I see. She writes that you have met her son.'

'But hardly at all. He is the gentleman of whom we spoke yesterday. We met him at the cliffs. A Mr Hobday. Mr Henry Hobday.'

'Cassy! You are smiling!'

'I certainly am not. And I assure you, I do not know him, not properly. I was not even aware that he had a mother, indeed.'

'Most men do, on the whole,' said Jane. 'And this one has a mother who is very keen to meet you. That does seem to set him apart from the rest.'

Cassy remembered her scheme. 'Will you not join me? Mr Hobday himself might be there, and I do believe you might find him very much to your liking.'

'No thank you.' Jane was already back at her pages; pen in hand, mind elsewhere. 'I am busy with this. It is going well this morning.' She wrote a few words, and added absently, flicking her pen: 'And I shall not.'

'Shall not what?'

'Find him much to my liking. You know that I never do.'

'Mrs Austen! And I take it you are *Miss* Austen.' Mrs Hobday smiled and nodded. 'Yes. I see at once. Quite charming. And how very kind of you to call on me. I am finding it difficult to leave the house at all this week. My poor lungs.' She patted the pearls on her bosom. 'I am here for the sea air, yet this wretched body of mine will not let me outdoors.'

As soon as word of the note reached her chamber, Mrs Austen was up and dressed and ready to leave. A naturally garrulous woman, she needed no coaxing. New company was to her always delightful, but especially company of the invalid sort. So much to talk of! She settled down and pitched in forthwith.

'Oh, how I do sympathise. When we arrived here, just a week ago, I was immediately struck down with my bilious complaint. That is my weakness. Lungs do not trouble me – but the stomach! Oh, Mrs Hobday, you would not believe . . .'

Cassy sat in a mortified silence and studied her hostess. She was a younger woman than one might expect. She must have had Henry – Mr Hobday – quite early. He took his good looks – well, his looks – directly from her. Fine hair of the same rich, dark colour framed a strong, intelligent face, a similar aquiline nose. From time to time, as Mrs Austen moved through a long litany of symptoms, Mrs Hobday glanced over at Cassy with twinkling green eyes.

At last she was able to get a word in. 'I see you are studying our books, Miss Austen. Do novels interest you?'

'Oh, very much so. You have some of my favourites there. My sister and I never go anywhere without Sir Charles Grandison beside us.'

'Then on that recommendation, I shall ask my son if we can do that one next. These all belong to Henry, you see. He is so good to read to me nightly, and I am very grateful. But in truth, I do believe the enjoyment is more his.'

'Mr Hobday enjoys the works of the Mesdames Burney and Edgeworth?' Cassy was startled. 'I do not know why, but I had presumed he was of the more scientific persuasion.'

'Oh' – his proud mother smiled – 'he is a scientist, an artist, a philosopher, an aficionado of the novel . . .' She flicked a hand at the universe. 'I believe he could take over the world, if he did not insist on caring for his invalid mama.'

It was as if he had been created by some novelist to Jane's own specifications. Cassy's mind worked busily: one part was occupied with the practical matter of effecting a meeting; the other, with the register of her own growing irritation. Was it possible that Mr Hobday had in fact too many perfections? It could all quite get on one's nerves.

'We are very close. I think, sometimes, too close. You see' – she turned to Mrs Austen, with an instinct that this fact might be of interest – 'we lost his father five years ago.'

She was right. 'I am so sorry to hear that.' Her mother leaned forward, alert: a dog in the hope of a bone. 'Was it anything particularly—'

'A tumour.'

This met with great gratification. 'A tumour!'

'We saw the best men, but there was nothing to be done.' Mrs Hobday gave a sad smile. 'It has left me with a certain distrust of the medical profession.'

'Indeed. However, I would recommend the local apothecary here. I do not know if you have tried him since being in Sidmouth?'

'I fear it is too late for that.'

'Oh! Mrs Hobday! I am so very sorry!'

She laughed. 'Do not worry, Mrs Austen. I am not dying, or not yet awhile. No, we depart first thing in the morning, taking the diligence to Exeter. My son despairs of Devon curing me. He has already arranged for us to head off to Europe.' Here, she looked at Cassy. 'Though I suspect he is regretting that now.'

'To *Europe*?' Mrs Austen was aghast. 'But, my dear lady, there is a war on! You cannot *possibly*—'

'Yes, we are aware, thank you, Mrs Austen. And let me reassure you, we do not intend to travel through France. Though, should it be necessary, my son is not the sort of man to let a wretch like Napoleon get in his way.' There was more than a hint of self-satisfaction in Mrs Hobday's smile.

'I do not doubt it. Well, then: that is a pity,' said Mrs Austen, with feeling. 'When we have only now made your acquaintance.'

'Quite so. It seems a little previous to us, too. But perhaps your family might be here next summer?'

'Sadly, not. Oh, it is indeed remarkably pleasant. We are very much enjoying ourselves. But it is our retirement, you see, and we mean to travel quite widely. Dawlish is the top of our list.'

Soon after that, Cassy found she was tiring of Sidmouth. The pleasures of the beach were exhausted; society brittle, empty-headed and too fashionable; she had no desire to revisit the cliffs. Even the weekly assembly did not seem worth her while. What, after all, was the purpose of dancing? She could not remember. So she stayed home with Anna, and read.

The weather caught on to the mood of disappointment and reflected it back at her. The clouds rolled in; the rain poured down; the blue vista was consigned to history. The wind that whipped off the sea brought a chill with it. Yellow muslin was now quite inappropriate. Cassy went back with relief to her hot, heavy black.

CHAPTER 15

Kintbury, April 1840

Cassandra needed air. Frail she might be since her illness, shaken she surely was, but she could endure that small room, these letters, those memories no longer. Society would offer distraction; some small act of usefulness would restore her spirits. She resolved to go up into the village and help Isabella.

As soon as she alighted in the hall, Pyramus put on a show of welcome so exuberant as to be almost demented. Cassandra was disquieted to find how much this moved her. It had been years, decades even, since she had elicited such a response from any living being. She patted him fondly and rubbed at his ear. Of course, he was still but a dog. Yet, within the limitations of the species – for which he could be held in no way accountable – he was clearly an exceptionally fine one. This time, she made a point of inviting him to accompany her, and was delighted when he chose to accept.

Together, they walked out of the vicarage and on to the lane. Cassandra's hope was to catch

Isabella at the Winterbournes. The family lived in the warren of mean dwellings behind the shops, near the cliff that hung over the canal. Her progress was not easy – this hill was a lot steeper than she remembered – but it was not an unpleasant outing. There was sun on her back and the happy sound of birdsong. Pyramus matched her pace in the fashion of a gentleman and her mind cleared with every slow step.

Up on the street now, she exchanged greetings with the blacksmith and asked after his boy – the inevitably full answer allowed her to take a discreet rest – then she turned on to the rambling path through the cottages. Here, families were squashed, haphazardly, into every free inch so that an outsider could not hope to find his way through. Miss Austen, though, knew exactly where she was going. She always made a point of visiting when she was here.

William Winterbourne had been a ringleader of the agricultural riots ten years before. Cassandra had not known him personally, but he was said to have been a mild-mannered, hard-working fellow and she chose to believe it. The fact that he swung at the magistrate with a hammer in the heat of the moment was clearly unfortunate, and it was hard to blame Fulwar for rounding him up and handing him in. No one could have anticipated that he should be hanged for his crime. But such was his fate, and he had ever since been a source of unease on the collective familial conscience.

She reached the dark corner that housed what was left of the family. The door was open, and she let herself in.

'Hello?'

She peered through the gloom, across the bedding laid out on the mud floor. There was no sign of Isabella or any children, just Mrs Winterbourne slumped a-heap by the damp wall with the calf's foot jelly beside her. Cassandra looked upon this sad remnant of a person and felt a cold anger. What sort of justice was this, that a good woman should be sentenced to a lifetime of misery for her husband's one thoughtless crime?

There came a sudden disturbance. A square, solid shape loomed at the threshold. A gentleman – or a man, at least – came into the room.

'Madam.' He acknowledged her with no more than a quick flick of the head and crossed the floor with a sure, firm step. He gained on her position. In the half-light, she could not quite see his face and began to feel apprehensive.

But then he dropped to his knees at Mrs Winterbourne's side.

'So now, me pet.' His accent was the broadest of Berkshire. He put down something that appeared to be a medical bag, and took her hand tenderly. 'How are we now then? Bin up at all since morning?'

Was this the doctor of whom Isabella had spoken, he who had nursed Fulwar so well at his deathbed?

Ordinarily, Cassandra would endeavour some conversation: perform that ritualistic exchange of social connection that we all do when meeting a stranger, in the hope of imposing some order on this vast, difficult world.

'Let's see if you can't take a bit of this nice jelly.'

But conversation did not seem appropriate. The doctor had no interest in her; he had made no introduction: his courtesy was no more than rudimentary. She could not, though, fault his manner to the patient, which was clearly exemplary. He was trying now to feed her as she turned her head to the wall.

'What is it that ails her?' Cassandra enquired quietly.

'What ails her?' The doctor sat back on his haunches and looked round. 'Nought I can cure sadly, though I wish as I could. Poverty. Misfortune. A system as treats those like 'er without any fairness.' He gave an apologetic smile – 'Forgive me, m'm, if you find me sounding too political' – and then a shrug. 'You did ask.'

'Indeed. Though I knew the answer already,' Cassandra replied. 'Our views are not wildly divergent. Thank you for ministering to her.'

'I'll not let her go.'

He turned back to his treatment. Cassandra watched him for a while – impressed by this man's dedication; moved by his kindness – then quietly retreated. She made her way back, emerging into the street in the sunshine directly in front of the

Plasterers' Arms. Was it not in its back room that Elizabeth Fowle ran her nursery? Then here was today's opportunity to be useful. She had been meaning to visit her.

She crossed and took the alley to the side of the inn. The yard at the back was piled high with old barrels and broken boxes, but there was a small path through it. Pyramus of course knew where to go. Cassandra picked her way along behind him, towards the swelling noise of infants in varying states of extreme emotion, and found the door.

'Miss Austen!' Isabella's sister, Elizabeth Fowle, stood with a child on each hip. 'Look, children, we have a visitor.' The only light in the crowded, dim room seemed to come from her radiance. 'Now' – she stroked a few heads and wiped a few tears – 'we must remember our manners. What is it we say to when people are so kind as to call on us?' She appeared, to Cassandra, as a saint in stained glass: aglow, blessed, redeemed.

A small girl toddled forward and wobbled a curtsey; a baby was placed in Cassandra's arms and studied her with interest. Pyramus lay down, accepting that he must now be a plaything, and a few older children obliged. The rest – how many were in here? Cassandra counted at least ten – carried on with their day.

'Elizabeth, my dear.' Cassandra moved forward and the two women kissed. 'So this is where you have been hiding yourself.'

'Indeed. And what a pleasure it is for me to be able to show it to you. I am sorry I am never at home now. My days are so busy here, I can never find the time.'

Elizabeth found Cassandra a chair and asked a helper to make tea for them. 'My charges arrive from five in the morning, you see. That is when their mothers have to get to the whiting works or the mill, and the women have to do such long hours.' She reached for a hard biscuit and put it into a small hand. 'By the time they have all left, I have no energy to do much but crawl up there to bed.' She gestured to a ladder that led to a loft. 'Before dawn it all starts again!' The rigour of it all seemed to delight her.

Cassandra listened. She could not help but be impressed, and as a consequence was forced to revise a long-held opinion – a process she never found pleasant. But credit must be given where credit was due and this previously meek and quiet daughter of the vicarage must be credited for transforming herself so.

'Come now.' Elizabeth picked up a crying baby.

These were not her offspring, and the room was mean and chaotic, yet she appeared now to Cassandra just like any good mother in her own nursery: she had the same patience and devotion, and that infinite well of maternal sympathy.

'There, there, my precious one.'

Somehow, and one had to admire it, Elizabeth had found the solution to the problem that was her situation. She had used her own spinsterhood as an opportunity and put it to public advantage. Her reward was long days filled with purpose – and even love, apparently. Here was living proof of the lesson that Cassandra wanted to teach Isabella: happy endings are there for us somewhere, woven into the mix of life's fabric. We just have to search the detail, follow the pattern, to find the one that should be our own.

The thought reminded her why she had come. 'I would love to talk to you about Isabella and her future, if you can spare me the time?'

'Ah, of course,' Elizabeth replied, setting clean napkins out on the table. 'The great conversation about Isabella and her future that never seems to come to an end. I cannot stop what I am doing, but I can offer at least one of my ears.' She started to strip down a baby.

Cassandra was astonished by her tone. 'Then this is something the family has already often discussed?'

'I try to keep myself out of it.' Elizabeth smiled through a pin. 'The great pleasure of my own grand establishment' – she gestured around the nursery – 'is that it is a haven from Fowle family politics. And indeed, there once was a time when they spoke of little else.'

'What – even before the matter of it became so urgent? But – I do not understand – why in such a straightforward matter would there be so much to say?'

Elizabeth looked at her. 'I think I have already made plain: I dislike being involved and am resolved never to be so. All I shall tell you' – she turned back to the napkin and a bare little bottom – 'is that there were, indeed still are, a few characters in my family who are known to be very persuasive. And my sister, of whom I am otherwise very fond, has the fault of being far too persuadable for her own good. Beyond that' – she stood up straight, nestling the baby into her neck – 'I will not go.'

Cassandra, baffled, tried to make sense of this sphinxlike pronouncement, but had never been one for the riddle. She gave up at once, and instead thought to revise her brand-new opinion: while one must admire a woman who looked after herself, one could never condone neglect of the family.

She resolved to say that which she had already planned. It had been weighing on her and she must unload it: 'Well, I cannot stand by and watch Isabella suffer from the insecurity of her current position. I must—'

'Why?' Elizabeth tilted her head to one side and looked quizzical. 'Why should it concern you?'

Cassandra was quite taken aback.

'Forgive me. Please do not think me rude. Mine is a genuine enquiry. You must know that we are not a family that would condemn a sister to the workhouse. Our father has left us each a little money. Isabella cannot look forward to much, but she is in no explicit danger. I suppose it is better put this way – why are you quite so concerned?'

That was, asked thus, indeed a reasonable question. Cassandra was forced to reflect on her own position. Was she being an interfering old woman? Oh, the horror if that were so! There was an invisible line between usefulness and intrusion and she well knew the perils of crossing it. She paused for a moment of routine self-examination until, satisfied with her own findings, she began her report: 'You, Elizabeth, are unusual and, perhaps, unusually fortunate in being happy in your work and indifferent to your home. Isabella is, as I saw at once when I arrived here, a woman for whom domestic stability is a prerequisite for function. It is breaking her heart to leave the vicarage; it is fracturing her soul not knowing what is to become of her.'

Elizabeth put down one baby to pick up another and lay him down to change.

'She reminds me, in that one regard, of my own dear sister,' Cassandra continued. 'We had many years, as you know – with your Aunt Martha too, of course – in which we went from pillar to post without ever settling properly. None of us enjoyed them, but they damaged Jane particularly and possibly profoundly. The memory of it all haunts me today. I do sometimes wonder whether, if we had had the chance to settle down sooner, she may not have – well, we might have had a few more years with her. The stress, I believe, took its toll.' She paused again, to gather herself. 'I could not help Jane – we had little money and no power – but I would like to help Isabella. Her contentment is there in our grasp. As long as you, my dear, consent to take a house with her, then she can stay here in the village. I can see that you are fully consumed here but, surely, she will find some occupation for herself. She has her pupils and her good works, I have noticed. So,' she concluded, brightly, 'then all will be well.'

'I am happy to do that,' said Elizabeth, with more than a hint of reluctance. '*If* that is indeed what my sister desires. But I will not be put in the position of forcing such an arrangement upon her, nor am I able to be very much help. I am, as you say, very busy. Now – if you do not mind – we are coming up to the children's tea and . . .'

All at once, Cassandra and Pyramus were out of the door.

The dog led her back towards the vicarage. Cassandra knew not by which route, took no notice of landmarks: there was too much to think about, and too much that was troubling. She would have liked to decipher the cryptic messages about Isabella's wishes, but it was all too mysterious and, frankly, incredible. She had never heard whisper of any dramas before, and was quite sure that Eliza would have shared them. Elizabeth Fowle, she concluded, was a somewhat hysterical woman – no doubt provoked by too much exposure to the works of Sir Walter Scott. The only fact to hold on to was that she had agreed to live with her sister. So there, Cassandra's work had been done.

Which left the unsettling memories of her own sister, stirred up first by her letters and then the stuff of that interview. The exodus from the vicarage, the uncertainty ahead . . . For the first time, Cassandra realised why she was so affected by the predicament of the Fowle ladies. What was happening in Kintbury was so redolent of what had happened in Steventon. It took her back to those turbulent first years of the century.

Jane had been shocked by their father's retirement and removal to Bath, but had seemed to rally in Sidmouth. Decline set in though, that following winter. Their father was still alive then; they still had his pension to keep them. There was no sign of the financial privations that were soon to assault them; they were not then forced upon the goodwill of their brothers: their caps were not yet in their hands. But still, Jane could not settle and found no comfort in society or tranquillity at home.

By the following summer, she was beginning to show signs – even to Cassy, who watched through a prism of unqualified sympathy – of becoming that most unwelcome of creatures: the unhappy woman, who refused to pretend to be anything but.

CHAPTER 16

Dawlish, 1802

The last bell had chimed and, in the small village church, the service was already under way as they hurried in and found a back pew.

'After you, my dear.' Mr Austen ushered his wife into her seat, but his courtesy did nothing to please her.

'This is most unsatisfactory.' Mrs Austen sat down, red-faced from her exertions, and quite out of breath. 'I shall not see anyone poked away here.'

Cassy and Jane took their places, found their psalm books and each silently prayed that their mother might be quiet for the rest of the service.

'Nor can I hear. Can you hear him, Mr Austen?' It was always a wonder of science that a whisper could travel so far and so clearly. 'Is this man any good?'

A year had passed, and the family had once again chosen to take summer lodgings close to the sea.

The ancient church, though, was set back in the country and could only be approached through gardens and fields. No one had expected Mrs Austen to make the effort that morning – the distance was such that God might excuse her – but she was determined.

For Dawlish, it turned out, was no Sidmouth when it came to society. Its fresh air and beautiful bay were certainly enough to attract visitors. It was ambitious to be an elegant watering place and not just a fishing village, but its transformation was not quite complete. So while it could boast of plenty of bathing machines and doctors for those preoccupied by their own ill disposition, it as yet had no assembly or other entertainments to amuse those who were well.

'I was hoping to see some new faces. I only have view of the back of their hats.'

It was only their first week there, but already Mrs Austen was worried by the resort's limitations. This was, of course, not on her own account. She would be perfectly content to spend a quiet summer in the company of her beloved husband and pursuit of their better health. But for her daughters, she felt that a pitiful prospect. The girls must make new acquaintances – perhaps (she would never give up hope) some even deeper alliance. With so little else on offer here, it would clearly be foolish to pass up the social opportunities of a full Sunday service. And once she got word that the parson was a bachelor, well: the walk of a mile suddenly seemed no distance at all.

The unmarried man began his sermon for the morning.

Mrs Austen leaned across: 'How does he look?'

Cassy studied him. She too would dearly like the season to yield some person of interest, although he would have to be very interesting indeed to wake Jane out of her doldrums. Could this be such a man? It was not easy to tell from an ordinary face coming over a pulpit. But then he got into his stride.

And Jane turned to her, rolling her eyes to the conventional Anglican heavens. Another evangelist! Must they be everywhere? There was the end of it. Cassy sighed. He would not do.

In time, and it passed slowly, they were able to brush away the brimstone and walk into the sunshine. Out there in the churchyard they would at last get their chance to evaluate the company. Mrs Austen moved slowly, stopping all the while to look around, keen to see and be seen by as many as possible. Cassy and Jane drifted a few paces ahead, pretending at patience and warming away the cold damp of the church.

'Mrs Hobday!' Their mother's voice rang out over the crowd. 'I do believe you have followed us!'

'Mama!' Cassy spun round. '*Please.*'

He was there.

'Oh, dear heavens. It was only my little joke. Why must our offspring be so alarmed every time we dare speak? I am sure your son is not so hard on you, Mrs Hobday.' Mrs Austen looked at the gentleman before her. 'And is this he? How do you do, Mr Hobday. Well, I believe I *did* see you in Sidmouth, eh? I thought I had not, but I remember it clearly. On the Mall, with my eldest daughter.' She reached out and grabbed Cassy, pushing her forward with force. 'One evening it was.'

Mr Hobday bowed. 'I could not forget.'

'And may I present my younger daughter,' Mrs Austen added – covering all options, just in case, should the age difference of three years be an issue – and all the remaining introductions were made.

'Well, this is a coincidence and I must say quite the happiest. How delightful to meet you again. You do look well this year, Mrs Hobday. The winter clearly agreed with you. They have been to *Europe*, Mr Austen – can you imagine? It puts our own adventures quite in the shade. Although we are even now hatching a plan to go to North Wales.' Mrs Austen paused, and then added, 'Which is also very far away.'

'Thank you. The Alpine air was exactly what was needed.' Mrs Hobday patted her son's arm. 'My dear boy was, as ever, quite right. I am so fortunate to have such a protector. His judgement in all matters is never less than impeccable.'

Now it was his turn to look thoroughly awkward. Cassy should have liked him a lot less if he had not.

'How did you come here this morning, Mrs Austen? I confess the thought of the walk defeated me, so we brought a trap. But Henry, I am sure, would be happy to give up his seat to you for the return. Why do not we, the two senior ladies, travel in comfort and the rest of the party go back on foot?'

This scheme clearly delighted Mrs Austen on every possible level: the ease of the journey; the time alone with the pleasant, well-bred lady whom she was determined to befriend; and, of course, the opportunity for this fine gentleman to become more deeply acquainted with her two girls. She looked from one to the other, and Cassy read her thoughts as she did so: the choice could be his, according to his own preference. She would not much mind either way.

'And how did you find the service this morning, sir?' asked Mr Hobday.

'I thought the young man did well enough.' Mr Austen flicked his cane as he got into his long stride. They left the crowd behind them and moved on to the meadows. 'It cannot be easy to have a parish with such a fluctuating congregation. Full this morning, but no doubt in the winter there is little more than one man and a dog.'

'Then that might explain his histrionics in the pulpit.' Jane put in with some scorn. 'Perhaps he is nurturing his own fame to drum up more trade.'

'Now, my dear,' her father cautioned. 'He is

entitled to preach in the manner he wishes, and we have no reason to doubt his fervour.'

'My father is being polite,' Jane told Mr Hobday. 'The sermon was not in our preferred style.'

'Jane!' Cassy exclaimed, putting hand on her sister's shoulder to signal restraint. 'We do not know Mr Hobday's own feelings on the subject.' She dropped her voice. 'We would not wish to offend.' Then she turned to Mr Hobday: 'Sir, you must forgive my sister.' The first time she had ever properly addressed him, and it was to beg forgiveness for her sister! How very unfortunate. 'She is not ordinarily quite so outspoken.'

Mr Austen roared with laughter: 'I am afraid that she very much is!'

'Please do not worry on my account. I have no fear of plain speaking, I assure you. Nor was that sermon quite to my tastes, but when one travels as much as we do these days, one can hardly pick and choose.' Mr Hobday's smile was broad and quite unaffected. 'Now, while we are embracing the spirit of mutual honesty, what think you all of Dawlish?'

'Very pleasant,' replied Cassy politely.

'As a resort,' Jane cut in, 'it is lacking.'

'Indeed it is!' Mr Hobday exclaimed. 'I tried the library yesterday, on our first afternoon. A pitiful business. If I did not travel with a good supply of my own books, I do not know quite what I should do with myself.'

Cassy smiled in anticipation, for here was the

perfect opportunity for a meeting of minds. Her sister's fury at the persistent flaws of the circulating library had been a constant refrain since their own arrival. So she waited now for the inevitable urgent agreement, but the wait was in vain.

At last, her father stepped into the breach: 'Then I envy you, sir. I had to surrender my own library when we gave up the rectory last year, and much pain did it cause me. To surrender one's books, well: it is to surrender part of one's soul.'

'And without them we are reduced to being no more than mendicants,' sighed Jane theatrically.

'Jane!' Cassy admonished, yet again.

But Mr Hobday seemed only amused. 'It is not many mendicants who have the good fortune to take a house in Dawlish for the length of the summer.'

'Oh, we shall not spend the whole summer here,' Jane dismissed him. 'My brother will arrive soon—'

'Captain Charles Austen RN, on the *Endymion*,' their proud father put in then. 'He has been at sea for a few years, seeing off Napoleon.' As if the war had been a duel between the two men. 'The blessing of this peace has come at just the right time. He is already on his way.'

'—and I dare say, Papa, he will not put up with *Dawlish* for long. He is a Man of the World now and accustomed to all manner of excitement. A place like this, in the company of no one other than his *family*, could never be enough for a strong character such as *his*.'

Cassy grabbed Jane's arm then, pulled her ahead and they walked back across the fields towards the sea and their lodgings, in silence.

Once home, Jane at once sat down to her writing with an air of great satisfaction. She had repulsed Mr Hobday with an expert efficiency. She could return to her invented world.

'I have given it much thought and concluded I rather approve of your Mr Hobday.' Jane spoke into the glass while Cassy brushed her hair for her that evening.

'Well, you certainly had a most interesting way of showing it,' Cassy scoffed.

'Oh, Cass.' Jane pressed her lips together. 'Was I terribly rude?' It was almost as if she might care a jot.

'Yes! You were frightful!' Cassy tugged at her locks playfully.

'As rude as I was to Mr Blackall?'

'No,' Cassy conceded, laughing. 'Nobody has ever, in the history of social intercourse between the two sexes, been as rude as you were to Mr Blackall. You set impossibly high standards with him, for all womankind.'

'Hmm. So would you estimate this morning at' – Jane held out her thumb and forefinger as if measuring – 'say, half a Blackall?'

'Not quite half a Blackall, perhaps more of one-third. But if our mother had been there and caught it . . .'

Cassy could not stay cross for long. The days here followed the same pattern. Jane had only two moods: sullen and silent, or brittle and wicked. Neither was easy on the household, and only Cassy could manage her. Mrs Austen was quite close to despair. But then she did not notice that which had struck Cassy. Those foul moods persisted only until the moment when Jane was free to pick up her pen. After an hour or two alone with her thoughts and her writing, she returned – as if purified – to something almost like calm. And at night, when it was just the two of them in their room, she was the happiest of all.

Cassy passed Jane her cap. 'Anyway, I do not know why you will call him *my* Mr Hobday. He is nothing of the sort. Indeed' – she moved to the side of the bed and knelt down – 'I had rather thought' – she hid her face in her hands – 'he might do for you.'

Jane climbed straight into bed and talked over Cassy's prayers. 'I assure you, he is very much your Mr Hobday. That was apparent from the way he looked at you this morning. Do not tell me you could not feel the warmth of his admiration.' She plumped up her pillow. 'So, on reflection, I should not have been quite so hostile. It can only have come from sheer force of habit.'

Cassy pulled back the cover and got in beside her.

'I condemn my own behaviour.' Jane turned, put an arm around her sister and planted a kiss on

227

her cheek. 'It was quite unforgiveable and I confidently expect you to forgive it at once. Anyway, I doubt that it affected your Mr Hobday one way or t'other. What matters a bad sister off in the background? He did not strike me as a lover who could be deterred by—'

'Lover!' Cassy pulled back in horror. 'What on earth can you mean, *lover*? Jane, you have it all wrong. He has all but ignored me at every opportunity. His lovemaking, if that is what you call it, is directed at everyone *but* myself – first Anna, then Papa, and today, I rather thought, you.'

'Precisely! There is my evidence – that, and the unmistakeable ardour. I am quite sure I saw sparks flying off him. I think one caught my bonnet. Because of you and your charms, I might have gone up in smoke. Oh, Cass, you can be so slow. Why do you suppose he has fetched up in Dawlish at all?'

'Well, I cannot say I know enough of the Hobdays to arrive at an answer, but I can only presume it must be no more than coincidence. There are not so many watering places on the South Coast—'

'And not many gentlemen of Mr Hobday's calibre in this one.' Jane blew out the candle and settled down. 'He is here in pursuit of the enchanting Miss Austen. You have him quite in your powers.'

Cassy laughed. 'How can you be so foolish? I have no powers to speak of.'

'Oh, but you do, my dear. And that you are

unaware of them only makes you more powerful still. Our poor Mr Hobday has fallen.'

'Then I am sorry for it,' Cassy replied firmly. 'You of all people must know me to have lost the only one I could ever marry. I have no possible interest in him, or any other gentleman now.'

'Is that so?' Jane turned on her side and nestled her chin into her sister's shoulder. 'Poor, beautiful Miss Austen, condemned to eke out a sad life with nothing to do but care for others and control the temperament of her difficult sister.' She pulled up her knees, preparing to sleep, yawned and then muttered: 'Let us just wait and see.'

CHAPTER 17

Dawlish, July 1802

Cassy had hopes for a return of her mother's poor health so that she could stay home and nurse her in blessed obscurity. But the next morning, to her profound disappointment, Mrs Austen arrived down in the parlour and pronounced herself well.

'What an excellent day it is out there! And I am pleased to report that I passed a good night and awoke feeling unusually robust. Now, Cassy, while your father and Jane are out, I think we should take a walk together, do you not agree?'

Cassy knew her agreement to be no more than a formality, and collected their bonnets.

'Oh, splendid,' said her mother, setting off from the threshold. 'The tide is still low and we can take to the strand. It is a pity that Dawlish does not yet have a more permanent promenade.' She squeezed Cassy's arm. 'We shall have to make sure that we seize every opportunity for walking and talking, eh? Let us not miss our chance.'

It was a dazzling day, all brilliant sun, clear air

and variegated blues. Cassy drank it in and prayed it be peaceful.

'Perfect conditions for bathing. Perhaps a good dipping will improve your sister's spirits. We can but hope, we can but hope. That girl is all sharp edges at the moment and it worries me greatly. Your father reported back to me on her conduct with our charming Mr Hobday and I do not mind telling you that I was most displeased. Of course, your papa thought it amusing, which irked me yet further. His excessive indulgence does nought to alleviate things and I have told him so often. But why she herself must endeavour to appear as unattractive as possible, that I do not understand.' She paused to take breath and they greeted a few passing neighbours. 'Mind, I have my own theory about Mr Hobday.' Mrs Austen's voice did not drop, but merely transferred to its booming and audible whisper. 'And that is, it is *you*, my dear, who have caught his eye.'

In her embarrassment, Cassy studied their feet as they took up walking again.

'His mother said something rather interesting to me on the way back from ch— *Mr Hobday!*' Mrs Austen stopped. 'With what pleasure it is that we meet again. It did not occur to me as we set off this fine morning that we might be so fortunate. The coincidence is quite startling. Tell me, what accounts for you being out here today?'

'Mama,' Cassy, curtseying, was compelled to introduce a calm to the histrionics. 'Mr Hobday is staying here in the village. It can hardly be pure serendipity. Most of Dawlish is enjoying the weather.'

'I beg you, madam' – he bowed – 'do not cheat me of such an effusive reception. It is not what I am used to, but must confess to finding it most pleasant.'

Mrs Austen chuckled. 'There. My daughter chiding me again, for no reason. You can be assured, Mr Hobday, you can always expect a warm welcome from me. Now, which way are you headed? We are merely pottering in an aimless fashion. Perhaps you might like to accompany us for a while?'

'Mama.'

'How delightful. I, too, am only taking the air and enjoying the view while my mother takes her sea bath.' He turned and started to walk alongside them.

'Forgive me for being so personal, Mr Hobday – it is my way, you will no doubt get used to it. People have to. I am too old to change now – but I must say that you are an exemplary son to your dear mother.'

'It had not occurred to me to be otherwise.'

'Nonetheless, not all young men can boast of such a clear sense of duty. Such filial devotion is a pleasure to witness. You remind me very much of my daughter here.' She patted Cassy with fondness. 'She, too, is in possession of the most remarkable qualities.'

'Mother, I fear you are tiring,' Cassy put in quickly. 'Perhaps you should rest on this bench for a while.' She settled Mrs Austen. 'Sir, please do not feel obliged to wait with us. Our progress is a little erratic, is it not, Mama? Oh!'

'You were correct, madam.' He smiled. 'Your mother must indeed have been tired. She has fallen asleep at once.' He sat down beside her. 'Please, allow me to wait with you until she has recovered. I do not like to think of you alone.'

'That is kind, but, truly, I have no need of the company.'

'Then let me think only of my own pleasure.' He pulled his cane towards him, and studied its top.

Cassy sat in silence and affected a calm, demure exterior that belied the raging torment within. A thin, warm summer breeze was all that held them apart. It played on her skin. Oh! He had only to reach out his hand and her senses would fire up, as they had fired up the first time she saw him. She quailed at the memory: that scalding, quicksilver flash . . . It was too much to bear. Her life was set, decisions made; her promise had been given and still there came danger. She had manoeuvred herself into a place of tranquillity and believed she was settled. Why should her resolution come now under such heavy assault?

She determined to freeze him away. He might converse on any subject that pleased him – thoughts on the picturesque or peace with the French; his incomprehensible love of the fossil – but could hope for no sort of success. He would find it as blood from a stone.

'May I enquire after the health of your dear niece, Anna? I think of her often and that pleasant morning we enjoyed on the beach.'

This was not what she had been expecting. In her shock, Cassy softened to putty. 'Thank you for remembering her, sir. She is quite well, I believe.'

'And I hope happy? There seemed a streak of melancholy, or perhaps insecurity, that was troubling to witness in a child of that age.'

'She lost her mother when still very small and is, I fear, scarred by it. Though I am surprised it should be perceived by a stranger.'

'Ah. The loss of a parent is a heavy burden to carry,' he sighed, 'especially in one so young.'

'Mrs Hobday told us last year of your own bereavement, for which I am sorry.'

'Thank you, madam. My father was an excellent man, and is much missed. My mother was badly struck by the grief of it, and that explains our peripatetic existence. She found it too painful to stay in our family home for a while. But I think, and pray, that her strength now recovered, we shall be returning this autumn to our estate.'

Cassy felt her mother twitch as that small but all-powerful word pierced through and pricked her innermost mind.

'For myself, I believe our mourning has gone on long enough. It is not only because I am keen to take up my inheritance, more that the pull of Derbyshire is too strong to resist.'

'Derbyshire!' exclaimed Cassy.

'*Derbyshire?*' In her excitement, Mrs Austen clean forgot she was asleep.

'So you know it?' Mr Hobday seemed pleased.

'Alas, not at all.' Cassy felt foolish. 'It is just that my sister has it in her head the place is some sort of perfection.'

'Then your sister is a lady of great intuition. It is God's own country, I sincerely believe.'

Mrs Austen struggled to her feet. 'And we would very much like to hear all about it, would we not, Cassy? Come now. Let us walk again.'

They both rose, on order.

'You can describe everything to us in the greatest of detail. We are country people ourselves, Mr Hobday, with an excellent sense of the land. My daughter here is quite a hand with the poultry, although – dear me! How foolish – I suppose you have people for that, yes? Well, of course. An estate, I heard you say. Now, how many acres?'

The tide had turned. The thin spit of sand – so wide and firm on their outward journey – was still desperately holding out, as if it had a choice in its future. Though it knew, from experience, that the sea was bound to overcome it, in time.

'Ah, that *is* extensive,' Mrs Austen was saying. 'And how much is farmland, and how much is park?'

Their return to the village had to be hurried. Cassy chose not to contribute to the conversation, but nobody noticed. Mrs Austen had too many questions to ask of Mr Hobday, and Mr Hobday was all too keen to reply.

With the excitement of Charles's arrival, the family became introspective. They each, individually, preferred the company of Austens above any other. With enough of them assembled, there was no need for society. They were a party unto themselves. And if they could not all be together, then this, for the ladies, was the perfect arrangement. Among their brothers, they each had their favourites, but on Charles they both equally doted.

The evening was warm, preserving the memory of the heat of the day. Jane sat by the open window, reading aloud to them. A light breeze sauntered through and lifted the hair around her face.

'I say, your Thorpe is the devil of a bounder.' Charles jumped up and strode around the small parlour. He could never be still for long. 'If that is the Oxford Man, I am grateful not to have gone there myself. I dare him to try and come on to my ship: we should have him run up the yardarm at once.'

Jane lowered her pages. 'He never would be on your or any ship, Charles. Mr Thorpe has neither the heart or the head for it. We all know that our sailors are the very best of our men.'

'Hear, hear,' said Mr Austen. 'As the French now know to their cost.'

'You say that, and yet my sister here continues to insult me!' Charles retorted.

'I?' exclaimed Jane. 'My dear Charles, you are surely teasing! What can I have done?'

'Is it not obvious? You will persist in writing these stories, full of splendid fellows of all different sorts, but never once have I heard one of your heroines to be blessed with a dashing sailor brother whom she admires and adores.'

'That is true,' laughed Jane. Cassy looked up from her sewing and smiled to see her sister so at ease. After a successful reading of her own work to the family, she glowed as she never glowed otherwise. 'But to do so would defeat my own purposes. It would strike right through the narrative. You must see that if a young lady is so fortunate as to have her own dashing sailor brother, she is spoiled then for any other hero I could create for her. For how, with such an example in her own background, could she fall in love on dry land? No man could match him.'

'Aha!' Charles bounded over and knelt at her feet. 'So that is why I return to find that you are still yet to be settled. Tell me, truthfully now.' He took her hand. 'Is it as I fear? That you *despair* of finding a man who could match me?'

'I certainly despair of finding one so adept at playing the fool.' Jane batted him away. 'But Charles, it is Cassy who betrays you. She has a new suitor, and is now far too grand to give thought to a subject as dreary as her dear sailor brother.'

Mrs Austen sat up, giving a round chuckle.

Cassy dropped her needle and looked up again in horror. 'Jane!'

'Oh, I am sorry. I have spoken in error. Ignore me, Charles. Cassy has, after all, *no* suitors. And I would particularly like to point out that she has no suitors who go by the name of Hobday. Specifically, Mr Henry Hobday . . .'

'. . . who happens to be both exceedingly agreeable *and* heir to a Derbyshire estate,' joined in their mother.

'No indeed. She has bewitched no gentleman who could answer to that description. No man at all.'

Cassy, blushing, was silent and resentful. She enjoyed these family jokes only when she herself was not the butt of them.

'You are making your sister uncomfortable, Jane,' Mr Austen reproved. 'And I must add that I have seen no evidence of this romance of which you speak.'

'That, Papa, is because it is a very deep secret. So deep that it is known only by all of Dawlish.'

'And Sidmouth?'

'Yes, you are right, Mother. I have heard there to be pockets of Sidmouth in which people talk of little else.'

'Oh, enough. Please,' Cassy begged. 'You see,

Charles, that Jane has become no less outrageous since your last visit. Her love of fiction has spread from the page and into our lives. I am sad to report that now she routinely spouts nonsense. We can no longer believe a word that comes out of her mouth.'

Charles, although he had been enjoying himself hugely, was never anything other than kind. He knew that it was the moment for a change of conversation, and with a captain's skill he steered it away. He entertained them all with stories from his ship and descriptions of faraway places.

And the sun set on a parlour that was all familial contentment. Cassy, recovered now and calm, looked about her with love. Her father asked learned questions and basked in the detail of the son's answers. Her mother rocked gently and smiled at her own thoughts. Cassy hoped that they were not straying into the district of Derbyshire, although she feared it most likely they were. And Jane? Jane looked happier and more alive than she had for months. Here in this room was all that her sister needed: good conversation in which she felt no inhibition; time and space to write, with an intelligent audience to listen; her family around her, with whom she could be her own self. These were the conditions upon which her happiness, or her equilibrium at least, depended. Were they altogether too much for a single woman to ask? Just these small things. She required nothing more.

*   *   *

It did not take long for Charles to lose patience with Dawlish. As Jane had predicted, this gentle village did not offer enough distractions to detain him. He was a young man of great energy, who had been away at sea and had little hope of this peace lasting. He craved a summer of society: fashionable crowds; no doubt, too, fashionable ladies of his own age and regular assemblies at which he might meet them. With that in mind, the Austens agreed to remove themselves to Teignmouth forthwith.

The prospect brought Cassy enormous relief. Of course, she had no craving for fashion or society, nor was this place too tame for her tastes – quite the opposite. For her, here lurked danger, and she had become almost desperate in her wish to escape it. She had feigned headaches, avoided calls, retreated to darkened rooms and ignored the entreaties of her mother for as long as could possibly be tolerated. Her behaviour was attracting attention and all of it negative. For once, Jane was left in peace to act as she pleased. Mrs Austen had shifted her focus of maternal concern. Cassy, of all people, was her new problem now.

'And how are you today, child?' Her mother's eyes narrowed as she peered over the breakfast table. 'Recovered at last, I do hope?'

'Thank you, Mama. Perhaps I am a little better.' Cassy dared not say otherwise, and indeed, she did feel much calmer. Her sense of threat was diminishing. After all, what could possibly happen? They were to leave Dawlish the following morning.

'Splendid!' exclaimed Charles. 'I suggest we three take our young legs out for a good walk, up over the cliffs and into the country beyond. What say you?'

'Nothing would delight me more,' Jane replied. 'It has been such a sadness to me, having an invalid sister. You cannot know how I have suffered, Cass, left all alone. Let us take a good picnic and we can celebrate your return.'

The matter was settled without waiting for Cassy's agreement, and she was soon caught up in the flurry of necessary arrangements. Neither of her siblings could be trusted to remember all that they needed and so, of course, she had to take over. There was an art to overseeing the composition of a good picnic. It happened to be one of her skills.

They set out. This was the first time she had taken the air in more than a week, and her senses could only delight in it. Yes, the sun was behind clouds and the wind was a little fresh, but then were these not the perfect conditions for walking? And she could think of no better companions than her sister and this brother. They proceeded along the seafront, turned, followed the brook up to the village and by now Cassy's spirits were completely restored. She was laughing and happy – any onlooker would have to presume carefree – when the others stopped and looked around. As if they were waiting.

'What is it?' she asked of them. 'I assure you we need nothing more for the picnic. We have all we could possibly want.'

'There he comes!' Charles raised his hand and his voice. 'Hobday, my good fellow. Here we are. Delighted you could join us. What a fine day we have for our outing.'

'Good day to you all.' Mr Hobday lifted his hat. 'And I am equally delighted to be invited. Ladies. Miss Austen, my particular pleasure. I have not seen you about lately. I do hope you are well?'

'Thank you, sir,' Cassy stammered. Her curtsey was not all it should be. She was not quite in control of her limbs.

'Capital!' Charles exclaimed with great satisfaction, as if all was well in the world. 'Let us sally. I am told that if we take this stream as our guide, then a picturesque splendour awaits us. Tell me, Hobday, where do you stand on this picturesque business? Not sure I quite grasp it myself.'

The men strode ahead and Cassy hung back. She did not want to hear Mr Hobday's opinions, on that or any other matter, for fear they might meet her approval. A morning of mutual agreement would prove most unhelpful. Better to live in ignorance, and hope him to be stupid and wrong.

'Do you mind terribly?' Jane, walking with her, put a hand on her arm.

'Yes, Jane. I mind very much.'

'It was all Charles's doing.'

'Of which you knew nothing?'

'No,' Jane conceded, trying to be serious, but too cheerful for that. 'Of which I knew all, and in which I could not see any malice. While you have been sickening with, well, whatever it is that *has* sickened you, the two have become friendly. Charles seems to like him exceedingly well.'

Another conquest, Cassy thought irritably. Why could he not just leave all well alone?

'Indeed, no one can find any sort of fault with your Mr Hobday. It seems he is the very model of masculine perfection. The universe has met and agreed upon it. It is all most infuriating.' Jane sighed. 'You know that, as a woman of many faults, I abhor faultlessness in others. What is there to be done with them if they cannot change or improve?'

Cassy laughed. 'You are faultless in my eyes.'

'No, I do not think so. But you do bear me better than anyone else ever could.' Peace was made between them. 'My dear Cass, it is you who are faultless, or as close to it as I could tolerate. You deserve something better than this wretched future of ours. This denial of your self is completely absurd.'

'Jane! Why must you make such drama from nothing? Our future is not *wretched*. We have our parents – at least for the moment, God willing. We have five fine brothers who will never neglect

us. Most important of all, we have each other –
unless or until you meet someone good enough.
And even then, I should not starve.'

'Not to starve! Is that your ambition? "Here lies
Cassandra Austen. *She did not starve.*"' Jane's
mocking tone at once became grave. 'I have no
crystal ball and cannot say yet exactly what will
become of us, but this much is certain: we must
be poor. We must, in no time, be old. We
must find ourselves become objects of pity or –
worse even! – comedy. This must be *my* fate and,
though I dread it, I have now reached acceptance.
But it does not have to be your own. Cass, you
are so dear to me. I love you above all. But we do
not have to live as one. We are two different
women. I beg you' – she stopped and grabbed
Cassy's hands – 'if you are offered some means of
escape, *do not refuse it.*'

'How goes it back there? Is it not splendid out
here today?'

The gentlemen had paused their walking so that
the ladies could catch up.

'Indeed!' cried Jane. 'We are loving it, are we
not, Sister? We were just celebrating our own good
fortune, to be surrounded by such spectacular
beauty on this particular day. How blessed are we?
Our hearts runneth over! What an excellent scheme
to come out here. What excellent men you both
are to think of it. Our gratitude is so great as to
be beyond all expression!'

This was such un-Jane-like behaviour that

Charles, rather letting the side down, barked with delight. 'What say you to that, Hobday? Not effusive enough, to my mind. Do you not agree?'

'Very poor, indeed.' Mr Hobday was smiling. 'Most wanting, as a response to such excellence as ours. I am starting to fear that your sister is hardly grateful at all.'

'Perhaps you should offer up a sonnet or two, Jane? In praise of us. That might be appropriate.'

'A mere sonnet? Too short, and too easy. I demand an epic poem, Miss Jane, long and heavy, very much in the romantic style. If it could be delivered to my chambers sometime this evening?'

'I shall start composing at once. *On Dawlish*, it is to be called.'

'Make sure you include that mill wheel down there,' Charles put in. 'I feel rather poetic m'self when I look at it. Sort of . . . moving like time . . . sort of thing.'

His sisters erupted in mirth. 'Charles, you are hopeless.'

'Well, what about that old fellow in the field, tilling the soil? Dashed back-breaking stuff, that is.'

'Ah, Austen,' Mr Hobday cautioned, 'you are failing to appreciate the relationship between the peasant and the poet. I am afraid that whatever his pain or his misery, whether his children be dead or his belly roaring with hunger, poetry can record only his unaffected happiness.'

'You see?' Jane cried. 'Mr Hobday understands

the craft perfectly. I think I shall not bother with people at all in my epic. They always appear to me too complicated and ridiculous. I shall get caught up in their dramas and it will interrupt my flow. Mind,' she added, glancing sideways, 'do you see how that shaft of light falls upon the face of my sister? That might be worth a line or two.'

'Oh, surely a stanza all to itself?' Mr Hobday smiled at Cassy. Cassy blushed back. Then Jane and Charles walked off at high speed.

And they were left there, alone, on the hillside. The sea sparkled beneath. The clouds of the morning had cleared and the sun seemed to bless them. There were no other walkers around.

'What happened?' Jane blew into their bedroom. 'Tell me, Cassy, now! Did he speak?'

Cassy lay on the bed, willing her heart to calm down. Her bonnet lay abandoned on the floor; her hair was all over her face. 'He spoke.' She turned on her side, away from her sister, and wept.

'And? Well?' Jane leaped on to the bed and grabbed her shoulders. 'Your answer? What was your answer?'

'I refused him.' Her words were muffled into the pillow.

'*Refused him?*' Jane screamed.

'Hush, Jane. Mama is downstairs.' Oh, her poor mama! She must never hear of this. 'Yes. I refused him. I do not appreciate you conspiring to leave me so undefended. But there.' She sat up and wiped her face with her handkerchief. ''Tis done.'

Jane got up and began to pace around the bedroom. 'I do not, I *cannot* understand you. What fault could you possibly find with him? What more could you ask for? A match like that, at your time of life – it is a story almost beyond fiction!' She stared out of the window, silent for a moment; then she returned and took her sister in her arms. 'Please, at least, do try and explain,' she begged tenderly.

'I – I . . .' Tears fell again. 'I cannot marry him. It is impossible. I promised Tom I would not.'

'Tom?' Jane was now genuinely puzzled. 'But Tom had no knowledge of your Mr Hobday.'

'On our last day in Kintbury, just before he left. We were in church.' Cassy struggled. She had never before admitted this. 'In front of the altar. We stood before *God*, Jane. And I promised him, faithfully, I would marry him or I would marry no man at all.'

Jane pulled back in horror. 'And Tom dared ask that of you?'

'No. Of course he did not. He begged that I not feel beholden.' She blew her nose. 'But beholden I most surely am. I cannot go back on my word. I should be punished again.'

'Cassandra! Punished, indeed. Punished *again*? What is this Old Testament nonsense? Who is this cruel God of whom you speak? I have a mind to call in Papa.'

'Our parents must never know any of this!' Cassy was urgent. 'They will not forgive me. And it would be useless. I shall not change my mind.'

The sisters lay down together then. Jane held Cassy tight in her arms while she sobbed and until she was calm.

Presently, when it was safe, she could not resist asking: 'Pray, Cass. Tell me all that he said to you. Did he ask well?'

Cassy pulled back and smiled. 'You will not be surprised to hear that he asked *perfectly*. He has loved me since the first time he set eyes on me. He was good enough to pay homage to my beauty, but only in passing. He spoke more of intelligence, mind and spirit and my, well . . .'

'Go on.'

'. . . character and – what *he* takes at least – its excellence. That he has perceived a gift for improving the lives of those I have around me.' She flicked her hand as if to brush away such a fancy. 'Though how he has come to that conclusion I really cannot say.'

'He is right, though. You do, my love. And here was a man capable of seeing it.' Jane sighed. 'How did he take your refusal?'

'Oh, *perfectly*, of course. He was grim, but respectful. He did not try to persuade me. Though he did beg for permission to write in the future.'

'And you granted that?'

'Yes, though I now deeply regret it. In the

moment – Oh, Jane! It was dreadful – it seemed the least I could do.'

'So he still must have hope.' Jane brightened. 'He could ask again.' She got up, collected herself and went to rejoin the family, to tell them that the headaches had returned, that she had seen for herself how much Cassy suffered.

Her report must have been accepted without question. Cassy stayed in her room, and was left alone.

CHAPTER 18

Kintbury, April 1840

It was now late in the afternoon. Pyramus guided her down the path through the graveyard to the porch of the church, and sat down as if to wait. Feeling herself to have been delivered for a reason, Cassandra opened the heavy oak door, entered – and was at once overcome.

The House of God, when empty, behaved in a quite different fashion from the houses of men. This was not sunken; this was no shell dependent upon people for its personality and atmosphere: quite the opposite. Free of worshippers and busyness, it stood solid in its own splendour; confident in its own purpose: cold, damp and simple, yet rich with magnificence.

Cassandra walked down the aisle, alone with her God, and lowered herself on to a pew, to keep His company for a while. She studied the altar, bleak in its Lenten attire, and thought back to that winter's night long ago, when it was dressed up for Epiphany and she had stood there with Tom. Her mind's eye conjured up that Cassy

– slim and handsome – making that promise she had no need to make. How rash she had been – impulsive, intemperate – to play games with fortune; it was quite out of character. There had been moments – in Dawlish, and after – when she had railed at God for letting her act so. He had been there, as her witness: could not He have stepped in and held her younger self back?

But, sitting there now, Cassandra had her own small epiphany. On reflection, she could see that the promise had proved a gift, provided an alibi. It gave her the power to refuse good Mr Hobday. It led her, through a serpentine route, down many dark and blind alleys, to her own eventual happy ending. So, one could argue, it never had been the wilful act of a foolish young woman, but instead the centrepiece of her whole life's design.

Cassandra rose, left the church and made her slow return to the vicarage, pondering the mysteries of events and their outcomes. The ambiguity of it all made her head hurt. She felt weak and depleted and longed to sit down. But when they came to the gate, her faithful canine friend did not lead her into the house, but instead set off for the bridge.

'Pyramus!' She could not walk any further. 'Here, Pyramus!' Nor could she leave him out here alone, unattended. No doubt he knew his way around – he was blessed with more sense than most humans – but still, he was too precious a creature to lose. She took a deep breath and followed.

Beyond the bridge was the Avenue, a long, straight lane, lined with good horse chestnuts, that led to the Manor. And there, halfway down it, was the small figure of Isabella in deep conversation with a tall man in black. Pyramus must have heard his mistress's voice. As they drew nearer, Cassandra divined this to be a conversation of some awkwardness. Pyramus must have sensed her distress. At last, she came upon them.

'Oh, Cassandra.' Isabella was trembling, almost tearful. 'I am pleased to see you.'

Not more Kintbury dramas! Cassandra did not have the energy.

'May I present to you Mr Dundas, who is to take over from my father as the new Vicar of Kintbury. Mr Dundas has just informed me that he would like us to remove ourselves from the house within the next fortnight.'

'Within the next fortnight?' Cassandra repeated. 'But that is too soon. Two months, Mr Dundas. The retiring family is always granted two months. That is a custom as old as the Church.'

'With a *family*, yes, I can see that is appropriate. But in this case, there is no family left to speak of.' Mr Dundas spoke with the confidence of one all too aware of his own winning charm. 'There is only Miss Fowle, so I foresee no difficulty. I am keen to get on and do the best for the parish, Miss . . .?'

'Miss Austen.' Cassandra had learned to be wary of charm. Too often had she seen it abused by the charmer in the ruthless pursuit of his own advantage.

'Miss Austen?' Mr Dundas bowed. 'You are perhaps some relation of the *actual* Miss Austen – the great lady novelist?'

She agreed that she must be.

'Oh, but then this *is* a coincidence! For I am her greatest admirer.'

Cassandra proceeded to revise her opinion of the gentleman. There was clearly more to him than manners.

'Allow me, please, to kiss the hand that must once have touched our dear Jane. There. It is as close as I will ever get to the real, proper thing.'

She re-revised it, immediately, and placed it back, firmly, into its original position.

'You cannot imagine my despair when she was taken from us so early. I was quite sunk for days when I heard.'

'Then it only leaves me to say how sorry I am for your great personal loss,' Cassandra said calmly.

'Thank you – most kind. I have read all of her works. Well, perhaps, most of her works. What is the one with the clergyman?'

'Well, it is hard to say which you mean. She rather went in for clergymen . . . They all—'

'*Mansfield House!* Yes, that is the one. My favourite above all. I read it and read it again. The thing about your sister, and so few people grasp this, is that her understanding of people, and a certain milieu, was so profound as to be almost unique.'

'Is that so?' Cassandra started to walk back in the direction of the house. Mr Dundas fell into step beside her. Isabella lagged behind.

'And it seems to me that she must have somehow been the beneficiary of the great education that is ordinarily the preserve of the English gentleman. Perhaps she was lucky enough to have a master, and not just a governess?' Cassandra could sense this was more of a muse than a question. 'I also feel – indeed, I am certain – that she travelled considerably and was the all-seeing guest in a great many drawing rooms of all the best people. I *can* tell you, definitely, that she was once in Bath, for my brother was fortunate enough to meet her there.'

'Was he indeed?' Cassandra remembered the occasion with clarity. She had gone to the Pump Room alone with her parents; Jane could not be persuaded to come out that day. The senior Mr Dundas had met only this *other* Miss Austen. As so often, poor, weak truth must lay down its life for the triumph of anecdote.

'He reported that she was the most sparkling creature he ever did meet!'

Well, that was most gratifying. She did recall, thinking about it, that she had been on rather good form.

'Your situation interests me. It must rub, does it not? I often find myself pondering on the random way in which blessings are scattered in families. There is your sister, a woman of genius, who, if there is any justice, should be the subject of interest for future generations. And there beside her is you, madam, whom, by the vagaries of fate . . .' He paused, and for the first time showed a little uncertainty.

'. . . am rendered of interest to no one at all?' she finished for him, helpfully. 'I think we are going this way, are we not, Miss Fowle? If you are off to your church and the very great importance of its ministry, Mr Dundas, please do not let us detain you.'

They made their farewells and he swaggered off into the distance.

'Isabella,' Cassandra said gently, once they were alone, 'do you intend to comply with this outrageous demand?'

'I do not feel I have a choice.' Isabella sniffed as she walked. 'He spoke as one most sympathetic to my predicament, and of course the parish must always come first. Mr Dundas is a man never less than impeccable in all matters. He was very flattering about your sister, was he not?'

'Indeed. I was quite charmed. But, my dear, have you yet found a place to which you might go?'

They had arrived at the drive of the vicarage.

'No, not at all.' Isabella sighed and sniffed again. 'Oh, it is all my own fault, I dare say. It generally is. That is what my sisters would tell me. I have been too happy to let others decide on my behalf. I am a wretched creature, all abject and prone.'

They were met at the door by Dinah, who stood waiting to take their outer garments.

'Surely there must be somewhere to suit in the village.' Cassandra untied her bonnet. 'You have *some* money, Isabella: the means of providing some sort of roof for your head. My dear, do remember that. All is not lost.'

Isabella unfastened her cloak. 'Yes, of course. A place. I shall find a place.' Her self-pity resurfaced as she looked around the gracious hall. 'Though I may never again have a home.' She retrieved her handkerchief from a pocket, dabbed at her nose and brightened a little. 'Indeed, I did hear yesterday of a house here in the village.' Her face fell again. 'No, that will not do. It is beyond my slender means. I could only take it if both my sisters came with me. Thank you, Dinah. That will be all.'

Dinah stayed where she was.

Cassandra's heart lifted. A house of three women, and all deeply connected: this was the best possible outcome, the one she had hoped for since her arrival: the Holy Trinity of Domestic Perfection. And now she could share her own intelligence.

'I spoke to your sister Elizabeth only this afternoon!' she declared with great satisfaction. 'She is willing to share with you if you would like it.'

They moved through to the drawing room. Dinah followed them.

'And I am quite sure Mary-Jane, too, can be

persuaded. She seems to feel a little insecure in that cottage.'

Dinah fled from the room, Cassandra hoped to make their tea.

'Oh, I do envy you. A new place is always a matter of tremendous excitement, and this will be the first of your own,' Cassandra went on. 'Think of that, my dear. So many women end up perched on the edge of their extended families, trying not to get in the way. You will have a parlour! Possibly even a garden. We have so loved our garden in Chawton. A patch of earth of one's own, to tend as one wishes; one small corner of the glory that is an English country village: it is the most we can wish for in this life of ours.'

She was subsumed with joy at the future to which Isabella could now look forward. Living alone, for the first time, these women would discover the true bonds of sisterhood and learn that this was, in fact, the happiest of all possible happy endings. After all, mere men were no requisite to contented—

A loud crash came from the pantry. Isabella rose and rushed through. Cassandra sat alone for a while, mildly curious as to what was going on in there now. Dinah was certainly not one of those servants who made life easier for the household, and Isabella's apparent devotion was hard to explain. Still, there was no reason to get involved in any backstairs business. She had more serious matters to concern her.

She returned to her room, reached into her valise

and retrieved that extraordinary note from Jane. *My sister is deeply in love!* Once again, the words leaped out from the page, and struck her right to the core. What was Jane thinking of, to write in such terms? Cassandra was horrified anew, and yet quick to comfort herself. Surely, this was scrawled out in the mood of a moment. Of course, there would be no further assault on her privacy.

Steeling herself, Cassandra reached for the next in the pile.

Teignmouth
July 10th, 1802

My dear Eliza,

You begged to be informed of the next stage in the saga, and it is with a heavy heart that I comply. For the news is that – despite all previous excitement and optimism – it seems, once again, we are to be left disappointed.

I hasten to tell you that the gentleman himself was by no means the agent of this disappointment – indeed, the reverse. Over the length of our stay, he proved himself as good a man as those who love her could wish for; on our last day, he declared himself, just as we hoped. It was already clear that the attraction was mutual and that it was almost too good to be true. Yet Cassy refused him! The sheer madness of it drives me to distraction.

As you well know, I am no advocate of marriage for its own sake, but I am all for a good match and this would be – could have been – a splendid one. Imagine, Eliza! My sister had the offer of a comfortable future – wealth, stability, love and respect – and she opted for more insecurity. I must say that I struggle to comprehend it. Bereaved fiancée, dutiful daughter, caring aunt – these are the roles she embraces. Esteemed object of a gentleman's heart, though? <u>That</u> she would rather reject.

I know that we – my parents and I – weigh on her. She fears we cannot manage without her and though that is true – I am guilty of an over-dependence, as is our mother – I shall endeavour to persuade her it is not. But she speaks, too, of a whole other reason – if my sister has one fault it is that of a wanton appetite for the denial of self – and it is for this that I write to you now.

It appears she feels beholden to Tom – some business of A Promise, though I suspect it is also connected to the fact of the bequest that he made her – and to your family. We have been so grateful that you have continued to treat her as one of your own, and the warmth, the kindness, the inclusion that you have shown to her in these dark times has been exemplary. But I am sure you would be happy to see her build a new life for herself, as would we all. Should the occasion arise, might you see your way to offering some Fowle absolution?

If we both play our part, then I am sure he will need but the slightest encouragement to ask her again. He is a man of some pride, but not too proud to be malleable. Some of the very best marriages require at least two proposals – do they not? – to get them on to the right foot.

And if that does not work, well then: I shall be forced to do something drastic. I would sooner sacrifice my own happiness than watch Cassy martyr herself so.

With fondest wishes,
J. Austen.

CHAPTER 19

Manydown, December 1802

'The very prince of days, and in the very king of counties!' Jane exclaimed, linking arms with her sister. 'Oh, the joy of being back on Hampshire soil.'

They were staying at Manydown, which happened to be one of Jane's few favourite places, with the Misses Bigg, who were both on the very short list of her favourite people. A combination of a little good fortune and considerable conniving had brought them here for three blessed weeks. They should be with James and Mary at Steventon, that was the arrangement, and had survived almost ten days under the rectory roof. But the effect on Jane – the livid grief of revisiting her childhood home; the irritations of being under the rule of its new mistress – had been such that Cassy had become quite concerned.

So Cassy had taken it upon herself to have a quiet word with Catherine and Alethea, and those excellent women had come to their rescue. This gracious house, with its spacious estate, had at once worked its magic. Jane was now almost restored. Together, the four friends strode out over a field made crisp by the dry winter, and Cassy breathed deep with relief at the lift in Jane's mood.

'Can you have any idea of your own privilege, girls? To have this limitless acreage at your disposal. To walk and to think in unqualified peace. One cannot quite appreciate the wondrousness of it, if you have never known anything other.'

'Oh, but we do, Jane. I assure you.' They had come to the ha-ha. There was a bridge further up, but they had never used it in their youth and they eschewed the use of it now. Alethea lifted her skirts and jumped the ditch. She landed with grace and, while waiting for the others, spoke on: 'There is always that threat hanging over us, to aid the concentration of the mind and the counting of blessings.' She held out a hand to help Cassy. 'We cannot forget that one day our brother will want to bring his own wife here and *she* is unlikely to want all these sisters lurking about, getting older and crosser.'

'You are the least cross women I know! But then who can be cross when in Manydown? Even I seem to have forgotten the knack.' Jane, too, leaped across the ha-ha unaided. 'And I am sure that were *I* the future Mrs Harris Bigg-Wither, I should make room for as many sisters as were available and then take to the streets and petition for more.' With a firm, quick step, she led their way across the pasture, scattering sheep in her path. 'Anyway, your brother is still a young man. He could be years yet off marriage and while your father is alive you can count on this as your home. We have a new and deep understanding of that small word now, do we not, Cass?'

'Oh.' Cassy took her arm again – a gesture that hoped to ward off the demons. 'Our life is not so bad, Jane. Bath certainly has its diversions.'

'Indeed!' Catherine joined in now. 'You forget, Jane, how bored you had become with Hampshire society. The same old faces at the Basingstoke Assembly . . . We hardly bother with it these days. Without you two there to laugh with, the evenings seemed simply interminable. There you at least have fresh meat to pick at.'

'Ugh.' Jane tossed her disgust over her shoulder. 'I should not dare, for fear it might poison me.' They crested the hill and she stopped to soak up the vista unfolding before them. 'Behold! A view for the ages. This is the stuff of life. Here is the place for proper contentment.'

'That is all you require?' Cassy asked, smiling. 'A mere one-hundred-and-fifty-acre slice of your own rolling country?'

They all laughed at her.

'I am a simple enough soul, Cass.' Jane laughed with them. 'Modest in my ambitions. Something like Manydown would do me quite well.'

Dinner that night was uncommonly cheerful. They were not a large party, which was lucky for Jane

263

could not always be relied upon to enjoy those. But they were a happy one: just the Austen and Bigg ladies, their father, Mr Lovelace Bigg-Wither, and his only son.

Fortune had been most specific in the division of gifts to the Bigg-Wither family: the daughters had received intelligence, grace and charm in abundance; the son had been blessed with a more grandiose surname and would one day receive the estate.

Mr Harris Bigg-Wither was the youngest in the family and as a child had suffered the indignity of a terrible stammer. Now one-and-twenty, he was not quite the miserable specimen he had been when the Austens last saw him. He had grown tall, and the strange distortion of his mouth become less apparent. The improvement was noticeable, and the Misses Austen duly approved it. Whether his mind had developed also, whether his opinions had become interesting or his reasoning sound – these things could only be guessed at. For although Mr Bigg-Wither had learned to talk well enough and was able to do so without causing undue embarrassment to himself or his listeners, he still talked as little as possible. His youthful affliction had left him shy in company, and the company that evening required no sort of contribution from him.

'Such a pity for the neighbourhood that your family has left us,' Mr Lovelace Bigg-Wither was saying. 'Why your dear father should even think of retiring I shall never understand.'

Cassy caught Jane's eye across the table and they shared a small smile. How could a landed gentleman appreciate the pleasures of retirement, if he has never before known the discomforts of work?

'I believe it had all become too much for him,' Jane explained. 'Not only the responsibilities of the church and his parishioners, but the running of the glebe too, I fear, took its toll.'

'Well, if you say so, dear girl, though I have often thought rector of a small, country parish to be the most enviable existence, without the onerous responsibilities of having too much of one's own land.' He took a mouthful of beef and ruminated for a moment. 'But still, why could not your parents have settled here in Hampshire? Bath – Bath of all places! It makes no sort of sense.'

'Ah, there we are in agreement, sir,' said Jane warmly. 'I now know to my cost that cities in general have not much to recommend them. The noise and smoke and the press of other people! All very well for a visit or two, but no longer than that.'

'Quite so, madam.' Mr Bigg-Wither pointed his fork at her to express his agreement, and peered with approval through a forest of eyebrow. 'Many a time my dear, late lady wife would drag me to London, promising a dashed good time. I would hide in my club for a day or two and then scuttle back here as soon as I could.' He took a potato. 'Never go near the place now. *London*, indeed. Makes a fellow quite ill.'

'My parents', Cassy put in, 'felt that the winter in Bath would make a pleasant change, and they are very much enjoying taking their summers at the seaside.'

'The seaside! *The seaside*?' The gentleman harrumphed. 'Then it is as I feared. They have quite lost their senses. What business can anyone have with the seaside? That is the beauty of our neck of Hampshire. We cannot see it. Thank the good Lord, we cannot smell it. We can all but pretend that it is not even there.'

'Papa, the sea is greatly in fashion,' said Alethea. 'They now say that it is of great benefit to one's health.'

'Ha! It will kill you as soon as it looks at you.' He bellowed his warning. 'Only a damned fool would trust it.' He sank into his chair and returned to his dinner.

'Sir, I must say that I have every sympathy with your position. Once one has known Manydown, then one need never travel again. If you have met perfection, why go in search of inadequacy?' Jane's words, though all true, were carefully designed to restore her host's humour. 'I feel just as strongly about Steventon. While I am very grateful to my parents for showing me other, different places, all that I have learned on our travels is this: there is no county to rival Hampshire, in my own affections at least.'

The ladies left the table so that the gentlemen could enjoy their port in peace. They walked through the hall, where the white marble was softened by firelight and candles, and the stone staircase stretched like a dancer out and up in an elegant curve. Jane sighed and squeezed Cassy's arm. 'Is this not heaven?'

'It is all very lovely.' Cassy patted her, soothingly. 'And you may have had a little too much wine.'

Jane giggled. 'Then who can blame me? It is very good here, and no one can predict when we will next sample its like. I intend to stock up like a camel, so as to somehow survive the oncoming drought.'

Once in the drawing room, Cassy settled herself with the others on the sofa while Jane walked over to the pianoforte and lifted its lid.

'What a fine instrument.' Her fingers brushed the keys.

'And wasted on we sorry creatures,' said Alethea. 'Will you play for us, Jane?'

She sat down. 'I fear I am no longer the pianist I used to be. All this unsettlement means not so much practising. You may find you regret having asked me.' But she started to play anyway, a Bach prelude of which Cassy was particularly fond. It took her mind back to their dressing room in Steventon, to their own safe, closeted little world.

Jane was still playing when Mr Bigg-Wither Senior came in and approached her.

'Miss Jane. Do excuse me. I come bearing a message. If you would be so kind, my son is requesting you join him now in the library.'

Cassy stiffened, looked around and caught Catherine and Alethea exchanging glances. She was seized with a sense of foreboding.

Clearly, her sister was not. 'The library? How charming.' Jane rose and giggled again. She really had drunk too much wine. 'I am always delighted to go into a *library*.' And she swayed out of the room.

'What is this?' Cassy asked of her hosts, while remembering to appear calm. 'What is this mystery?'

'We could not possibly say,' returned Catherine with the most knowing smile. 'No doubt all will be revealed.'

They did not have to wait long. The young Mr Harris Bigg-Wither soon entered the drawing room, with a flushed-looking Jane upon his arm.

'Father, Sisters, madam. It is with great pleasure that I announce' – he paused, either for theatrical effect or to control his stammer – 'that Miss Austen has kindly consented to be my wife.'

The family swarmed about the couple in great celebration. Cassy was unable to move. This was madness! A toast was suggested, glasses were filled, health was proposed and still she sat watching. Could not anybody else see that this was sheer madness? Everything about it was wrong! Oh, as proposals go, it looked the part, certainly. The evening, the drawing room, the candlelight, the couple – dazed and yet beaming. Yes, the stage was set exactly as it should be.

All as it should be. And yet, in Cassy's eyes, nothing as it ought.

It was sometime later that they were able to shut the door on their bedroom and talk openly.

'Jane! My dear, what on earth have you done?'

'Well, there is a response. Are you not to congratulate me on the splendour of my match?'

'Yes. Of course. I shall speak of my joy and express all the right sentiments and kiss you and bless you. Once you have assured me that you are in love with Mr Bigg-Wither.' Cassy's voice rose. 'And that you admire him above and beyond all other gentlemen. That he is your one chosen companion for the rest of your life.'

'I cannot do that, of course.' Jane sat on the bed, a hard smile fixed on her face. 'Nor could he with me, I dare say. Indeed, I am not entirely convinced he likes me particularly. But when manna does happen to fall down from the heavens – which it has singularly failed to do upon *me* before this very evening – then it would be foolish to squander it.'

'Of course he must like you. Why else do you suppose he would—'

'Oh, Cass. A dull boy growing up with such

intelligent sisters can hardly be expected to own his own mind. I suppose I just happened to be on hand, he thought the arrangement might bring pleasure to the family and that I may do as well as any civilised woman of their acquaintance.'

'Then what are you doing?' Cassy knelt down at her feet. 'This goes against all that you feel and believe in. It makes a mockery of everything you have ever said on the subject of marriage and love – love, in particular.'

'And what did I know? What did I know about love or any other matter?' Jane cried out. 'In truth, I now look back on my erstwhile confidence and shudder at it. Before we left Steventon, I had no understanding of the world and its malice. The things I once wrote!' She put her face in her hands. 'What a silly, *silly*, naïve little child.' She thought for a moment. 'This after all, need not be such a stretch of my so-called principles. I have always maintained the impossibility of love without money, but there must still be the hope that, with money, love can perhaps grow, over time.'

'And you truly believe that could happen here, that you could one day love Mr Bigg-Wither?'

Jane sighed. 'I cannot, of course, predict any such thing. I admit it unlikely. But this much I can say, and I have said it before.' – she grabbed Cassy's hands – 'We cannot go on in this fashion. One of us has to do something that might release us from this pitiful state. What should I care the sort of man he is in thought or in habits? It may

270

hardly matter. He is from a good family. He cannot be all bad. And think of it, Cass: his sisters can stay here. We will all be safe! And together!' She looked at Cassy then and stroked her face. 'And you, my best girl, are now free. Free to marry your Mr Hobday.'

'Jane!' Was this what was behind it? She pulled away and stood up. Was Jane truly willing to enter into a disastrous match so that she could enjoy what might be a better one? Cassy could never know *freedom* in a strange place like Derbyshire, while her own sister was miserable and miles away . . .

She sat down again. This was Jane's first proposal, the closest she had ever been to marriage, and she was too excitable, right at that moment, to look at it seriously. Cassy had been there twice now, and had the presence of mind, the time, the experience to peer in and see enough to know fear at all it entailed. The image of Tom's dirty shaving rag swam up before her . . . Of course, there was a chance that it might work out well with Mr Bigg-Wither . . . but all evidence pointed against it. If Jane was sure and determined, then Cassy would not prevent her. But to be the cause of the marriage, to know herself to be its true justification? That was unthinkable. Cassy could be no part of this story.

'I can tell you now that whatever you do will not make me marry Hobday. I have refused him. It is over. I never think of him even.'

271

That was untrue. Of course she thought of him. Often. Through his letters, he had become less the unknowable stranger, and something approaching a friend. But, if needs be, for the sake of her sister, she would resolve never to think of him again.

'And how could I leave our parents now?' Cassy went on. 'Papa is old and ailing. Mama cannot be left by herself. There is my duty—'

This, at least, was the truth. If Jane was indeed gone, then Cassy could not possibly think of leaving.

'Oh, Cass. You and your infernal sense of *duty*! I beg you, lay it aside and think of yourself for once.'

'But I could not *be* myself if I did that! Without it, I should be nothing – or some other woman whom I could never respect.'

Jane flung herself back on the mattress and started to cry.

Cassy opened her arms and cradled her sister. 'If you can be happy here, then I shall be happy, just in that knowledge.'

They lay together, each in her own thoughts. In time, Jane asked, in a voice so quiet that Cassy at first did not hear it: 'And will I be happy here, do you think?'

'Well.' Cassy sat up to consider the question. This was a strength she had over her sister: to analyse, assess; bring a rational head to the complexities of a problem. 'You love Manydown, and place is of particular importance to you, to your sense of well-being. But then you would be its mistress, with all the little issues of the day-to-day that are entailed. *That* may not suit you!' She smiled. 'Though Catherine and Alethea would, no doubt, help shoulder the burden.'

'As you do for me?'

'Possibly not quite as much as that, my dear. The control, all the decisions of the household, must fall upon you, or you should be failing in your wifely duties.'

Jane was pale.

'And then, of course, there will be children. I presume Mr Bigg-Wither would hope for a lot of them. Men are prone to when there is an estate to consider, and so many bedrooms to fill.' She offered up a prayer that her sister would somehow prove strong enough to survive it.

'I shall be in pig for the rest of my years!' Jane wailed.

'Yes, but you love children,' Cassy countered. 'You have a gift with them.'

'With other people's.'

'You will love your own even more.'

Jane sat up; she leaned her head on Cassy's shoulder. 'What else? What other factors should I consider?'

Cassy was reluctant to continue. The conversation was heading for trickier waters; it would be wise to drop anchor now. 'It is a bit late for any further consideration beyond that, my love. May

I remind you that you have already accepted? The family knows. The deal is struck.'

But Jane's mind went on alone. 'I will have no time to myself, for thinking. For writing. I shall not write more than a letter again.'

'We do not know that,' Cassy insisted, though she feared it was true.

'I shall have a husband. A master.'

'Come now! You talk as if you are entering service, not marriage. Mr Bigg-Wither is hardly a cruel man and not overbearing.'

'Under-bearing, if he is anything.'

'Time for bed.' Cassy said briskly. 'It has been a most eventful evening. I think we could both do with some sleep.

An hour before dawn, Jane shook Cassy awake. 'I cannot do it. I have thought all night and, Cass, I cannot do it.'

Cassy sat up with a bolt. 'But you *have* done it, Jane. It is already done!'

'No.' Jane was white and close to hysterical. 'It was all a mistake. The most hideous error. I do not know what I was thinking. I shall tell him this morning.'

'Oh, my dear.' Cassy fell back on to the pillow. 'Oh, but this is a calamity. The girls. The father. Mr Bigg-Wither himself, the poor boy! Are you quite certain? You cannot go through with it?'

'Certain.' She rose and marched to the wardrobe. 'We will leave here this morning.'

'And go where? Back to that life you so hate, that you cannot abide? Remember now your reasons for accepting.'

Jane was removing her nightcap and pulling at her hair. 'They are not enough. This is not the answer. I shall stay with you. Together, we will survive it, somehow.' She turned then and smiled at her sister. 'To quote a philosopher of my acquaintance: I shall not starve.'

They dressed, sought out Alethea and prostrated themselves before her. In that moment, the latter proved her worth, as a very good woman and an even better friend. Mr Harris Bigg-Wither was fetched and he and Jane left alone for their interview. Cassy did not enquire of the details; she did not want to know.

Then, at once, the carriage was called and the Austen ladies returned to Steventon. The rectory was stunned by their sudden appearance and the distress of their countenance. Mary, in particular, was all agog.

'*What* is this *new* drama? Austen! What have they done *now*?'

To her fury, the sisters said only that they must leave for Bath and begged James to escort them.

'On a Saturday?' he exclaimed. 'But of course, I cannot. I am impossibly busy.'

But such was their upset, Mary stepped forward and suggested he manage it. And then he could only agree.

Once back with their parents, in the comparative

tranquillity of their lodgings, Cassy sat down to address a last letter to Mr Hobday. After careful consideration and in spite of her previous words on the matter, she must insist that they cease all correspondence. She had been grateful for his attentions and, if his disappointment was heavy, then she was sorry.

Neither could pretend that she was his one chance of happiness. She wished him well for the future, extended her warmest regards to his mother. This was her final decision. She would not write again.

CHAPTER 20

Kintbury, April 1840

Cassandra sat in her armchair and thought for a while. Her purpose in coming to Kintbury had been to remove all that might reflect badly upon Jane or the legacy: that was the brief she had given herself. But the letters about Tom and Mr Hobday were incriminating to neither, merely deeply intrusive upon herself. Was that justification enough to remove them, too?

She pictured her sister-in-law Mary reading them, spreading the contents, passing them on. She imagined the next generation examining her own traces as if she were a South Dorset fossil. They would wonder, even laugh, at the idea that their desiccated old aunt might have known such romance. They would know that she had not, after all, been so very faithful to the memory of dear, good Tom Fowle.

Worse yet was the fear that these letters might somehow fall into the hands of a stranger. Cassandra could never surrender the hope that there would one day be a greater appetite for Jane's novels; that this could bring a new interest in the life of their author had long been a matter of dread. Now, in that moment, she felt the dawning awareness of a whole other danger. For was there not a chance – remote and, yes, possibly ridiculous – that even her own life might then be trespassed upon? After all, Jane's story and her own could not be separated: they were bound tight together to form one complete history. On the fortunes of the other, each life had turned. A chill ran down her stiff spine.

She had but one choice: as soon as she was back home in the privacy of Chawton, alone and unwatched, she would burn them. Lowering herself to her knees, Cassandra pulled out the trunk from its place under her bed, opened it and secreted away all the letters she had so far found troublesome.

And now for the crux of the matter: the difficult, second act of the drama: the unmentionable business. This would be painful to read about, hard to revisit, but the job must be done. And for it to be done properly, Cassandra now needed her own letters to Eliza. She knew full well how much she had once shared, and she knew she must censor it. Their retrieval was imperative. She would soon leave the vicarage. There could be no more delay.

Determined, she hurried downstairs to the door that led through to the domestic offices. Sounds of spirited conversation came from within. The voices were Dinah's and that of a man which Cassandra did not immediately recognise. She stood for a while, summoning the courage to enter. Then the door opened on her.

'Can I help you, m'm?' Dinah asked.

'Ah, Dinah.'

Cassandra caught a glimpse of the table, upon which sat a slab of pork pie with an egg in the middle.

'I wondered' – Cassandra withdrew into the hall, so that Dinah might follow her – 'if I might have a word?'

Dinah came out and stood before her, with that particular air of respectful impudence that she had made quite her own.

'I had, as I believe you were aware, some private papers in my chamber.'

'Is that right, m'm?'

'And while I was ill, they were somehow . . . mislaid.'

'Sorry to hear it, m'm. A body interfering in another body's business? I don't hold with that, m'm. Meddling, I call it.' She tutted. 'That would never do.'

Cassandra pressed on, regardless. 'I wondered if you might know of their whereabouts?'

'Me, Miss Austen? You think *I'm* one for meddling?'

It was now perfectly clear that Dinah was the culprit and that she, Cassandra, was being punished for some reason.

'Heavens, no! Not at all, Dinah. But perhaps you have some idea of *why* they might have been removed?'

'Can't say as I do, m'm.' Dinah looked her full in the eyes. 'Unless . . .'

'Yes?'

'Well, unless there was someone who thought that you, m'm, was going in for a bit of interfering yourself . . . Oh, of course, *I* would never think such a thing . . . Just, you know, other people . . . Nasty thoughts, some of 'em.'

The woman was an outrage. There were no 'other people', and Cassandra was interfering in nobody's business but her own.

She decided to play her trump card. 'Of course, I would very much like to be free to leave you all in peace at the earliest possible opportunity. I am well aware that this is a difficult time. But I have come to say that I cannot possibly consider my departure until the letters are returned.' She turned on her heels, and withdrew.

Dinner that evening was pleasant, for her niece Caroline was come to join them, but short. Dinah was absent, so Fred served them a quick meal that held no ambition beyond the continued conjoinment of body and soul. Cassandra, thinking with some longing of that pork pie out in the pantry, picked at her plate, while discussion ranged over the lives of various Fowle relatives. She took no part in it; her interest was limited. This was a failing of hers in old age, but she would not correct it. Members of her own family, all of them without exception, seemed so much more interesting, their stories more engrossing, their characters elevated and distinguished. Those other mortals, whose poor veins must somehow pulse with no Austen blood in them, always appeared to her comparatively pale.

Once in the drawing room, she pulled out her patchwork and sat silently sewing while the two younger cousins talked together on the sofa, until Isabella, tiring of their subject, leaned across.

'Your patchwork looks most impressive, Cassandra. When first you arrived, I thought you were doing nothing more than stitching together odd bits of stuff. But I see now there is more to it, is there not?'

'Oh, a good patchwork always *starts* with odd bits of stuff. Therein lies the glory of the process.' Cassandra was sewing a sprigged square to a blue one. 'With sharp vision and no little imagination, those random elements become a thing that is quite other, and with its own intricate, inherent beauty. This will have one hundred and forty points of symmetry by the time I am done – if I live long enough, that is.'

'Goodness. I cannot imagine! Do you work with a pattern?'

'No, not at all. I do not need one.' She tapped the side of her head with a thimbled finger. 'All is in here. I shall not actually see it until I am finished. It will be too large to spread out in Chawton. I have not the space in the house. In the summer, I shall take it in the garden, put it out on the lawn and enjoy how it looks then.'

'So you have all that complexity in your mind's eye? You can look upon those small pieces and somehow see the whole?'

'Well, not at first perhaps, but as it evolves I can see my way through.'

'Oh you are clever, Cassandra.'

She was too old to be bashful and would not deny it. She *was* clever, and had been fortunate enough to grow up in a house in which cleverness in its daughters was valued, and no apology was made for it.

'Is your aunt not clever, Caroline?'

Caroline did not enthuse, but merely replied: '*All* Austens are clever.'

Cassandra smiled: that girl was turning into her mother.

'My own dear papa' – Caroline spoke with complacence – 'had the most formidable intellect, as does my brother James-Edward.'

'*And* my sister, of course.' Cassandra licked at her thumb. In the annoyance of the moment, her needle had slipped. 'And what is cleverness when put beside brilliance? We are all in the shade of those who shine brightest. As I have always been – and quite contentedly so – in the shade of your dear Aunt Jane.'

'Oh, yes,' Caroline conceded. 'And Aunt Jane.'

'We are halfway through *Persuasion* now, Caroline,' Isabella put in. 'I must say I wonder at it. I had no idea a novel could engross me so. It is a thing of genius, or it seems such to me. I now find myself wishing I had taken more notice of your aunt while she was still with us. I have vague memories of her visits, but no clear recollection. Tell me, what was she like? For genius often comes, does it not, with a difficulty of temperament?' She shrugged. 'Or so my father used often to say.'

Cassandra put down her sewing and shifted in her armchair, preparing to answer. There was no subject on this earth in which she could find the same pleasure, or on which she was most qualified to speak, though of course she must choose her words carefully. 'Well—'

But she was interrupted by Caroline. 'Oh, Aunt Jane was the very best of aunts. Quite my favourite of all and, I am lucky to say' – now she was blushing – 'I myself was a particular favourite of hers. We shared an uncommon bond, I remember, even from my earliest years.'

Cassandra was dumb with astonishment. Jane was fond of all her nieces and nephews, and certainly did have her favourites: Anna, of course, and Edward's daughter, dear Fanny. But she used to worry that Caroline might show traces of her mother – and, clearly, she had been prescient on that, as she was prescient on most things.

'I would send her my own stories, and she would take them so seriously, as if I were her natural heir.' Caroline smiled. 'I must look them out. James-Edward might be interested in them as family documents.'

I would not do that, Cassandra thought to herself. You might see their true merit and suspect that they were received with no more than a patient indulgence.

'And her temperament?' Isabella nudged.

'Oh, her temperament!' Caroline clapped her hands. 'On that your dear father was quite wrong. Yes, she was a genius, and yet a stranger to mood, other than cheerful good humour. I always so looked forward to my visits to Chawton, when Aunt Jane was still there. One would know, with certainty, that there would be such fun and games. It is not the same any more. I do miss those days, I confess. Nowadays, every time I approach Chawton, I do so with sadness, a sense of dread almost. As do my cousins. It is hard to be reminded of the joy that cottage once held.'

Isabella, horrified, looked over at Cassandra. Cassandra, Chawton's one remaining and apparently joyless inhabitant – the object of dread for a whole generation – was trying not to laugh. Of course their cottage had been a place of great joy when they had lived there together. But that joyfulness was Jane's natural and dominant emotion was far from the truth. Oh, the power upon reputation brought by an untimely death and a modicum of fame and success! Still, she thought as she gathered her things, she would

284

not contest that legend, if that was what they chose to send out to posterity. The moodless Jane Austen. What a splendid image. She rose from her chair. Now it only remained to destroy all evidence to the contrary. She did hope those letters had been returned.

'I must leave you, my dears. I trust Caroline to give you a full picture, Isabella. Your interest is safe in her hands. I shall turn in now.'

'Oh, but I was hoping we might read more of *Persuasion*,' Isabella protested. 'We have just got to Lyme.'

'And you will enjoy it enormously,' Cassandra said smoothly. 'Do read on with your cousin. I know it too well.'

She opened the door, strode into the hall and into violent collision with the crouching form of a human.

'Oh!' Cassandra gasped, then: 'It is you! What on earth—?'

Dinah drew herself up, but made no excuses.

'Yet *more* dusting?' Cassandra smiled. 'Please do not overdo it. Goodnight.'

On the long, steep return up the stairs, Cassandra pondered the value of duty. She had given years in service to Caroline and her family, as she had given years to all Austens. That it counted for so little came as no surprise, and provoked no self-pity or rancour. She had never acted in the pursuit of fame or appreciation, but only in the interests of her own conscience. Cassandra was dutiful, had possibly been born dutiful, certainly could only *be* dutiful: she knew of no other way. In her own – for want of a better word – virtue, she had found an endless reward.

She was not unique in this. The world, she well knew, was full of good women like her, who dedicated their time, their bodies, their thoughts and their hearts to the service of others. And if they, and she, were rendered invisible: well then, what of it? Let us just pity those who had not eyes to see.

Back in her room, she put down her valise and looked about her: nothing was altered. She shut the door and, with a quiet confidence, lifted the corner of the mattress. What a surprise! The letters were there. Now for her service to the one whom she loved above all other people, who had loved her in return and never failed to acknowledge her worth. She settled down, determined to make quick, sharp work of it.

It was not an uncomplicated process. They spent eight years without an address of any real permanence – or, as Jane would refer to it, 'out in the wilderness' – but they were not all unhappiness. Far from it, indeed. Cassandra leafed through the papers, caught passages detailing short, happy stays in Manydown and Kintbury, long weeks of luxury in Kent with dear Edward. She revisited the great news of April 1803, when Jane sold her novel, *Susan,* for a princely ten pounds – oh! The excitement of that! She stumbled across references to Jane's high spirits, remembered and smiled. That those spirits were, sometimes, perhaps too high; that the happiness had an almost hysterical edge to it; that this tended to happen when they were in the comfort of the stable, established homes of their family and friends: these were not observations that Cassandra had shared with Eliza. She had chosen to keep them to herself.

But the other extreme of Jane's temperament, the seemingly endless days in the darkness: these she had written of, for she had to tell someone. Cassandra licked a finger and flicked through, searching for the letters of danger. There. January 1805. That was when it all began. She pulled out several, put down the rest of the pile, and began.

Green Park Buildings, Bath
January 24th, 1805

My dear Eliza,

Your expressions of sympathy and respect were all that we might have hoped for from you, and brought us much comfort. Yes, we have lost an excellent father and are still almost numb with the shock of it. But, though his sudden death has been hard on those who loved him so dearly, it was at least peaceful for himself. He did not suffer unduly, he did not linger in pain, he was not given the time to reflect upon those he was leaving, and for that mercy we give thanks to God.

Of course, it is with some trepidation that we all now must embark on a life without him, his wisdom, his tenderness and his humour. You ask after my mother, and she bears it bravely, though these are early days and the future can only be hard. The burial is on Saturday, in – such awful symmetry! – the same Walcot church in which they took their vows forty years ago. Forty years! They were blessed with such a happy and fruitful union as is not often witnessed, and she has known hardly a day without him by her side.

All my energies at the moment are directed in support of her, as well as the many practicalities that a sudden death must entail – it is quite all-consuming. Yet there is another aspect which, I must confide, also preys on my mind when I have a moment for it and it is this: my sister shows signs of taking it all very badly. At first, I charged her with writing the letters announcing the news to the family, which she did beautifully, of course, and their composition seemed to give her some sort of comfort. But now that is done, it is as though she is sinking away from us. She was devoted to her father, as you know, and is quite overcome with the grief of it. More than that, I fear that our new insecurity is affecting her adversely. That there will be a change in our circumstances is sadly inevitable. Yes, we shall be moving again soon, but then – just three ladies – we should not need or expect much to accommodate us. Jane knows that, understands it, but cannot yet make peace with it . . . I shall not write too much now in the hope that time does its healing but will say that I am more than concerned by the depth of her distress.

Yours as ever,
Cass. Austen.

CHAPTER 21

Green Park Buildings, Bath
February 14th, 1805

My dear Eliza,

Your kind letter was, I suspect, prompted by some intelligence from my sister. I do not doubt she has told you of my low spirits, I am sure she has asked you for some advice. Please believe me when I say that, at the moment, there is nothing to be done for me. Were there a way out of my gloom, I should find it. I am acutely conscious of being a drag on the household. My poor mother and sister have enough to concern them without tearing their hearts further. I am a poor wretch. All these potions and recipes create yet more work for Cass, and make no earthly difference. They cannot heal me. I beg that you offer no further suggestions, I wish only to be left alone.

Yrs,
J. Austen.

'Dearest?' Cassy sat on the edge of the bed in their Bath lodgings and gently shook her sister's shoulder. 'There is news. We have now heard from our brothers. Jane?' It was late morning, but the curtains were closed. 'You must try and rise now, my dear. We need to talk with Mama and make all sorts of decisions. Come now. Neither of us wishes to do it without you. These matters concern us all.'

Jane stirred, turned and looked up. Her white face appeared like a moon in the darkness. 'You do it, Cass. I am sorry. I cannot. I simply cannot bear . . .' Her voice was reduced to a hoarse whisper. 'I cannot see what there is to discuss on the subject of poverty. It brings with it no choices. If we have options, then I opt not to be poor. Anything beyond that, I trust you to decide on my behalf.'

'But the news is good! That is what I want you to hear. Please. This is our future and we must face it together. Nothing will be as bad as you fear.'

Jane turned away again. Cassy, surrendering, went back down to the parlour. Her mother, whom she had only ever known to be the most talkative, busy and bright of women, now sat, bleak in her mourning: quiet, crumpled, defeated, alone. It was two weeks since the funeral, but still, every time she caught sight of such a sad alteration, it shocked and tugged at this fond daughter's heart.

Cassy stood for a moment to gather herself. Truly, there was within her a well of love and tenderness for these two women, so deep as to be unfathomable. She prayed too that there was also the strength, somewhere, to lift up and carry them both through this difficult period.

'Mama,' she said quietly. 'It is time now, I think, for us to discuss our business, if you do not mind?'

Mrs Austen started out of her thoughts, blinked and looked up at her. 'Forgive me, my dear. Yes. Our business.' Her chin wobbled and Cassy feared another outburst of grief. But then she swallowed, controlled herself and rose to sit at the table.

Cassy drew out a chair for herself and collected the letters of the morning, when her eye was caught by the appearance of a figure in the doorway. 'Jane!' she cried out in relief. 'How good to see you downstairs.'

Her sister was still in nightgown and robe, with a shawl pulled round her shoulders. Her hair, which had not been brushed for days, hung about her face. Pale, thin and wild-looking, she was more ghostly apparition than human. Cassy guided her to the place nearest the fire.

'This should not take us long.' She returned to her seat, determined to be brisk. None of them needed to dwell on this subject. 'Now, of course, we can no longer rely on our dear father's income and annuity.' She spoke hurriedly. 'They stopped with his death and left a little – a little – er – deficit in our finances.' Understatement was such a useful tool in these sorts of moments. 'But, Mother, I am happy to say that your sons have risen to the occasion, as all we who love them could only expect. I hope you will be most touched by their proposal, which I received just this morning.'

No one else spoke. Cassy wondered if anyone really was listening.

'At first, Frank was insistent on offering us one hundred pounds per annum.'

'Oh, the dear boy!' That aroused her mother. 'But that is too magnificent from him, even with his new promotion. Cass, I am sorry I cannot accept. He will want to be married soon, he cannot afford to waste that on *us* and should not commit to that which must soon be taken away again.' She wiped her eyes. 'Tell him it is enough for me to know that he offered it. Such a good, fine man! His father would be so—'

'I agree, Mama. We have all agreed. But I can now tell you that his generosity has been matched and shared among his brothers. It is now arranged that Frank, James and Henry will each pledge fifty pounds per annum to your – and our – welfare. And from Edward, we are to receive a further one hundred a year!'

'Oh, was there ever such an excellent set of children as these!' Mrs Austen exclaimed.

'Indeed. Altogether,' Cassy continued, feeling rather like a king in his counting house – albeit a king of somewhat limited munificence, 'it means that—'

'Sorry, Cass, to interrupt you.' At some point, it seemed, Jane had come to and now sought to contribute. 'But am I to understand that Frank, the hard-working sailor who has not yet known a home of his own, offered one hundred pounds and Edward Austen of Godmersham, Kent, agreed to the exact same and no more?'

It had not occurred to Cassy to make the comparison, and she would prefer not to examine it too closely. She could, though, choose to take comfort from this evidence of Jane's acuity. Her sister was not, after all, losing her mind. There was something on which to hold. 'Are they not generous?' she replied. 'We must always be grateful to them for their willing and fulsome support.' She returned to her sheet of numbers and sums. 'So that is a full two hundred and fifty from the men, then . . . To which we can add the yield of your own money, Mother, and mine . . . Which should leave us four hundred and fifty clear for the year!'

'To which I contribute nothing.' Jane gave a low moan. 'Not a farthing. What a wretched creature I am!'

Cassy pressed on. 'We shall be comfortable enough on that, will we not? Of course, some changes must be made. We cannot stay here in Green Park Buildings, but then these rooms are more than we need now. I think, Mother, you are set on staying in Bath for the winters? That seems entirely sensible. We can find somewhere smaller and cheaper, and then if we are able to visit our family and friends in the summer months, that will cut down on our expenditure considerably. We need only to think of our transport, and then trifles such as—'

Jane rose and drifted, weightlessly, out of the room.

'You have done very well, my dear.' Mrs Austen put a hand on Cassy's. 'You are a great strength to me, as your father always knew you would be. We shall manage quite handsomely, I am sure.' She moved back to the armchair by the window. 'Oh yes, we will always get by. Three women alone' – she swallowed – 'require so very little.' Cassandra arranged a rug around her knees. 'And soon God will remember to send for me. He cannot intend to leave me down here much longer.'

'Oh, Mama. Please.' Cassy stayed for a little to comfort one mourner, before setting off up the stairs to deal with the other.

Jane was lying, face in the pillow, and weeping. Cassy got up beside her and gathered her in.

'It pains me, my dear, to see you in this much suffering. Tell me, what can I do to help you?'

'Nothing.' Jane turned and laid her head in Cassy's lap. 'There is nothing anyone can do to help a woman who has spent thirty years on this earth yet has nothing to show for it.'

'But that is not true!' Cassy cried. 'There is your ten pounds from Mr Crosby. Forgive me. I omitted to mention it. It was cruel of me. Those ten pounds were *earned*, dearest, not the profit of a legacy. That is a great thing indeed.'

'They were not worthy of a mention, as I have spent them. And I am at last facing the fact: nothing will ever come of it.' At that, the tears poured down Jane's cheeks.

Cassy stroked her hair. For the first time, she could see through to the heart of Jane's crisis. It was not just the loss of their father, but also her writing – and perhaps some interconnection between the two.

After the debacle with Mr Bigg-Wither, Jane had not, as Cassy had feared, slumped into regret and dismay. She had returned to Bath with no backward look but in its place a renewed, almost furious energy. She tidied up her latest manuscript, asked Henry Austen to see if he might sell it on her behalf and – to universal delight and no small pride – this he had done. A Mr Crosby of London, whom none of them had met, had accepted *Susan* and promised its 'immediate publication'. There was an advertisement in the press, which they had all pored over and exclaimed upon. Jane, now officially An Authoress, acquired a great confidence and began the composition of a new work, to be called *The Watsons*. Her mood was good, her industry estimable: the household was calm.

But it was to turn out that this Mr Crosby was a man of bad faith. Cassy did not approve of hatred in general, and had no previous experience of the emotion, but she now hated Mr Crosby of London with the depth of passion that only sisterly devotion could bring. For although Jane watched out for her novel's appearance, seized every periodical and notification from the circulating library, *Susan* failed to appear. The family chose not to mention the fact, not wanting to shine light on the humiliation. Instead, they had watched on, with sadness and sympathy, and prayed.

Almost two years had passed, and now Jane, vulnerable in her grief, sharp in her vulnerability, had at last, it seemed, accepted that it was but a false dawn. She lay in Cassy's arms, weak and wounded as a mistreated animal: clinging reluctantly to life though in mortal pain.

'Hush now,' Cassy urged. 'Many a writer has known disappointment at some stage.' In truth, she knew nothing of the fortunes of writers, but the words had a plausible ring to them. 'And as you certainly sold one book, then you have every chance of selling another. Anyway, may I remind you: you do not write only for profit. You write too, surely, for your own pleasure, and that of your family. To us, it is priceless. Do pick up and continue with your new one. We were all enjoying it hugely, Papa – may God rest his soul – particularly so. And you must never forget, now he has left us, how sound his judgement was on these matters and how much he valued your work.'

'You fail to understand, Cass – or you are refusing to do so. This "change in our circumstances" of which you talk in such practical fashion. Can you not see? That window of time which allowed me to pursue my writing: it is closed now.'

'I do not see why—'

'With our father's death, our mother has lost her true companion. It now falls to us to replace him.'

'Of course.'

'So we have lost the little independence we once enjoyed. We can no longer rely on being able to make visits together. You will still be invited on long stays to Godmersham, and I shall be in sole charge of Mama. You, no doubt, will take over our father's duties to the household. I cannot permit you to bear the brunt of the housekeeping on top. Those afternoons I spent alone with my pen are gone now. I shall be paying calls with our mother, and dealing with Cook. The rest of our time will be spent as *guests* in other people's homes and there I can never work.' She drew a weak, tremulous breath.

'You have protected me for so long, Cass. You have allowed me to be alone in my own head and' – she squeezed Cassy's hand – 'I thank you for it. But we embark on a new period in our lives and I must face up to my own responsibilities at last. I have had my years of opportunity, and I have squandered them.' Jane sighed, turned her back to Cassy, returned her face to the wall. 'Allow me to grieve for that, and our father. I beg you. Strength will return to me. Please just give me time.'

* * *

The next weeks were desperate. While the immediacy of death throws up many distractions, the business of mourning outlawed any at all. Cassy and her mother stayed in their lodgings, going through the motions of life but hardly living, in any sense of the word. The four walls pressed in on them. Meals were discussed and then eaten, letters received and returned. Eliza wrote regularly, with remedies and recipes for potions. Cassy climbed the stairs six times a day with beef tea, arrowroot and herbal infusions; Jane took them in, like a well-behaved, sickly infant. She did not, though, come down.

Mrs Austen was the first to recover her spirits. Cassy had always known her mother to be a woman of great personal strength, but still she was pleasantly surprised, and impressed, by the manner in which she accepted the challenge of widowhood and rose to it. Together, they selected their next inferior lodgings and, when the time came to move, Jane seemed to take that as her signal. She left her bed and resumed her duties to both mother and sister.

'So this is our new palace,' she said, looking around the dark, small apartments. Her eye caught the patch of damp, but she did not remark on it. 'Twenty-five Gay Street. Such an exquisite name.' She was still frail, pale and thin, but in her eyes was a return of that twinkle. 'It will serve not only as an address but also an instruction. I promise to be only gay while we are here.'

Cassandra's whole being loosened. She let out her lungs and felt her shoulders descend. The depression was over. It had been misery, but now they could put it behind them. Together, they had survived the worst blow that could strike. There was no reason to fear that it could come again.

Southampton
15th October, 1806

Dear Eliza,

We are arrived in Southampton for the start of our new venture and with a whole different household: we three Austen ladies, your dear sister, Martha, plus Frank and his bride. One must hand it to our new straitened circumstances; they do bring with them all sorts of unexpected developments. We are certainly kept on our toes! It seems this is our future: to team up with the myriad others who share our limitations and try to make some sort of go of it. This is the first of no doubt many such combinations – what a curious concoction of a family we shall always appear to our new neighbours! – but I have every hope it will work happily enough, in time. It is certainly a great comfort to have a man about the house again – we cannot count on having that privilege very often, if ever again – and of all my brothers, Frank is the most practical and useful. The new Mrs F. A. seems a mild, easy person and Martha is, of course, a delight and support to us all. She will always have a place with us, wherever we land. You must never worry on <u>her</u> account, I can promise you. Martha is one of us now.

As a place, Southampton seems pleasant enough, though our current lodgings less so. We are a little cramped, which I do not mind so much while the weather remains mild and we can get out and about, and I am now so used to domestic imperfection that I hardly notice it. My only real concern is for my sister, who is struggling again. Jane finds change very difficult – which is unfortunate, as change comes at us so often and without the courtesy of warning us of its arrival – and I fear she may be on the brink of yet another bout of melancholy. Sadly, I have witnessed enough to read the all the signs. I had hoped, in my foolish way, that they were brought on by Bath and its winters, and that by quitting that place, we could leave them behind us. I begin to despair of that now . . .

'Look at this!' Martha's broad, pockmarked face was alive with pleasure and slapped pink by the cold wind. 'Are we not blessed, to have this on our doorstep? To think that we can come and look at the sea when so ever we wish! We are fortunate women, on that we can agree.'

The three ladies walked arm in arm along the

seafront, with Jane in the middle. No doubt, Cassy thought, they looked like happy friends, united in their afternoon excursion. In truth, she and Martha were all but holding Jane up.

'Oh, Martha.' Jane sighed and sagged between them. 'Your gift for contentment, your stubborn cheerfulness, your relentless good humour – I confess that they all baffle me.'

'I fear that is simply my nature.' Martha laughed, undeterred. She was the best possible partner for Cassy at these moments. 'And will continue to be so, whether you comprehend it or not, Jane. You must simply find, in that cruel heart of yours, the grace to forgive it. I can be only contented and cheerful wherever I am.'

Cassy smiled fondly. Martha was blessed with far less than the Austens. Indeed, she really had nothing at all. The legacy on which she lived was so small as to be negligible. As the one spinster daughter, she had spent her good years nursing her mother, with much devotion and very little thanks. And when old Mrs Lloyd was released from her suffering and called to a better place, this Miss Lloyd was then left in a highly precarious state. She was by then forty – a most dangerous age – and though her sisters were most welcoming when she was needed, neither had offered her a permanent home.

Had the Austen ladies not stepped forward and taken her in – and when the time came they had done so with delighted alacrity – it was uncertain what might have become of her: a back bedroom somewhere, companionship to an elderly lady. Yet she had never shown fear, not once complained.

'And to be with you two dear girls in this charming town brings most extraordinary pleasure. I marvel at it, truly. The fun we shall have!'

Despite her refusal to acknowledge it, there was, in fact, one quite glaring imperfection inherent in the Southampton arrangement. Back in the past, there had been an Austen scheme to marry Martha to Frank. She had been most strongly in favour, and refused to think of any other gentleman during her critical, marriageable years. He, though, had not been tempted. It was a cruel disappointment, to which was now added one final indignity: now here they both were – Frank, with a new bride; and Martha, obliged to help keep their house for them. Soon enough, that bride would be bearing his children, with Martha, no doubt – who was to stop her? – acting as nurse. But if she was suffering, she suffered invisibly. And to the running of the house and the care of Mrs Austen, she found enormous enjoyment in contributing more than her fair share.

'Which way shall we take? I must not be out long. I promised your mother I would walk with her later. She wants, I believe, to watch and assess Southampton society.'

'There. From the list of your previous faults, I forgot to add selflessness,' said Jane. 'Southampton society? The very thought of it makes me want to take to my bed. Those endless acquaintances that can never be friends. What is the point of it all? This is like Bath all over again.'

'Come now,' urged Cassy. 'Our situation here is very different. We have Frank with us, for instance.'

'Yes,' Jane conceded. 'We do have Frank, and he is a joy.' She sighed. 'Though we might all enjoy each other a little more in better accommodation. There is not really room for so many of us, and the walls are so thin! I swear I heard every twist and turn of each plum and dumpling on their progress through my mother, as I lay sleepless last night.'

'You slept perfectly soundly.' Cassy was crisp. 'And this place is not permanent. We shall find better soon.'

'And when summer comes around,' Martha joined in, 'you will no doubt be once again in residence with some grand relation.'

'Ah, yes. And then I shall be happy once more!'

Martha laughed. 'You are all Lizzy Bennet – one glimpse of "beautiful grounds" and everything changes.'

'You flatter me twice, dearest.' Jane kissed Martha's cheek. 'Comparing me to Lizzy *and* quoting my words back at me. You know the way to a novelist's heart.'

'I wish you would compose something new for us.'

'I cannot. Not here.' Jane sank again. 'All that is behind me.'

'Then let us start *First Impressions* again, after dinner.'

Through all their journeys, as Jane travelled from visit to visit and from one temporary home to the next, her writing box had travelled faithfully with her, each treasured manuscript tight by her side.

'*Again*? You both know it by heart!'

'And yet it pleases us anew every time,' said Cassy. As they made their plans for the evening – a reading, followed perhaps by a game or two – Jane's demeanour improved. They followed the river, chatting and laughing, and all was, for the moment, peace and harmony. But, still, Cassy could never quite stop feeling fearful. It was as if a monster were stalking their threshold. She was on permanent guard, her weight against the door, her eyes ever vigilant: desperate to keep it at bay.

CHAPTER 22

Godmersham, Kent
12th January, 1807

My dear Eliza,

It has come again! Of course, I am in Kent and Martha with you, so my only source of information is the tone of her letters, but – I have every reason to fear Jane has slipped into yet another bout of melancholy. This is now the fourth such occurrence and grieves me particularly, for I feel responsible. I should never have come away and left her alone.

I had thought that, if she were surrounded by family, all would be well. It was so kind of James and Mary, offering to go and stay with my mother and sister while they were alone in their lodgings after Christmas, and I am sure that they both did their best to bring cheer to the season. Unfortunately – and I cannot think why, the reasons are not known to me – their visit seems to have sent Jane over the edge. I was too much the optimist.

The worst of it this time – oh, Eliza! I am frantic! – is that I am so far away from her here and cannot see any way in which I can return. I am beholden to my brothers to deliver me back, and none is at present minded to do so. They are enjoying such good winter sport and – though I have not dared to ask – would be quite heartily sick if they had to leave now. So I can do nothing but sit here – in splendour, certainly, but such is my impotence I cannot enjoy it.

I was wondering – and do forgive me for asking, you must know I would not were I less desperate – if you might be able to spare Martha soon? Should you still need her in Kintbury, then I quite understand, but if instead it would be easy for you to release her back to Southampton, I would be so grateful, Eliza. She is the only other person I can trust.

With love,
C. Austen.

Cassy wrote the Kintbury address, sealed up the paper and put down her pen. There was nothing she could do now but hope. That morning's letter from Jane – an anguished cry from the darkness – had distressed her enormously. What would she give to be by her side now! She hid it away in the bosom of her dress, and rose from the writing table.

Elizabeth Austen looked up from her place by the fireside. 'All well, my dear?' she asked kindly.

'Quite well, thank you,' Cassy replied. 'Though I believe my mother and sister are missing me a little.'

'Oh, do not worry yourself on their account, Cass, truly. You are too much in the service of others. No one can object to you enjoying yourself here for a while.'

Elizabeth had, just before Christmas, been delivered of her tenth baby. With each new addition, her fondness for Cassy had grown incrementally: the more crowded the nursery, the greater occupation for the mother, the shorter-lived the governess, then the more welcome the sister-in-law found herself to be. It was a simple enough formula, which Cassy well understood. It was also true, though, that through these epic years of heroic breeding, the two women had formed a genuine bond, and a deep affection had grown up between them. Each matched the other's devotion to the children, both were patient and even of temper: they shared the same mood.

'How goes it upstairs, do you suppose?' Elizabeth wondered aloud, without stirring.

'You stay there, Elizabeth, and gather your strength. Allow me to go up and see.'

Cassy left the warmth of the library and swished her way busily across the impressive hall and up the grand staircase. However sunken her heart, her artistic eye could never fail to catch and acknowledge the beauty of these surroundings.

Edward and Elizabeth were ensconced now in Godmersham, a large, fine, winged house, seventy-five years old, which presided over its park with the grand manner of one sure of its own great importance. Each window framed a charming vista; every interior wall was adorned with exquisite plasterwork. Cassandra was acutely aware both how fortunate she was to be staying here, and also how perverse that she wished she were not.

What other woman of such limited resources would be so ungrateful? She crossed the landing and took the long corridor. Christmas here had been splendid, and joyful, the dear children delirious in their excitement. Cassy had eaten too much – more than was good for her; they had made merry and played games every evening; she had laughed fit to burst.

Yet, throughout, her mind had been distracted by thoughts of Southampton: how was Jane coping with running the household in her own absence? Jane had lately had the whooping cough and by rights should still be convalescent. Could she get sufficient sleep to maintain her strength? Here, in her well-appointed chamber, alone in her stately comfort, Cassy lay awake each night, worrying. If only Edward had asked Jane here instead. She would gladly change places, for then she would at least know true peace of mind. But she herself was always the Godmersham favourite, particularly when there was a new baby around.

She climbed the stairs up to the attic schoolroom, in which the governess was teaching the older children.

'*Bonjour, ma tante!*' Fanny exclaimed at the sight of her.

'*Et bonjour, chérie,*' Cassy returned. '*Tout va bien?*'
'*Très bien, merci.*'

Mrs Morris clearly had them under control. Elizabeth took her children's French very seriously; Cassandra would not disturb them. She moved on to the day nursery to check on the small ones – all was well – and, thus released, she decided to take the air.

It was a fine winter's day, after a long dry spell, but whatever the weather, there were always good walks to be had here. Mud did not trouble the Godmersham parkland: that was for other, less gracious places; mud would not dare. She returned to her room, collected her cloak and, down in the hall, let herself out through the door to the garden. The sharp cold hit her face and banished the clouds from her brain.

Daytime solitude here was a rare and precious commodity – there was always someone demanding her time – and Cassy determined to use it. By nature, she was a practical woman who did not enjoy feeling out of control. This issue of Jane's melancholy was challenging all of her instincts. It tended to strike at the least convenient moment and refused to respond to rational argument. So far, Cassy had treated it as any other illness – with nursing and potions and care. It was true that, after a few weeks, Jane had each time – so far – recovered. But was that due to Cassy's own offices? Did she herself cure it? Or was it anyway of a limited period, like a phase of the moon, and it simply moved on with time?

She walked, eyes to the ground, ignoring the views, across the lawn in the direction of the river. Surely, rather than stand by waiting to physic, she should concentrate instead on prevention: establish what were the things that brought on the misery, deal with them and then it might not reappear.

She made a list in her head. The first and most obvious cause was, of course, instability. They had moved house four times since the death of their father, and each had been difficult. Cassy, now in the coppice and out of the sunlight, shivered and sighed. There was nothing she or anyone could do to prevent more change in the future. They would not be long in Southampton, she was sure of it. Soon, no doubt, they would be off again and who knew where next?

Then, there was lack of peace. Jane had been right on that count. It had all turned out as she feared. Cassy and Martha were often called away to help with their families, and Jane was left, as she was now, in charge of the household, shunted between mother and household and cook. It was true, too, that she had no time – or no inclination, certainly – to work on her writing. She had put down *The Watsons* in Bath and not once looked at it since.

Emerging from under the trees and into the clearing, Cassy saw that there was only one solution to all of these problems: a permanent home of their own. If only, if *only*, she had the power to provide one. The river shimmered before her, and there at its bank, was Edward.

'Cassy, my dear!' His face was ruddy with the morning's excursions; a noble hound stood by his side. 'A capital day, what?'

Linking arms, they walked along together.

'I could not resist it,' Cassy replied. 'What have you been busy with this morning, Brother?'

'Been off seeing a couple of the farms, just checking up. With fifteen of 'em, there is always something to worry about.'

'You have so many responsibilities: I cannot imagine you ever know a quiet moment. The house, the estate, not to mention all those children. How many are there now? One hundred, two?'

'Ha! I lost track years ago. You jest, but we might make it to one hundred, you know, if Elizabeth gets her way.'

'I think you should. Not every couple can produce such perfect offspring. You owe it to the world to produce all that you can.'

'Well, we certainly have the space, in that we are fortunate. Indeed, we will soon have yet more of it. The lease is up on the Chawton estate, and I have decided not to let it for a while. We shall use it ourselves this year, for high days and holidays – a bit of Hampshire in the mix will be just the ticket.'

Cassy's brain lit up. Chawton. Estate. Cottages – Edward owned cottages galore there, as she understood it. And all in their home county! This could be the solution to everything. Here was the answer to her prayers.

'Oh, how we miss Hampshire – your sister, your mother and I.'

'But you are already there, surely. Southampton is within the county, is it not?'

'Of course, but not the *country*, Edward. It is the villages we miss, places like Chawton, for example, with hedgerows and pastures . . .'

'Then it will be a short hop for you to come and visit us there, on occasion.' Edward was expansive. 'You will always be welcome as our guests, as you know.'

They both fell silent for a while as they followed the curve of the river.

'And have you heard from Southampton lately? How goes it?'

'I had a letter this morning, and I confess, it has left me a little concerned. I fear our mother is finding it hard to settle there.' In truth, Mrs Austen was quite splendidly robust, and took every decline on the chin. But surely the way to a man's heart was through his mother . . .

313

'Mother! You astonish me. She can withstand anything. It is probably the post-Christmas lull. I expect she loved having James, Mary and the family. What fun that must have been. And what a pleasure for her to share a house with young Frank again – and the bride and a baby on the way.'

'Oh, Frank is a treat,' Cassy conceded. 'He is currently employed in fringing the curtains! Still, it cannot last long. He will go back to his ship, and mother and infant will go to her family. Then we shall be off again, no doubt.' She paused, to select her words. It would not do to push Edward too far. He was a man of business; he liked to make the decisions. This plan must be his idea, or it would not come to pass. 'I think she mentioned Alton as our next stop.'

'Alton! But that is so close to Chawton, most convenient, and there are many good townhouses there.'

'Oh, indeed.' Cassy spoke quietly, as if thinking aloud: 'Not that we shall be able to take one, of course. Once Frank's family is growing, we can no longer take money from him.'

'Quite so. Look there! A kingfisher.' Edward's interest in the topic of poor ladies was waning. 'That is the bliss of this river. Always something to catch the eye.' He threw a stick, and the dog leaped in to retrieve it. 'I do look forward to Chawton. Change is as good as a rest, is it not?'

The dog emerged sleek from the water, and shook his wet coat.

'I say! I have had an idea. Why do you not take one of my cottages there?'

Cassy sat in the library in blissful reverie. Replete from her fine dinner, pleasantly exhausted by an afternoon outside with Fanny and her pony, now she could allow herself time to think of their Chawton cottage. How big would it be, she wondered, and with how many rooms? There must be space for Martha – oh, they would make space for Martha somehow. Then who could be as happy as they? She could not wait to write to Jane in the morning. The relief would surely bring her out of her bed, and give her some faith in the future.

'My love,' Edward said then, from his armchair, 'I was thinking about the summer, when we go to stay at Chawton.'

'Ah,' sighed Elizabeth. 'I forgot we had all that commotion ahead of us. Do you not pity me, Cass, having to live with this man and his taste for seemingly permanent revolution?'

Cassy could think of other, more deserving, objects of pity, but smiled back all the same.

'It has occurred to me to give one of the cottages to the Austen ladies.'

'To the *ladies*? Oh, Cass. Are men not funny? Ha ha! So very amusing.' Elizabeth returned to her embroidery and adopted a voice of great patience:

'The last thing the ladies want is a *cottage*, my dearest. Theirs is an enviable existence, to my mind. They can fetch up in any town which pleases them, enjoy endless changes of scenery. I cannot keep up with all their different addresses. A cottage, indeed. What on earth do you imagine they would do with themselves there?'

'Well.' Edward at once looked uncertain. 'Live in it? Work in the garden? Whatever it is ladies do.'

'And die of boredom, I should not wonder. To whom should they talk? What company might they keep, in a village of all things? Oh, it might suit your mother, although she too has a strong appetite for good conversation. But your sisters need society, Edward. They require diversions. Assemblies. They need to *meet* people.' She looked over fondly to her sister-in-law. 'It is never too late, my dear.'

'In truth, Elizabeth,' Cassy said gently, 'it *is* too late, and we are perfectly at peace with it. I must confess, we have grown a little tired of dances and calling and so on.'

'Then you must pull yourselves together and simply resolve to get on with it,' she replied, rather sharply. 'Believe me, Cassy, you have no idea of the trials of running a house of your own. For example, what would you put in it? You enjoy this footloose life, from one furnished lodging to the next. You have not your own furniture! You know nothing of the responsibility!'

'We could donate some furniture, my love,'

Edward offered, but Cassy could sense his grand idea was already collapsed and in pieces all over the plush library rug.

'They do not require furniture, Edward, because they do not want a cottage and there, I hope, is the end of it.' Elizabeth picked up her scissors and cut her thread with some violence. 'You see, Cass, I have done you a great service. Your sister will be most grateful to hear of it, I am sure.'

Cassy was no stranger to Disappointment. He – Disappointment was surely a he – was a regular visitor, and she greeted this latest appearance in her customary manner: with a rebuke to herself for inviting him in. There was nobody else she could blame.

Elizabeth had spoken from genuine concern for the family, and was informed only by her life and experience – as were they all. Truly, how could a woman in her position be expected to understand their own, very different one? Of course Edward, who had been so generous to think of the scheme in the first place, would always accept his good wife's opinion, which was in itself testament to his excellent nature. No, it was her fault, for being so selfish, ambitious and demanding in the first place: her fault entirely. At least Jane had known nothing, and her hopes were not raised. Cassy vowed never to mention or think of it again.

Still, despite all that strength and resolution,

Disappointment stayed with her, settled, weighty and immoveable as a Sidmouth beach boulder. It rested somewhere in the region of her stomach, just below the anxiety that raged in her breast. The letters from and to Southampton came thick and fast – more often, certainly, than could be afforded – confiding the misery of one, begging the return of the other. Cassy could do nothing about either, beyond burning the evidence in her own fireplace every night.

However much she might long to leave Kent, she was powerless to do so. Her journey depended on the will of a brother to escort her, and it was inconvenient for any brother to do so before the spring. Martha did not return, nor did Eliza respond to the request that she should. So there was nothing to be done but occupy herself with the children, play games in the evening, make calls and receive them. Live well, dine well and wait out her sentence: an unhappy prisoner in the happiest of homes.

In February, finally, Jane's darkness lifted and the chatty, merry tone returned to her letters. They had found better accommodation, larger, with a garden! She and her mother were busy with the planning of it. In March, Cassy was able to return there and look after them. She was done with the future, and designing and scheming. Instead, from now on, she would live in the present, whether it be easy or difficult, and deal with each day in its turn.

CHAPTER 23

Kintbury, April 1840

Night had fallen and still Cassandra sat alone in her mean, narrow chamber, gazing down at the papers spread out on her bed. She had identified ten letters of danger, testifying to Jane's distress and Cassy's dismay. They were not so incriminating in themselves, perhaps, when put in the context of a lifetime. But Cassandra well understood the powers of the written word. She knew, too, that the powers of editing were yet greater still. One could influence the other, mangle and distort it: persuade it to alter its shape and its purpose.

In isolation, these documents could be taken as proof of a disturbance of mind. Even put together with all other evidence, they would point to a character most complex, fragile and awkward, whose weakness and frailties battled against its strengths. Removed, though, destroyed – here, Cassandra quickly checked once again that she had them all, folded them up – then they had no powers whatever, for no eyes could see them nor any such judgement be made. All that remained would speak, for eternity, of a sweetness of temper. What was that phrase about Jane she always used when talking to the nieces and nephews? 'Few changes and no great crisis ever broke the smooth current of life's course.' Ah, yes. Very good. Extremely well put. She rose, stretched, concealed them in the depths of her trunk and let out a sigh of immense satisfaction. Back in Chawton, she would have an excellent bonfire – oh, she did love a bonfire. She could look forward to that.

There still remained one final letter from Jane to Eliza – written from Winchester, in July 1817 – but Cassandra could not yet find the strength to read it. That, she slipped into her valise for safekeeping. Bundling together the rest of the correspondence – all happy nothings – she went to return it to its place in the settle

Silently, Cassandra opened her door and moved out to the landing. It was now very late; all was quiet. Caroline had left and Isabella was surely asleep. Eliza's room was in darkness, but she groped her way across, put the bundle back where she had found it, and headed back to her room.

There came a sniff.

'All done then, m'm?' Dinah, again, stood sentry at the bottom of the attic staircase. Did she spy all night? Cassandra wondered. Did she never go to bed?

'Goodnight, Dinah. Sleep well.'

'And you, m'm. You'll be off soon, then, is it, now? Nothing left for you 'ere? That is a shame.'

The next morning, Cassandra opened the curtains on a blue sky and sun that suggested it was already mid-morning. She smiled, amused at her own indolence. That was not like her, not like her at all. Miss Austen, famously, rose with the lark. The strangely long sleep could only be put down to a clarity of conscience and deep sense of accomplishment, for those were two things she had not known in a while. Well, it was most restorative, certainly. Galvanised, with something quite close to energy, she dressed and went out. There was no need to bother the household with her breakfast. All this well-being could be put to good use and the service of others. She must see Mary-Jane, on Isabella's behalf.

The trees in the churchyard were heavy with blossom; its pale colour and light scent made her heart sing. She had arrived here in winter, depleted and burdened with the problems ahead of her. Now, behold the change in the world! Behold, too, the change in herself. She wondered how her own garden was faring. What a pleasure it would be to sit in it again.

A maid opened Mary-Jane's door and pointed her into the parlour with no further comment. Cassandra stood in the doorway, and was also, at first, stuck for words.

In the middle of the room, beneath the watchful

gaze of her many exotic artefacts, Mary-Jane was floating around in circular motion, waving her arms: dancing, though not a dance Cassandra immediately recognised. Her body was swathed in a long, red, loose-fitting gown; an expression of rapture adorned her odd, square face.

'Do not mind me, Cassandra. I am whirling.' She did not look across. 'Come in, sit down. I will be with you shortly.' She continued to whirl.

Cassandra perched on the skin of a tiger, not without some discomfort, and waited politely.

'Have you heard of whirling, Cassandra?'

Cassandra had not. Mary-Jane whirled a bit more.

'Do you know of the Dervishes?'

'The Dervishes?' They were presumably some local family, though she could not quite place the name. 'I do not believe I have had the pleasure of their acquaintance.'

'Of the Sufi.' Mary-Jane stopped then and settled down cross-legged on the floor. 'There, that is done for the day.' She reached for her pipe. 'I came across them and their practice on my journeys – Whirling Dervishes, that is. Fascinating business. Decided to try it for myself and now simply cannot do without. Very spiritual, I find. You should try it. I shall teach you.'

'Thank you. I think I would prefer not.' Cassandra shifted a little against the tiger skin's bristles. 'I have always found the established Church more than sufficient for my spiritual needs.'

Mary-Jane lit her tobacco and drew on it. 'It is only when you go out into the world that you see how small England is, and how limited. Believe me, Cassandra, there are customs and religions and ideas out there that make . . .'

Cassandra stifled her irritation. This visit threatened to be an unnecessary challenge, when her time was so short and – she felt a pang – her stomach so empty. Why travel was said to broaden the mind, she could never quite fathom: the company of those whom travel had blessed was often so splendidly dull.

Mary-Jane was now talking some nonsense about Yogi, whatever they might be. Cassandra did not want to know. She must interrupt.

'On the matter of travelling, or moving at least, I was wondering if you have had contact with your sisters of late?'

'Are *they* to go away? Best thing for 'em. Isabella would love it. There is so much—'

Cassandra stepped in and outlined her plan, cloaking it in the apparel of a suggestion.

'What, leave *my own house*?' Mary-Jane shouted, puffing smoke in the manner of a very cross dragon.

'You had given me to understand you enjoy new adventures?'

'Well, yes. *Abroad.* What part of the village is this house in? I told you before, it can be dangerous around here.'

'Perhaps not quite as dangerous as India, or the

land of the Sufi?' Cassandra suggested. After all, what caused them to whirl in the first place? 'And you would not be so much alone. There is safety in numbers.'

Mary-Jane chomped on her pipe stick. 'I could take my things with me?'

Cassandra looked around at the trophies and swords – the venomous snake – allowed herself a moment to think of Dinah, obliged to dust them each morning: there was a sweet, small revenge. 'Of course. I am sure of it. There will be plenty of space.'

'Well then. Perhaps the idea does have its merits. Those girls are vulnerable. I can protect them. I have my gun.'

The matter was settled. Cassandra endured a short lecture on Middle Eastern food and its superiority, promised – in good faith – that she would certainly try it when the opportunity arose and the two women parted cordially.

As the door closed behind her and she emerged, blinking, into the sunlight, it occurred to Cassandra that she might never see Mary-Jane again. She could not know how many years, months or weeks, even, were left to her. Still, not every experience must be tinged with regret.

She made her way home, thinking with some amusement of this new Fowle establishment. Were there ever such three different sisters? But then, they had spent too long apart, each let herself stray into eccentricity. Mary-Jane, in particular, had gone really quite mad. It would be good for them, in the long run. No birthing was easy; no change came without some discomfort or difficulty; even when – especially when – it was all for the best. As she passed through the gravestones, each daffodil seemed to nod its agreement.

It had been late September, in the year 1808, when the eleventh child of Edward and Elizabeth arrived in Godmersham – just a few hours before his most useful of aunts. Having missed the event, Cassy was left with little to do but peer into the cradle, pronounce him an Austen in both bounce and vigour, settle his proud mother and take over the nursery.

She went to her room, repaired herself and took a moment to look out at the park, exquisite in autumn. This time, Cassy was delighted to be here and determined to enjoy it. All was easy back in Southampton: her mother was healthy, Jane's spirits were good and Martha was with them to ward off disaster. No worries tugged at her; there was no reason not to look forward to the few months ahead.

Truly, she must be, of all single women, among the most fortunate. At least once a year, she could come here to Godmersham and pretend to the life of a privileged gentlewoman, enjoy the gift of important employment – a large and gracious household to run, a host of young children to teach and amuse – and the pleasure of a gentleman's company every evening. And all without the trials of regular confinement. Eleven babies – imagine! Elizabeth was the most remarkable specimen, but her plight was not one to be envied. Cassy had the better deal of the two: she could play-act the role regularly and then walk away free, back to those she loved above all.

'Aunt Cass!' Fanny burst through the door with excitement. 'You are here! Have you seen the new baby? Is he not fine?'

'My dear child. Come here at once.' Cassy folded her niece into her arms and squeezed tightly. 'He is most fine indeed, but you are still my finest. Let me look at you.' She pulled back. 'No, I am sorry. You have grown up too much for my tastes. What are you thinking of, becoming such a young lady so soon?'

Now fifteen years of age, Fanny had a fresh and pure beauty: a hot-house lily on the cusp of its bloom. But for all her new height and refinements, she still giggled, and sat down to bounce on the bed. Cassy smiled, listening to the chatter of news as she arranged her things and made herself quite at home. Of all the joys to be found here, Fanny was surely the greatest. She had charm, a quickness of mind and, of course, a happy disposition – for how could this particular Miss Austen fail to be happy? Hers was the most enviable lot.

'Aunt, I am reading Mrs Burney's *Camilla*.' She was become almost another sister.

'And enjoying, I hope?' Cassy closed the last drawer and looked about her with satisfaction.

'Oh, indeed. Later, when the little ones are asleep, shall we read it together? I have only just begun.'

'Of course, I should love it. There. I am done here. Shall we go?'

Holding hands, they went up to the schoolroom. Each enjoyed nursery duties as much as the other, as well as reading and needlework and family business.

How very pleasant it was all going to be.

For a full eleven days, all was indeed as busy and cheerful as had been hoped for. Disaster then struck on the twelfth.

It was the evening, and Cassy was in the library, with Edward and young Fanny. The daughter was keen that they should read aloud from *Camilla*; the father was keen they did not.

'I must say, I am looking forward to having your mama back with us downstairs,' Edward was saying. 'Thankfully, she and I are in total accord on what makes for an evening. Alone with you two *bookish* ladies, I feel as a stranger in my own home.'

'It will not be long, Papa,' Fanny soothed him. 'Mama is quickly regaining her strength. She has tonight eaten a most hearty dinner.'

Suddenly, Cassandra sat upright, her ear cocked. 'What is that?' she cried out with urgency. Sounds of running feet, shouting voices came down from above. At once, she was up and rushing for the stairs. Halfway up, a maid flew towards her.

'The doctor! It is the mistress! We must have the doctor!'

Cassandra lifted her skirts and ran to the chamber. There, lying halfway out of the bed, was Elizabeth in the most hideous contortion. Her colour was high, her eyes were bulging: that once pretty face polluted by a look of pure, mortal terror.

'It's a seizure!' cried the nurse. 'From nowhere! I never saw anything like it!' She was jabbering, all professional competence seemingly vanished.

Cassy grabbed a wrist and felt a pulse: it was wild. 'How long?' she asked urgently. 'How long has she been like this? When did this start?'

'I cannot be sure, m'm . . . Five minutes at least.'

Five minutes? What had the woman been *doing* all that time? 'Give me the laudanum,' Cassy demanded. 'Then help me to get her back on the bed.' And in a gentle voice now: 'There is no need to panic, Elizabeth. My dear, calm yourself. I am with you. Listen to me. I am going to open your mouth now.' But the tongue was so enormous, the neck horribly swollen; Elizabeth was writhing. Cassy had to struggle and fight to get the drops in. It took all of her strength. There! At once, Elizabeth slumped, her head lolled. Had Cassy succeeded? Had the drug worked its magic? Desperately, she searched for the pulse again.

Her search was in vain.

★　★　★

328

Godmersham plunged into darkness. The dearest of wives, most devoted of mothers – the radiant centre of this huge, happy household – was wrenched away, and replaced by a torment of suffering.

Edward was stunned by his grief, restless in his misery; the poor motherless infants bewildered and lost. Cassy worked tirelessly to comfort and see to them. So all-consuming was the present that she did not have time to stop and think of the problematic future. Until the night after the funeral, when Fanny appeared in her room.

'Oh, Aunt Cass.' Fanny climbed up into bed and the arms of her aunt. 'What is to become of us? How can we cope? I cannot do it. I am no equal for Mama.' She wept violently.

'My dear, hush now,' Cassy comforted, her heart bursting with pity. Oh, how she remembered this feeling. To have the one life you know torn away from you; to be forced into another against your will: that was bitter, indeed. 'You are an excellent daughter, a great solace to your poor, dear papa. And as an eldest sister, you are remarkable. You understand those children better than anyone. My love, you will manage. It will be hard, but you will. The Lord sends us these challenges in order that we rise to them and become stronger and better as a result.' She took the sweet, wet face in her hands. 'It is what your mother would expect of you.'

'But I am not properly prepared!'

'You are more prepared than you know. Elizabeth was a fine wife and mother, and she raised you, with her own impeccable standards, to be exactly the same.'

'Yes, in five years or ten . . . Not *now*, though, not *yet*. I fear I shall fail. It is too much for me. Please, Aunt Cass, I beg of you. Please will you stay?'

'I shall stay for a few months, until you are all settled.'

'No. Stay forever. It is you who should be my father's companion; you who must bring up the children. You must live here, with us. We cannot do it without.'

Fanny slept then, the shallow sleep of a soul in deep turmoil. Cassy held her close, awake and in thought. Long ago, she had seen Kent as her only solution. When she was here after Tom Fowle died – which baby was that? Number four, number five? – and searching for some means of survival, this was the one she had hoped for: to live on the edges of a young family as an invaluable, invisible appendage. How different she was now, how very altered. Ten years, it seemed, was enough to change every pore of one's being and corner of one's heart.

The next morning, Edward called her into his study.

'I believe Fanny came to you last night.'

'She did, the poor darling.' Cassy sat down in

the leather armchair. 'She was a little overwhelmed by the situation, but will rally in time, I am sure.'

'It is her suggestion . . . she would like . . . well, we would both like it if . . .' Poor Edward. He was as lost as the children; all that easy confidence vanished. 'Well, if it would suit you . . . to come and live among us here.'

'Oh, my dear brother. I feel for you all so deeply, and will do anything in my powers to help you all.'

'Yes?' He looked up, blue eyes encircled with shadows.

'And I shall come to stay with you as often as you would like. With great reluctance, though, I must refuse the kind offer of making this my permanent home. My true place is with my mother and sister.' She did not add that it was the place she preferred above all. 'My duty is there.' Duty was a good word to use here; no one could argue with duty.

'Ah, of course.' He cleared his throat gruffly. 'Yes. I do see.'

'In the next few months, we face yet another upheaval. Oh, please!' she exclaimed suddenly. 'Please do not think that I am belittling your own situation! Of course, your troubles are greater than ours and you have all our hearts and our minds and sympathies, truly. But . . .'

She paused. Suddenly, in all that blackness, her eye caught a light: the glimmer of a golden opportunity. It flashed, as if signalling. Seize me, it said to her: seize me now!

'We have to move again shortly.' She gave a deep sigh. 'Southampton is becoming too dear, and too much for my mother. It is time to find somewhere else and settle – yet again. It looks to be Alton. We have word of a place of some indifference that may be within our means. I hope it will work out, but it will not be without its difficulties. Our mother needs my support.'

'Indeed.' Edward hunched over his desk.

Cassy stayed silent, allowing time for his stolid mind to make its pedestrian progress. She had to wait a good while. Eventually, he spoke.

'Perhaps I could do something to help both you and my family at the same time? There is a small house on the estate here, in Godmersham, that comes empty shortly. Then you would be close by, and on hand for the children.'

Oh, Edward, she thought fondly, come, come. Your situation is very sad, but not exactly impossible. We all know you can do better than that.

'What a charming idea! That is too kind of you.' She pretended to consider it. 'But no – our mother is determined on Hampshire, talks only of living her last years upon her home soil. I can try, but do fear that she could not be persuaded away from it.'

He was crushed, forced to think yet again. 'Then, might you consider Chawton?' His voice was beginning to sound almost desperate. 'There is a cottage, opposite the duck pond – not so very large, I fear, and it does require work. But it is close to the Great House and then when I and my family are in residence, we could, I hope, see much of you? If our mother did not need you more . . .'

'Chawton?' she repeated, in a cool, measured tone and pondered. 'Hmmmm . . . Let me think . . . Hmmmm . . . That *might* be a more promising plan . . . A *cottage* in *Chawton* . . . I do believe we *could* entice her to that . . . Yes!' She jumped up, moved over to Edward and kissed him. 'What a clever and most generous brother you are. You may just have come up with the perfect solution!'

And, before he could think any further, she headed fast for the door, calling over her shoulder: 'I shall write straight away and suggest it.'

At last, in the autumn of 1809, the Austen ladies achieved their ultimate happiness, and moved into a home of their own. The cottage had once been the bailiff's, and was even more spacious than Cassy had hoped. Downstairs, they had not just one sitting room, but two, as well as six bedrooms in all. On top of that, it sat prettily in their ideal situation: in the middle of the village, close to the road, so that their mother could watch all the comings and goings and remark upon them from a position of warm comfort.

'Oh, this is perfection!' exclaimed Jane, going from one bedroom to the next.

'If we give this to Mama,' said Cassy, pointing to the best, 'and this here is Martha's, then' – she led her sister to the small pretty room at the end of the corridor – 'we can be quite comfortable in here, can we not?'

Jane went in and looked about her with great satisfaction. She peered out of the window, down on to the yard and the promise of garden beyond, clapped her hands, then turned and took Cassy into a tender embrace. For a moment, they stood in the sunlight, holding each other. 'It is over,' Jane whispered. 'The worst is behind us.'

'And there is no reason to think of it again.' Cassy pulled away, took her hand and continued the tour. 'That leaves this little apartment for our brothers and their children.'

'I wonder how often they will choose to visit?' Jane looked through the doorway. 'It will be so lovely when they do.' She turned then, and smiled. 'And so lovely when they do not!'

They walked down the stairs, taking a moment to stop by the window and admire the exterior again. At the foot, Martha stood, solid and smiling.

'Well?' she asked, eager.

'My poor Martha, I fear it will not suit you,' said Jane.

'No?' As if the air was punched out of her. Martha's experience of disappointment was deeper even than their own, and she must always fear its return at any moment.

'It is nowhere near grand enough for a lady of your expectations. You are bound to find fault with the house as well as everything in it. We know your troublesome ways.'

Martha beamed with relief. 'I have already been in to assess the kitchen. It truly has all we can possibly need. I have to keep pinching myself and cannot wait to get started.'

'We are so good to you, Martha' – Jane took her arm and they all walked through to the drawing room – 'that we are willing to give you total control of it and the cook. Are you not lucky? You have nothing to concern you but our taste buds, and how best to satisfy them.'

'Do not fear, my book of recipes is already unpacked and next to the range.'

'And I', Cassy announced, settling herself down on the sofa next to her mother, 'shall be running the house.'

'That is good,' said Mrs Austen, 'for I am taking the garden as my own private fiefdom. That vegetable patch is demanding attention. It is a very sorry affair at the moment.'

'Which leaves me with what?' Jane protested. 'Am I to have no employment at all? I demand some sort of equality.'

'You can be our entertainment.' This was Martha's suggestion.

'The Cottage Fool! There is a prospect to wake

up to each morning. "How shall I amuse them today?" And suppose you did not laugh at my jokes? It might sound ridiculous – after all, I am a very fine comic – but you are a particularly harsh audience. I fear I should find the pressure of it quite insupportable.'

'We could put you in charge of our breakfast?'

'Aha! There is real power. Add to that, the sugar stores – and perhaps the wine – and then we have a deal. I shall be all but an emperor.'

'Agreed. We shall all be at our work, of course, in the mornings and, no doubt, people will call on us. But after that, you still have plenty of time left to dedicate to our entertainment.' Cassy had been waiting for this moment. 'Those manuscripts you have been carrying around for so long can come out of their hiding place. The little table is sitting there, calling to you. The afternoons will be free. And so . . .' She paused, then burst out, 'You will write again! After all, what is there to stop you?'

'Splendid!' Mrs Austen exclaimed. 'You can read it back to us every evening, Jane. It is to be just like the old days.'

'And make our fortunes!'

'Martha!' Jane cried. 'Can you think of nothing but money? So tawdry in a lady. Your venality lowers you.'

They all laughed; Mrs Austen said, chuckling: 'You dear girls will be very happy here, I am sure. Of course, I cannot expect to be around for much longer. I have already exceeded my allotted time, and my troubles get worse every day. What God is thinking of, leaving me down here to get in the way, I simply cannot understand. But may you all, at least, be blessed with long years to enjoy it.'

'Oh, Ma-*ma*,' Cassy and Jane said at once.

CHAPTER 24

Kintbury, April 1840

'There you are!' Isabella exclaimed.

'Good morning.' Cassandra came into the vicarage hall and set about peeling off her gloves.

'We wondered what had become of you, did we not, Dinah?'

Dinah, who was on the half-landing with a bucket and mop, turned and looked at her. 'We are always wondering about you, Miss Austen. Quite the law unto herself, isn't she, m'm?'

'I am sorry. I do try to disturb you as little as possible.' Cassandra heard a sniff that was dripping with satire. 'I have been to call on Mary-Jane and I have some good news. She is willing to give up her cottage—'

And suddenly, all was noise and horrific commotion. Dinah was plummeting, head over heels over bucket and mop, down the whole length of the stairs. Cassandra gasped; Isabella screamed. Dinah fell to the floor, where she lay lifeless.

They ran to her.

'What happened?' Isabella grabbed a wrist and felt for a pulse. 'She must have fainted. Did you see it, Cassandra? Did she faint?'

Cassandra had indeed watched it all happen, though found it hard to believe her own eyes. It was as if Dinah had thrown herself, plunged down deliberately: pitched as one pitches only when confident that one will be caught. And yet they could never have caught her. She had endangered herself, and done so deliberately. What could possibly provoke such peculiar behaviour?

Pyramus barked, loud and urgent. Fred came at once to the door. Cassandra went to him, quietly commanded that he run – run quickly! – for the surgeon, then helped Isabella turn Dinah on to her side. She was unconscious, motionless, her face white as death.

'Oh, dear Lord!'

'There is a pulse,' said Isabella. 'She lives, but I have no doubt has sustained serious injury. Oh, Dinah,' she whispered, stroking her forehead. 'Oh, Dinah. Stay with us. Stay with us, please.'

'We must not move her until the surgeon is here.'

'Mr Lidderdale?' Isabella looked up, eyes wild.

'I have sent for him. This is serious. We need him here with us.'

Isabella looked over at Dinah. 'You are right, Cassandra. She cannot be put at risk on account of my own . . . While we are waiting, could you get me a cold, damp cloth, and the witch hazel?'

Cassandra did as she was bid and went through

the servants' door. She had certainly seen more efficient sculleries in her time – here, chaos had control of every surface and corner – but with her home-maker's instincts found her way around soon enough. She rushed back to the hall, cloth and bottle in hand, just as Mr Lidderdale made his own entrance.

'G'day to you, ladies. What we got 'ere then?' This was indeed the doctor she had encountered the previous day. 'Come on then, me pet. Let's be having a look at you.' He took off his overcoat, which was stained on the front, rolled up the frayed cuffs of his shirt and began his examination. With strong, sure hands he tested for broken bones, while Cassandra watched on, intrigued.

Now, in broad daylight, there was something familiar about this Mr Lidderdale. She fancied she had seen him on some other occasion, but could not quite place where. Average height, or below, but with broad shoulders that gave him the presence of one more – Was this the gentleman whom she had seen on the bridge with Isabella, back in the early days of her visit? That morning when Isabella seemed to return in distress? Possibly, though she could not be sure . . .

'Nought fractured, as I can see.'

'Just concussion?'

'About the size of it. We needs to get her to a more comfortable place, Isa— Miss Fowle. The bedroom be too far.'

'The sofa,' said Isabella. 'In the drawing room.'

'You take one side, me the other. Gently does it.'

Together, in partnership, they manoeuvred the dead weight and laid her down, tenderly.

'The witch hazel,' Isabella commanded, holding her arm out behind.

Cassandra stepped forward and made her small contribution.

'That's it. Nicely done,' said the doctor with approval. 'A good bump coming up there.'

'Salts?'

'Salts might help bring her round.'

They stood close, one next to the other, and – what was that? – did Isabella lean against him for a moment, or had Cassandra imagined it? There certainly seemed to be some sort of unity, a sense of partnership, between the two, no doubt provoked by a shared worry and concern for poor Dinah. It was indeed very terrible. Suppose, just suppose, she did not make it through?

A long-standing servant, suffering grave – possibly the gravest of – injuries in the line of one's service was too awful to contemplate. Cassandra knew nothing of Dinah's family, but there must be a person to call, a relative who was possibly dependent on her income. For someone out in the village – for Dinah, certainly, and poor Isabella – this was one of those days that were not to be forgotten, when life twisted its shape and sheered off into another dimension. Feeling powerless and useless, Cassandra sat down on the edge of the armchair, clasped her hands in her lap and silently prayed that the outcome be less grave than she feared.

'Thank you for coming to us,' Isabella said, quietly.

'You's c'n always count on me. Yer know that.' He laid a hand on her arm.

Cassandra felt, suddenly, as an intruder. They seemed to think themselves alone, and at liberty to speak freely. She kept very still.

'That is kind of you to say. But after – well – after all that has passed between us, you could be forgiven for refusing.'

'First, I'm a doctor. I shall not turn me back on a patient who needs me.' His hand moved to Isabella's, and took it. 'But I am also a man. And I shall never – not ever, me pet – turn me back upon you.'

'Oh, John.' Isabella turned to him; Cassandra caught her sweet face in half-profile. She was no longer monochrome but pink, as if lit from within.

A low murmur came from the sofa.

'Her eyes are opening! She is back with us!' Isabella fell to her knees. 'For delivering her, Lord, I thank you.'

'Oooof, my 'ead.' Dinah's voice was muffled and uncharacteristically soft. Cassandra could not quite hear her, precisely. The next words sounded something like: 'You came then. It worked. That's good.' But of course that made no sense. Was it the concussion talking?

Mr Lidderdale performed tests on Dinah's eyes and speech and was soon able to pronounce that, apart from severe bruising, the accident had left the patient unscathed.

'It'd take more than a topple, sir, to undo me.'

'Even so, best if you di'n't make a regular thing of it.' He closed up his medical case. 'Falls be nasty, Dinah. You been very lucky.'

Dinah begged that she be allowed to rest, and all energies were then directed towards her maximum comfort. She lay on the sofa with a self-satisfied air while the rest of the household flurried about her. Pillows were brought, and a blanket; brandy was found, served and appreciated. She was instructed, in the sternest of terms, to stay there for the rest of the day and forbidden from all further work. Strangely compliant, Dinah issued one final demand – that Miss Fowle take the good doctor back to the kitchen and feed him; they would find the pork pie in the pantry – and then settled herself down for a snooze.

Cassandra stayed to watch over her, in case of relapse, and sat quietly. Pyramus came to stand guard at her feet and rubbed his head against her legs, while she pondered. Was it possible – she hesitated, tried not to let the thought in, but such was its power it could not be held back – was it possible that she had misread Isabella's life story?

Suddenly, she felt sick to her stomach; her neck

prickled with heat; soon her whole face was aflame. For as she read it again, in the fresh light of the morning's events, she could not deny its new meaning. Memories of past conversations flooded her brain: of a father's last wishes; of a daughter's persuasion; of parents threatening to spin in their graves. This was not, after all, the age-old tale of a spinster who needed her family. There was a whole other hidden plot – of love, and obstruction.

And she had missed it. Cassandra·had missed it, completely.

Then how great was her own arrogance! How great, now, was her shame! She had taken the lessons of her own life and imposed them on the life of another. She had interpreted her own happiness and promoted it, relentlessly, as the only true happiness. Misled by an old woman's blind faith in 'experience' and 'wisdom', she had strayed on to the path of true love. And then – the horror of this part! – she had joined forces with those who sought to obstruct it and placed herself in love's way.

'Oh, Pyramus!' The dog's liquid brown eyes seemed to peer into her soul. She buried her face in the thick, reddish-brown fur at his neck and implored him: 'Oh, Pyramus, what have I done?'

CHAPTER 25

Chawton, 1813

It was an English summer's afternoon of middling perfection in Chawton, and Mrs Austen was alone in the garden. Eccentrically dressed in old clothes – although, these days, even her best clothes were old, for what did it matter? – she knelt at her strawberries, attacking insurgent weeds with a trowel. Within the cottage, the three other residents were to be found, as was their habit, in the drawing room.

Jane was at the little writing table, showing the same ferocious intensity in intellectual battle that her mother brought to the physical. Martha was copying receipts into her notebook. Cassy, in the armchair beneath the open window, sat in a wafting cloud of rose scent, and read that morning's letter again. It was the fourth such missive that she had received since living in Chawton, and she still did not know why they were written. What was the purpose of this communication? How could it change things? What is done, is done. Was the hope to inspire some sense of regret?

Their peace was disturbed.

'I am at the very end of my tether, and hanging on by no more than my fingernails.' Mary Austen appeared on the threshold. Anna, taller and lovelier than her *stepmother but sharing* the same cross demeanour, stood hang-dog beside her.

'Good afternoon, Mary.' Jane slipped her page under the blotter and looked up. 'What is it now?'

'I have reason to believe that *your* niece, *my* stepdaughter, is about to embark on *another* engagement! And this time with Ben Lefroy, of all people.'

The aunts offered cautious congratulation, and Anna returned an equally cautious smile. It was true that, as a match, Mr Lefroy was less than ideal, but he was at least better than the last one.

'Of course, obviously one does not want her to end up an *old maid*, but it is hard to have faith in her after what she has put us through. Honestly, I believe she just does it only to vex us.'

It was Cassy's belief that Anna was simply desperate to leave home and would do anything in her powers to effect it. Poor child, there was only ever one means of escape. She certainly did not have the air of a young woman in love. In fact, she was a study in misery.

Mary bustled into the middle of the room and, as was her wont – her mind buzzing like a bluebottle from one unpleasantness to the next – alighted upon a new subject. 'Each time I visit, I am struck by the same thought: your brother

Edward could have done so much better for you, had he so wished. Does it not peeve you, living here, when he has so many better properties in his gift? You have been too good-natured, and he has exploited that. It is my long experience that the undemanding single woman never gets her due.'

'And it is mine' – Jane rose – 'that the demanding gets nothing at all. Truly, Mary, do not worry yourself on our account. We are as comfortable as can be, and endlessly grateful. Can I offer you a cool drink?'

'Certainly not. It is very cold in here.' Mary shivered theatrically. 'Very cold and extremely dark.'

'Perhaps you are sickening, Sister?' Martha asked, worried.

'I never sicken. There must be a draught. Is there a draught? I fancy there is a draught. You should call out Edward's man to make him take a look.'

'We would never trouble him for such a thing,' Martha replied. 'And when work does need doing, then well: we can pay for it ourselves now. Jane is, after all, a very rich woman!'

Jane's new 'wealth' was much talked about in Chawton that summer, and dear Martha went to great lengths to drop it into any conversation. Since the week they moved in here, Jane had, as her sister had hoped, returned to her manuscripts. First, she revised *Elinor and Marianne*, which became *Sense and Sensibility* and – oh joy! – found a publisher and had sold really quite well. At the urging of the household, *First Impressions* was next to receive her attentions. With its new title of *Pride and Prejudice*, that was doing even better. It was the fashionable novel of 1813, and its anonymous author at the top of her tree. She was set to make more than a staggering one hundred wonderful pounds. They all fell on the reviews as they came out, exclaimed at the sales as they heard them. Jane was toiling, with enormous pleasure and absolute satisfaction, on something quite new: the adventures of a young heroine, rich in morals and low in income. There was nothing anyone could do to burst her bubble of delight. Nevertheless, Mary must try.

'*Rich?* Oh, Martha, you are so sweet and so foolish. Jane has had a little windfall this year, and we are all very pleased for her. But, as I was saying to Austen only last evening, popularity is no measure of quality – or longevity, indeed. Novels are a fad, nothing more, nothing less. Austen says so and who can know better than him? When I think of his poetry – oh, well, there I shall stop, for I do not wish to offend. Please bear in mind, my dears, that this *wealth* is, most likely, no more than a one-time occurence, and spread over a lifetime of seven years and thirty, what does it amount to? More or less, nothing.'

Again the bluebottle took flight, landing this time on Anna. 'Now, then. To return to more pressing matters, I have brought Anna to see her grandmother, in the hope of some old sense being talked into a silly young head. Come with me, child, and confess all.'

Off they went to the garden.

'Ignore it,' Cassandra said mildly, returning to her letter.

'Oh, I do.' Jane flicked her hand. 'But I cannot help but find what she says interesting. You know, she really, genuinely, in her deep heart of hearts, pities all three of us. Here am I, England's Happiest Woman – self-appointed, perhaps, but official nonetheless; the crown is secure on my head – and in comes Mary, assesses my lot, and can only see Tragedy.'

'She approaches the subject of Life with quite different criteria.'

'Yes, but is she alone?' Jane wanted to know. 'Does everyone feel that way? Do they all look at us and see three creatures as joyless and stiff as' – she looked around and her eye caught the cold fireplace – 'that poker? The fire screen? Some plank of dry wood? We took the sow's ear that fate offered us, and fashioned from that something quite wonderful. And I *do* wonder at it, truly. Yet perhaps, despite all that luck and conniving and ultimate triumph, we are still as old, poor and laughed-at as we always had feared.'

'Perhaps.' Cassy thought of an incident of the previous week. She and Jane had been walking through the village together, in matching bonnets. Their wardrobes had merged lately and their middle-aged garb was, more often than not, almost identical: like strange, superannuated twins. They were clearly a comical sight, for a group of young labourers had laughed when they passed them. Jane had not noticed – she was too busy talking. Cassy had, though – and not cared. For what do we live but to make sport for our neighbours, and laugh at them in our turn? 'And what does it matter?'

'It does not matter in the slightest. I was merely curious. We novelists are curious creatures. We can never cease in our examinations of character and situation.'

'Oh, Martha.' Cassy laughed. 'I think we are to be pitied, after all, are we not?'

'And on the subject of my curiosity and its insatiable nature,' Jane continued, 'who is your letter from, may I ask? And do not say "Nobody", for you have read it one hundred times this afternoon, and "Nobody" rarely warrants that level of scrutiny.'

'It is from a Mrs Hobday. I do not know if you remember: we—'

'*Hobday*?' Jane exclaimed. 'Why, yes: curiously, the name does ring a bell. It deafens me, in fact. What does she want, after all these years?'

'She writes to inform me that her son—'

'Your *Mr* Hobday.'

'The seaside gentleman?' Martha sat up.

Cassy shot a glance at Jane, who looked sheepish. 'Mr Hobday', she continued, 'has been recently presented with his third child. Very pleasant news, I am sure you agree.'

'We are all very happy for him,' Jane said drily. 'And why does she imagine that you might want to know that?'

Cassy sighed. 'That, I agree, is something of a puzzle, which I have been failing to solve. I could do with an astute lady novelist to shed light on the matter. If only I knew one . . .'

'At your service.' Jane walked to the window, looked into the garden and thought. 'Of course, the pride of any fond mother – and *she* was the fondest, if I remember correctly – would chafe at the notion of another woman rejecting her darling. Perhaps she is still smarting, even after the passage of so many years.'

'But if that darling is now settled, and blessed with a growing family,' Martha put in, 'that would be more than a little churlish.'

'Ah, you speak as one who is a stranger to churl.' Jane turned. 'If only the whole world had your talent for resilience and forgiving, my dear friend.'

The room fell silent. Cassy was thinking, and had no doubt that they too were thinking – for all three now had the power to read the minds of the others – of Martha and Frank Austen. She had loved him for so long and so deeply, and yet never once had that love refused her permission to rejoice in his happiness at finding love with another. She possessed quite the purest of souls.

'It is also possible', Jane then went on, 'that the

senior Mrs Hobday is less churlish, more calculating. Perhaps she worries that the *young* Mrs Hobday might not survive all this childbearing. She wants to ensure that the *next* Mrs Hobday is there waiting in the wings, preparing to take centre stage.'

'Heavens!' Cassy exclaimed. 'What a dark, strange place is your mind, Sister.' She folded up the letter and put it away. 'I cannot accept that theory. It is too sinister for words. And if you are right, then she can only be disappointed again.'

'Truthfully?' Jane moved to her side, and put a hand on her shoulder. 'You do not regret it? You would never go back to him? Even now, that you no longer have the worry of me and our mother? I do wonder sometimes. Both of you were made, surely, to be married ladies. I never was, of course. But you two: you would have been such excellent wives. Is there not, deep within you, some small, closed, secret chamber of disappointment?'

Martha smiled. 'I, for one, was never presented with a choice.'

'And I' – Cassy squeezed the hand that now held hers – 'regret nothing. Look at us. We have found our Utopia! I can imagine no better life than the one we have here.'

CHAPTER 26

Kintbury, April 1840

'Dinah?' A chastened Cassandra spoke softly from the armchair. 'You are awake. Thank the Lord! Are you feeling a little better?'

'Bit sore, m'm.' Dinah wriggled and shifted, checking gingerly about her body for tenderness. She winced as her hand met her forehead. 'Ouch. Still, not so bad considering. I think I got away with it, m'm.'

'You have been very lucky, from what I can see. Is there anything I can do to make you more comfortable?'

'Wouldn't say no to a cup of tea, Miss Austen. Course, only if you're going that way.'

Cassandra rose on command – 'I shall make it at once' – withdrew to the kitchen, and struggled back with a heavily laden tray.

'Ah, the good china, I see.' Dinah sat up. Cassandra rearranged her pillows. 'Nought but the best for the invalid.'

'It seemed a shame not to use it. You had not got around to packing it up, then?'

'Didn't have the 'eart, m'm. Miss Isabella's that fond of it.' She slurped her tea and sighed happily.

'Dinah, while we are alone' – Cassandra sat down – 'I have a few questions for you. First of all – and this is simply to satisfy my own curiosity – might I be right in thinking that you have been listening to the reading in the drawing room of my sister's novel, *Persuasion*?'

'And what if I 'ave?' Dinah narrowed her eyes. 'Law against it, is there? Servants hearing things thought too good for 'em?'

'Not at all,' Cassandra protested. 'Indeed, the reverse. Nothing could delight me more! It just occurs to me that your fall from the stairs was not dissimilar to a scene in the story. You remember, it takes place in Lyme?'

'Can't think what you mean, m'm,' Dinah rebuffed her. 'I'll take another cup of that tea, if you don't mind.'

Cassandra took the china and poured. 'Be that as it may, I would like to take the opportunity to applaud you both for your intelligence and your devotion to your mistress. You took quite a risk there, but it appears to have worked.'

Dinah looked smug and slurped loudly again.

Lowering her voice now, Cassandra leaned over. 'And now – well, this is a delicate matter. I hope you do not think me intrusive – about Miss Isabella and Mr Lidderdale.'

'So we got there at last, did we?' Dinah gave one of her sniffs – signifying deep contempt, if Cassandra read it correctly – then visibly softened. 'He loves 'er. She loves 'im. They been like it for years.'

'Yes. I understand that now. But why—?'

'The master wouldn't 'ave any of it. You know how he got sometimes. Stubborn as a mule. No budging 'im. There's not much wrong with Mr Lidderdale, I tell you that for nought pence. The whole village loves 'im, but he's not much in his origins, if you get what I mean. Not born a gentleman, and the Reverend wouldn't put up with it. Not good enough for Miss Isabella and that was that. Not even better than nothing at all, which is what the poor lamb ended up with.'

'I am so shocked to hear that.' Cassandra had never heard whisper of any such drama! 'As well as greatly saddened, on the poor couple's behalf.'

'So when Mr Fowle passed away, I of course got me hopes up. There! I thought to m'self, they're free. There's no one to bully them. And I kept saying all that to Miss Isabella, whispering in 'er ear. Then *you* turned up in the works with your spanner.'

'Yes, I am sorry. And if I had but known . . .' Cassandra was humble. 'But what of Mrs Fowle, and her feelings on the match? Surely she must have been most conflicted.'

'If she was, she never let on.' Dinah slurped her tea. 'She was a perfect woman, my mistress – too perfect, as I see it. Perfection!' She sniffed and shook her head with disgust. 'Perfection brings no end of trouble. Mrs Fowle would keep 'er thoughts to 'erself, which is a daft way to go on, if anyone wants my opinion. She never argued with anyone, specially not with 'im – and he wasn't always right on things, not by a long chalk. And nor was she one for meddling. Very strict on that she was, even when meddling was just what was needed. Wouldn't catch her at a meddle if the house was on fire.'

'So most unlike us, then: you, Dinah, and me.' Had she gone too far? Cassandra, covering her apprehension with a tentative smile, clung to Pyramus for some emotional support.

'The difference between you and me, madam,' Dinah said, archly, over her best cup and saucer, 'is *my* meddling's done all to the good.'

Cassandra found Isabella out in the garden, down by the riverbank.

'You seem deep in contemplation, my dear.'

Together, they stood by the newly green willow. Two swans drifted past, heads high and tails up, arrogant in their conjugal felicity. Tall iris promised, with a slight hint of flag, the fulfilment of colour to come.

'Today has left me with plenty to think about.' Isabella appeared dazed. She also, Cassandra noticed for the very first time, looked almost uncommonly pretty. Mourning had been replaced with a pale pink that lent a bloom to her face and revealed her fine, delicate form. The sun fingered gold strands in her hair. She appeared now as a woman of half her real age. All the marks and the wounds of those hard, long, lost years – how must she have suffered! – disappeared in the miracle of a morning.

'I have just now left Dinah, and can assure you that there is nothing to worry about on her account.'

'Dinah?' Isabella started, as if the matter of the accident was the last thing on her mind. 'Oh, yes. That is good news indeed.'

'It seemed that the fall was never as bad as it looked, though we could never have presumed it would be so. I hope you are not unhappy that I called the surgeon?'

'Unhappy?' Isabella laughed. 'Far from it, Cassandra.' She took her arm, and they started to walk back to the house. 'Who knows what more Dinah might have done to herself if Mr Lidderdale had not come out then? Chopped off her own head, more than likely. You did entirely the right thing, I assure you.'

At that, from the house, stomping across the lawn towards them in a most urgent manner, appeared the less-than-pretty sight of strange Mary-Jane.

'I came as soon as I heard.' Her boom pierced the tranquillity. 'What is the upshot? Dead, I suppose. Terrible business. Stairs can be dangerous

– wicked things – always said so. To be used at one's peril. That is why I sleep downstairs.'

'Good afternoon, Sister.' Isabella kissed her without any real warmth. 'Dinah is well, thank you, and recovering indoors. We were all very lucky. There is nothing to worry about.'

'Well, you can say that, but what is the extent of the damage? Is she to be well enough to help us move into this new place or not? If that is to happen soon, we cannot be down a maid.'

'On that,' Cassandra said calmly, 'may I make a suggestion? Loath though I am to interfere.'

The two very different Fowle sisters both turned to look at her, with a shared sense of wariness, for which Cassandra could hardly blame them. Had she not already interfered quite enough?

'Contrary to my previous advice, I wonder now if it might not be better to wait a while before committing to a lease on a new property? After all, it may be foolish to rush into a new arrangement in a time of great crisis. Is there not a case for Isabella to find a more temporary arrangement, to bide her time and take a month or so to think about things in more detail?'

This new solution was, unsurprisingly, met with ready agreement by both, as neither had been much keen on the old one. And as the threat of it lifted, so the mood took an up-turn. Happy in the knowledge that domestic intimacy would not be theirs; joyful that their futures might not ever be entangled; elated, indeed, that they need never meet again if they so chose it, they decided, together, to take a tour of the land.

'Strange to think that all this is shortly to leave the family,' said Mary-Jane as they walked towards the stables – once so busy and fragrant, now sadly deserted.

Isabella laughed. 'You have hardly been down here for years!'

'Perhaps not. It is not a journey to embark upon lightly – what with the churchyard and so on. But I always had the comfort of knowing it was here.'

'It is the loveliest garden in England, in my opinion,' Cassandra said warmly. 'The first time I came here, all those long years ago, it felt as if I were stepping into a storybook, of which I myself was the heroine.'

Isabella turned then and stared at her – astonished, perhaps, to hear such a romantic speech from one she no doubt saw as a dry, cold old lady. 'And then your story turned into tragedy. I am sorry for that, Cassandra.'

'Oh no, not exactly, my dear,' Cassandra replied. 'Indeed, it was a terrible blow to lose your dear Uncle Tom. His death brought enormous distress to us all. Your poor grandmother never recovered. But I – Please do not think me to have had a sad life, Isabella. After all, there are as many forms of love as there are moments in time.' She took her arm again, and smiled. 'Or as our good sage Dinah would have it: "each to her own".'

They skirted the coppice and headed down the slope and back to the riverbank.

'Your sister,' said Mary-Jane thoughtfully. 'I remember her coming here for her very last visit – ailing quite badly; we all noticed that. She wandered about, too, just as we now are doing, with the air, I then fancied, of one who never expected to see this place again. Which year would it have been – 1817?'

'It was the summer before,' Cassandra replied softly. 'That was very astute of you, Mary-Jane, to read her actions like that. You were but a young woman, and I – so much older and wiser – yet refused all such evidence. You see, I could not but have hope. Even though my sister herself, I believe, knew even then that all hope was lost.'

CHAPTER 27

My dear Eliza,

Thank you for your note, and I am most gratified to hear that you so enjoyed Emma. Altogether, her passage into the world has gone as smoothly as I might ever have hoped. Though there has been <u>some</u> criticism – each word of it piercing, a dagger to the heart – it has been tempered by enough appreciation to leave me moderately cheerful. Of course, I would be more cheerful still were her <u>sales</u> to improve, but there: I shall never be quite as rich as I should like.

Nor as lucky. As fortune gives to me with one hand, it takes with the other. And in confidence, Eliza – I would swap all hope of wealth and success now just to feel well again. I wish I could say that the Cheltenham waters are working their magic but – alas! – it would not be true. And for all the medical men who bustle around here – each other one is a doctor, or at least <u>claims</u> to be – there is not one who can put a name to my ailment. You cannot wonder at that, of course. I have, as you know, always enjoyed being a Woman of Mystery.

None of this is enough to deter my dear Cassy. She delivers me to the Spa every morning, confident that each dose will bring a miracle. And though I try very hard, and pretend for <u>her</u> sake that my symptoms are lifting, I feel weaker now than when we arrived. It is not only the discomfort – my back aches, my skin is all over peculiar – but the <u>fatigue</u> that most plagues me. Today is a better one, but some mornings, it is too much to lift my head from the pillow. And more lowering still is the thought of being such a burden to my most excellent sister. Oh, she does not complain and is ever good-humoured, even as she slaves in my interests. But she is so very <u>determined</u> on finding a cure for me, and I am ever more doubtful of her success. This poor, stubborn body of mine seems to be quite set on decline. What a miserable wretch I am become.

My spirits, though, rise at the prospect of calling on Kintbury on our return home to Chawton. We aim to be with you on Thursday, and that thought alone is enough to put a rose in my cheeks and return life to my legs. I hereby instruct my condition to ease off for a few days – take its own little holiday. It will <u>not</u> interfere with the enjoyment of our visit. I shall not permit it.

Yrs,
J. A.

Cassy stood with Eliza at the window, and looked out on the garden. The Kintbury drawing room was buttery with afternoon sun; the shadows were lengthening in the garden beyond.

'How is she now, do you think?' Eliza asked as they both studied Jane on her wander by the bulrush.

Cassy replied with great confidence: 'Oh, there is a definite improvement that I can discern. I am most encouraged. Her back aches a lot less, and I am sure her skin settles down. What do you make of her?'

'Me? I am sure you are right. I was a little alarmed by the strange patches on her arm, but of course they would not vanish at once, and it would be foolish to expect it. It is just that I had not seen her for a while . . .'

'She is very thin.' Cassy bit her lip. 'And those black marks are alarming, I agree.'

'We have fed you both up,' Eliza soothed. 'And really the marks are nothing. I do not know why I mentioned them. What marks? I ask myself now. And indeed that was a few days ago. No trace remains, now that I think of it.' She moved back to her chair and picked up her embroidery. 'We will send you both back to Chawton all pink and plump.'

'My dear.' Fulwar strode in. 'I hope you have remembered that I am out this evening? The Tory Dinner in Newbury. Forgive me' – he bowed to Cassy – 'for leaving you ladies all alone, and on your last night at our table. Too much to resist.'

'Please do not worry on our account, Fulwar.' Cassy bent her head deferentially. 'We will, of course, be most quiet without you, but I am sure one of us, at least, will come up with something to talk of.'

'Quite so.' He marched to the window. 'How goes your sister? I must say she is looking a pretty poor specimen. You will be out of your mind with the worry of it all.'

Eliza stitched on in silence.

'We were just saying, in fact, that Jane seems much better,' Cassy said firmly. 'Well on the way to recovery.'

'Humph. Got the melancholy that I often see in my line of work – the air of the mortally ill. Still, I gather you have had a run of bad luck lately. Perhaps that is the cause. It cannot be easy.' He went to the fireplace, lifted his jacket and rocked on his heels, even though there was no fire there to warm him.

Cassy sighed. 'One or two of my brothers have had their financial difficulties, it is true. But you know the Austens as well as anyone: we have more than our fair share of blessings in general but – alas! – money will always elude us. No doubt we will survive.'

'And those books of hers are all come to nothing, I hear. Sort of petered out, did she not, after that one rather good one? Shame for her. Still not much to write about, I should not wonder.'

'Jane has had four novels published, and all to acclaim!'

'No profit in 'em though, so Mary tells me. She reports that while the rest of you ladies work hard at your duties, your sister does nothing but write, and yet all for nothing. We did *try* that new one, that – er –um—'

'*Emma*?'

'Some lady's name. Could not find much in it, could we, my dear? Read the first chapter, skipped to the last. Quite got the gist.'

'And that gist was what, in your view?' Cassy asked, with a chill of a smile.

'That nothing much happened. Who is going to part with their money for that sort of performance? Best not to bother. Now, *Waverley*—'

'In fact, Jane is busy with a new work that I believe may be her best yet.' Cassy left the window to sit on the sofa, and prepared to expound. 'It is—'

'Tell Eliza all about it. She is a great listener, are you not, my love? I must dash to get dressed. Cannot be late. Those Newbury Tories are the best company I know. Top conversation – quite sparkling.'

CHAPTER 28

Winchester, 1817

'Dearest?' Cassy touched Jane's face softly. 'Can you hear me, my love? Are you there?'

No answer came. There was no sign of movement. She laid gentle fingers on a white, tiny wrist and felt the faint, fluttering pulse. Not yet then, thank God: not quite yet awhile. They had been granted at least one more day.

Cassy pulled back her shoulders, stretched and condemned her own weakness. What was she thinking of, falling asleep at the bedside? So she had not slept for days, so fatigue overwhelmed her: what of it? From now on, she would do all in her power – stick pins in her eyes – to stay awake until the end that she knew must come.

She walked to the window, parted the curtains and watched the summer dawn rush in and flood College Street, Winchester: the final address they would share. How very strange it was that they should find themselves here, all alone in these alien, insignificant rooms. How very poignant that such a dear homebody should be called to her Maker when she was anywhere other than home. Perhaps Jane no longer noticed; perhaps she was too ill to care anything for place and its meaning. Cassy cared, though. She cared very deeply. For forty-one years now, she had acted as staunch defender of her sister's interests. And in the forty-second year, she had failed.

A full twelve months had passed since they took the waters in Cheltenham, and enjoyed that brief stay with Eliza. It was now July of 1817; they were in Winchester, and had been brought here by hope. Cassy had found a new doctor, who had promised, if not quite a cure, then at least an improvement. That, surely, was something to reach for: something that had to be tried? But then hope had abandoned them, soon after their arrival. And at once, it was too late to get back to Chawton. Cassy sighed heavily, burying her head in her hands. She must reach acceptance. This was the last trick life could play on them in these the last moments of its mischievous game. There was nothing to be done now, but accept themselves beaten. And wait for the Good Lord to come.

'You have been here all night?' Jane whispered from the depths of her pillow.

Cassy ran back to her side.

'Cass, you do look exhausted. I am aware that my own beauty is not at its height, but you, my love . . .' She tried a weak smile, her neat little teeth rendered enormous – almost bestial – by the emaciation of her face. 'Why will you not let the nurse do the worst of it? I promise not to leave without you by my side.'

Cassy felt for her hand. 'I have let the nurse go. No, do not waste your breath! She was nowhere near good enough. I could not trust her. But help is on its way.'

'Martha? She is coming?' Jane gave a low flicker of pleasure. 'Then we shall all three be together.'

'I did ask for Martha,' Cassy said gently. 'But apparently it was decided – and we cannot know what is happening back there in Chawton – that Martha should stay with our mother. So Mary is now on her way.'

'*She* is to attend *me*? Oh, Cass. Mother is perfectly well, I am sure. Did I not always say she would outlive us all? I fear it is I who am now the main spectacle, and here is the proof of it. I can admit now to having harboured faint hopes of recovery. But if Mary is coming, I must face it: Death cannot be far behind.' She turned and winced as her back touched the soft mattress.

'Hush now. Keep calm. Try and take in some water.' Cassy knelt on the bed, cradled her sister – no more than a skeleton – and held a cup to her mouth while she sipped. 'There. Sleep for a few more hours yet. The doctor will call at around noon. Let us be quiet until then.'

⋆   ⋆   ⋆

'I came as soon as I could.' Mary untied her bonnet. 'How fares she now? What can I do?'

'Thank you, Mary.' Cassandra kissed her. It was such a relief to see someone from the family – such a relief to receive an envoy from the world of the well, even if it was only Mary. 'Her spirits are good. Her body, though, less so. The doctor was with us this morning. I now fear – well – he suggested . . . there is not long to go.'

Mary prepared herself for duty, and took up position by Jane's side. Thus released, Cassy went into the bedroom and lay down to rest. She would not sleep, she could not let herself . . . Just a short nap perhaps . . .

It was late afternoon when she rushed back into the sickroom, heart in her mouth, appearance all in distrait. Had she missed it? She could not, surely, have missed it. She heard low conversation, weak laughter. Mary and Jane were each enjoying the company of the other.

'This is a pretty sight,' said Cassy, much pleased.

'We were remembering when we were young,' replied Mary. 'When you were at Steventon, and we were at Ibthorpe. Oh, we did have such fun, then. Before I was married.'

Jane agreed. 'I have been so very fortunate in my family, and my friends. If I live to be an old woman, I am sure I would wish then to have died now: blessed in that tenderness, and before I survived either you all, or your affections.' She touched Mary's hand. 'You have always been a kind sister to me, Mary. Why do you not rest now, and let Cass take her turn?'

Cassy waited until they were alone, before speaking. 'That was touching, to see you two so cheerful together.'

'She is being really most pleasant, genuinely so,' Jane admitted.

'Mary is a very good nurse, like her sisters.' Cassy tucked in the blankets and made the bed tidy.

'It is not so much that, and she is no equal to you, dearest, or Martha.' Jane sank a bit deeper, her face white as her pillow. 'Disaster often brings out the best in her. It is success that disturbs her good nature.'

During the course of the next eight hours and forty, Jane was more asleep than awake. Her looks altered and she started upon the process of slowly falling away. On the Thursday evening of 17 July, there came some sort of attack: a faintness, an oppression; the sign of the end.

'Tell me what you are feeling. What is it now, my love?' Cassy held a cool sponge to her face, blotted the papery skin. 'What can I do for you? *Anything.* Do you want anything?'

'Nothing, but Death.' Jane's eyes were closed, her suffering immense but her words still intelligible. 'God grant me patience. Pray for me, Cass. Oh, pray for me, dearest. Pray for me, please.'

Throughout the following night – their last one together – Cassy sat with her sister's head in her lap, stroking her, whispering comfort. Until just before dawn, when she lost her.

And, grateful to be alone, thankful there was no other to share in this most private of moments, Cassy performed her last services. She placed the dear corpse back on the bed, closed each eye and kissed it, and then stood, in deep contemplation at the enormity of that which she had witnessed. Jane had been the sun of her life, the gilder of every pleasure, the soother of any sorrow. Not a thought had one ever concealed from the other. Cassy fell to her knees, and prayed fervently for the deliverance of this most precious of souls. Such a sister, such a friend, as could never be surpassed.

It was as if she had lost a part of herself.

CHAPTER 29

Kintbury, April 1840

'My 'ead doesn't 'alf hurt,' Dinah grumbled from her comfortable billet on the drawing-room sofa.

'I can believe it.' Isabella laughed. 'Mine, too, is throbbing quite horribly. It is nothing to do with your injuries of yesterday, I can assure you of that. It is because we drank far too much wine.' She gave a comical moan, and clutched at her forehead. 'That was a bright idea of yours, Cassandra, to liberate those few bottles from Papa's cellar, but I fear we are now good for nothing.'

'The morning after is never easy, my dear.' Cassandra smiled. 'We must just remember the fun of the evening before.'

The three women had spent it together in the spirit of happy celebration after the momentous events of the day. They finished *Persuasion*, drank slightly too much of Fulwar's excellent claret, and talked, far too late, of the future.

All was set fair. Isabella was convinced now

that love should prevail, and love's enemies must simply get used to it. There was no better man than her John, and that he had waited so long for her was the proof of his worth. She would make an excellent doctor's wife – on that, they were all agreed. And Dinah expressed every ambition to be an excellent doctor's wife's excellent maid – but on that, Cassandra chose to reserve judgement. She did, though, hope it might prove to be true, as well as know it to be none of her business.

And now it was time for her to leave.

She sat in Eliza's old armchair – cloak already on, bonnet tied around her chin, precious valise at her feet – and waited for the sound of her coach. There was, in the pit of her stomach, that familiar knot of anxiety that came with the threat of a journey. The driver had promised only that he would arrive by mid-morning. No doubt, Cassandra was, as usual, ready too early. They were now all in that moment of awkwardness, when farewells must be made, but one did not know quite how long one had for their making. There was so much to be said, but it should not all be said too soon.

'I shall miss you,' she said to Pyramus as he nuzzled her knee. 'You have been a great friend to me while I was here and quite converted me to your species.' She looked up as an idea occurred. 'I think I shall get myself a little dog when I am home.'

'That is an excellent idea, Cassandra!' cried Isabella. 'I hate to think of you living all alone.'

'Oh, I do not mind it. Do not worry on my account. Those whom I wish to live with are no longer around, but their memories keep me good company. No, God has been most merciful, truly. He spared my dear mother until she reached an uncommonly great age – eighty-seven years was a miracle, for one so dogged with ill health. And your Aunt Martha is not so very far away, still. I can go to her and Frank whenever I please.'

'Theirs is a busy household. I cannot imagine that you want to go there for too long. How she can find the energy for all those children at her time of life! It hardly bears thinking.'

'She is a stoical creature, and the best stepmother to them all that the family could wish for. It is never easy, when the fond, real mother is taken too soon, but we are all very pleased to see them married at last. You are right, though – my own visits do tend to be short.'

'Dear Aunt Martha.' Isabella smiled, fondly. 'I can never get used to the fact that she is now *Lady Austen*.'

'Nor can Mary,' Cassandra cautioned her. 'She finds the elevation most trying. It is best not to use the title when she is around.'

They were interrupted by the sound of wheels upon gravel.

'Ah, there is my man.' Cassandra rose, and embraced Isabella.

During the course of the visit, their relationship had grown from a wary acquaintance to the richness of friendship. They stood now together, in silent communion, each celebrating the worth of the other.

'Isabella.' Cassandra pulled back, took her hands, and began. 'I cannot begin to—'

'Mrs Austen, madam,' announced Fred from the doorway as Mrs Austen barged past him and bustled through.

'Mary!' Cassandra exclaimed. 'You have just caught me. My coach will arrive any minute.'

'And again, you travel without the courtesy of informing your sister,' Mary replied tartly.

'Forgive me. I was too keen to get home and leave the household in peace.'

'Not before time. What on earth are you doing lying down there, Dinah? Get up. Get up at once! There is not the time to malinger.'

Dinah rose, and sniffed disobligingly.

'I hear' – Mary now faced Isabella – 'that wretched man Dundas is throwing you all out prematurely. Unspeakable behaviour, if you ask me, but not a surprise. Oh dear, no. I have seen it all in my day, and enough to know this: there is no greater menace *on this earth* than the clergyman, newly appointed. Now then. Where do we start? I am aware that I have not yet addressed the matter of the letters, and I have been thinking on that. Unless there are items that you children want, Isabella, I suggest I take them all. Fred! Go straight to the mistress's room, remove all correspondence and bring it to me. There may well be something in there that is of interest.'

So she was right to have come here! Cassandra gave a breath of relief.

'Goodbye, my dear.' She stepped forward and took Isabella's hand. It seemed that, after all, they were not to be afforded their proper farewell. 'It only remains to thank you for having me here. It has meant a great deal, in a great many ways.' She leaned forward and whispered into her ear. 'By the way – the best china of which you are so fond. Keep some for yourself. No one will notice. Enough for two settings, at least.'

Isabella smiled, and planted a warm kiss on her cheek.

'There we are.' Mary put herself between them. 'Best not to make too much fuss of it. You can wait on your own now, Cassandra, can you not? We are busy, and do have to get on.'

She propelled Isabella out, but stopped then, and softened.

'So, this is the last time we will ever meet in this house. It is a profound moment. We have had so much history here, have we not? And now all is to be lost.' She looked suddenly pitiable. 'No trace will remain.'

'Dear Mary.' Cassandra bent down to kiss her. 'Surely our history is all in our minds, in our memories. We can do no more than pass it on to the next generation, with as much honesty as we can muster.' She smiled. 'And only hope that what lives on is true.'

'As if there were any interest! Oh, the stories of men will live on, I am sure: Fulwar, of course. My good husband; my fine son in his turn. But our own? Not a bit of it. There will be no one to care about us.'

Cassandra left as she had arrived: alone and unwatched. She settled herself down in her carriage seat, braced against the difficulties of the journey ahead, and looked about her for the very last time. There, in the background, were gentle undulations; to the side were the brick and flint cottages. And behind her now, never to be looked at again, the parsonage: solid and square.

The coach pulled out into the lane and the direction of the Avenue, and before it had reached speed, Cassandra caught a short, broad figure walking up from the towpath. She leaned forward and signalled to the driver to stop.

'Mr Lidderdale,' she called down to him. 'Good morning. Are you on your way to the vicarage?'

The doctor removed his hat and observed all the niceties. 'I'm not very sure, madam, if I am wanted. How fares Dinah today? Of course, I'll be there if I'm needed.'

'No, you are not needed at all. Dinah is perfectly well. But I have reason to believe that if you did find the time to call on Miss Fowle, you could be assured of a very warm welcome.'

'Thank you for that.' His broad face was lit by the broadest of smiles. 'Thank you kindly, Miss Austen.' He straightened his shabby coat. 'No time like the present, eh? I shall go there at once.'

The coach gave a lurch, trundled and swayed up to the turnpike, shaking Cassandra's old bones apart. Oh, how she longed to be back home in Chawton! She would have that bonfire, as soon as was possible: feed the flames with those difficult letters; wait and watch until the ashes were cold. And then, only then, all her work here was done; no duties remained. At last, she would be free to dwindle away, worrying for nothing but the roses, the chickens and the church.

Still, the journey would take several hours. How best to distract herself from the discomfort and boredom? It was then that she remembered the letter from Jane, not yet looked at. Reaching into her valise, fumbling her fingers among the pieces of patchwork, she found and retrieved it, and read.

College St, Winchester
10th July, 1817

My dear Eliza,
    An attack of my sad complaint has seized me again – the most severe I ever had – and reduced me so low that I now feel recovery unlikely. You must not pity me, though – I

will not hear of it. If I am to die now, I am convinced that I die as the luckiest of women. For how to do justice to the kindness of my family during this illness is quite beyond me! And as for Cassandra! Words must fail me in any attempt to describe what a Nurse she has been to me now, what a dearest, tender, watchful sister she has been through my life. As to what I owe to her, I can only cry over it and pray God to bless her more and yet more.

I cannot expect to have the strength to ever write to you again, but thank you now for your friendship, wish you and your family long health and happiness and beg you to please look after my dear, darling Cass. These next months and years will be hard. We have never borne separation easily, she and I. And, as I approach this final departure, I am selfishly grateful that it was never my fate to be the one who survived. For how could I? What sort of life would it be, if I did not have her by my side?

With my fondest affections,
J.A.

Cassandra raised the paper to her lips, closed her eyes and, as a pilgrim with a saint's relic, kissed it.

The wheels ground and turned; the horses pulled and panted. Through her tears, she looked out of the window. Berkshire started to fall away from her now, Hampshire was opening up: the soft contours of the country she had once thought her sure destiny yielding to the dear shape of home.

AUTHOR'S NOTE

It is a matter of family record that, in the last years of her life, Cassandra Austen looked over the letters that she and her sister had exchanged. All those she found open and confidential – the majority of them, then – she burned. We cannot doubt that there would also have been a long and deep correspondence between both Cassandra and Jane, and the Fowle family at Kintbury. None of this has, as yet, come to light. The letters in this novel are entirely imagined. The poetry is all by James Austen.

Of the favourite nieces: Anna did marry Ben Lefroy in 1814 but was widowed fifteen years later and left with seven children, a narrow income and indifferent health. In contrast, Fanny enjoyed a life of great comfort, becoming the second wife of the wealthy Sir Edward Knatchbull. She took on a host of stepchildren and had nine more of her own. In later life, she wrote dismissively of her Aunt Jane as 'not so *refined* as she ought to have been'. Nevertheless, her eldest son, Lord Brabourne, was the first to take the opportunity to collect and publish Jane Austen's letters.

In her last years, Cassandra enjoyed having a dog of her own, called Link. He would go with her manservant to the Great House to collect her milk, and carry the pail home in his mouth. Cassandra died of a stroke in March 1845, while staying with her brother Frank near Portsmouth. She is buried in the churchyard at Chawton, next to her mother. Among the beneficiaries of her will were the Fowle daughters. To Isabella, by then Mrs John Lidderdale, she left forty-five pounds. And to Elizabeth, the only one left unmarried, she bequeathed the extraordinary sum of one thousand pounds – presumably in reparation of that bequest she herself had received so many years before.

Gill Hornby
JULY 2019